SECOND SPRING

By
Sandhya Jane

COPYRIGHT INFORMATION

Copyright © 2014 Sandhya Jane
In US and India

SECOND SPRING
ISBN: 978-0-692-25932-0

9 780692 259320

All characters in this book are fictional and figments of the author's imagination.

Published By:
ANISAN Technologies Inc.
Email: info@anisans.com

Printed by:
Thomson Press India Limited

Distributed By:
India
India Book House
Mumbai - 400 071

Worldwide:
Ingram Spark & Amazon Inc

- "Go ahead and let the love blossom coming spring!"

I always admire strong females who choose to live life their way without compromising on their duties and responsibilities. She is the one, who has won my heart." By Priyanka Batra Harjai

- "The story of life is always this prayer of hope.
Literatures that speak of this hope are one of my favorite readings. That's why 'Second Spring' by Sandhya Jane touches my heart." By Biswanath Banerjee

- "Love is silent but strong." A second spring is a story of unsaid promises and unrequited love; the kind that sometimes takes years to get over with. This is a heart wrenching tale of pining for love and finding it in the unlikeliest of place!" by Indywrites

- "I have read 'Second Spring' and loved it. Well done on creating a novel that shows strength and power but of love, romance and the realities of life. I love the role reversal of powerful businesswoman falling in love with a man who is professionally beneath her. It is a refreshing change from the norm and you have done it so well." By Jennifer Douglas

- "An Exceptional read!" A Second Spring is extremely well written and I love the way the author wrote the story from the viewpoint of the characters.

- "This novel is a perfect summer read! The author tells a charming tale about the perils of love and how love can maim and revitalize the human soul.
The author excels in developing strong, dignified, and authentic characters. Avantika was the strongest of these characters and quickly became my favorite character." By an Amazon reader.

- "Touching. 'Second Spring' is a very gripping book that would take everyone to old and fond memories.
The language and the story build up is fantastic and par excellence.
Definitely a must read for people with taste to romance and love!" By

another reader…

- "A second chance sometimes a blessing or sometimes a curse/a lesson to be learned. In Avantika's life both happened and even a courageous person can't hold their tears for so." By Murali Thirumalai

- "A fresh take and a nice holiday book indeed, just curl up, this winter and read the book with a nice cup of hot cocoa. " By Dhara Kothari

- "First, I applaud you for the topics you have taken up of present day world & its intricacies, i.e. Single Mother, confident, smart, helpful, hardworking but Lady Boss and her traditional values.

Avantika is progressive, practical, fun loving, and determined person, with calculative brains. I really got involved with her and emotions" By Nandita Tiwari

- "It enjoys its own story-line and characters. Yet, it fits into the thematic mold of modern Indian women's writing rather well." By Sakshi Nanda

- "Second Spring, as the name suggests, is about grabbing at the second chance that life offers you. It is a good book for those who love romances with melodramatic twists and turns." By Madhuri Maitra

To
my Aryaman,
'you never failed to bring sunshine in my life…'
Love, Mom

PART I

CHAPTER ONE

Avantika

I got up with the first ring of the alarm at 4:30 a.m. To be honest, I didn't sleep at all. I tossed and turned all night, and kept looking at the clock every thirty minutes or so. I yawned broadly, stretched, and let out a long, exasperated sigh as I did my best to come to life. It was actually a relief to get up and get started.

With practiced precision, I showered under the hot spray, letting the liquid alarm clock awaken my senses. It was still dark outside when I dressed, but I knew it was going to be a dry, arid day. There had been no rain after the initial monsoon showers had hit Mumbai like a bolt of cosmic fury. The torrential downpour lasted a week, only to disappear without a trace, leaving us to swelter and wonder about its return.

I turned to look at the other side of the bed where my five-year-old son, Aarav, was still fast asleep. So, he had sneaked here in again. I knew it was a good idea to finish getting everything ready for the day before I roused him. The priority for the day's agenda was to drop Aarav off at my cousin's before leaving for a business meeting with clients in Pune.

There was a bizarre silence while I walked toward the kitchen, passing through the corridor that had two bedrooms on each side. Those rooms were occupied by my oldies, my aunts in their seventies, who needed care in their old age. However, this morning, they were visiting with a friend to celebrate the birth of their grandchild. Baku, my maid, had also accompanied them and Aarav's governess was on vacation. So, this meant only Aarav and I were at home.

We had a spacious apartment, by Bombay (Mumbai's) terms. With five bedrooms, large kitchen, dining area, balcony, and terrace, there was plenty of space for our needs. The central part of the apartment faced west, overlooking marshland and the cerulean beauty of the Arabian Sea. The dancing breeze from the water kept our home cooler in the morning and evening, and treated us to abundant warmth in the afternoon from the hot sun. There was a large study that I had converted into my home office. It provided me with much-needed privacy when I was working.

The important part of the home was the maid's room and the kitchen that occupied a small section of the apartment and was next to the entrance. It is important to note this, Baku, my maid mattered to me was a big contributor to my personal happiness. Her love for Aarav and her dedication toward our family made my life very comfortable. Otherwise, without her, my life—the personal one as well as the professional one—would have been miserable, as I had experienced while watching my couple of friends' lives closely.

Aarav's room was next to the master suite. Although it was done relatively well, in his favorite theme of *Spiderman*, he wasn't happy to leave Mommy's side. He would sneak into my bed almost every other night. He told me it was the spooky ghost that drove him out of bed. I wasn't sure if that was just a convenient excuse to be near me or if something was actually torturing him in his sleep.

I knew we wouldn't have time to eat on the way to Pune via my cousin's, so I decided to pack up a to-go meal for us to munch on. I quickly fixed a cheese sandwich and stuffed it into a plastic bag. Before turning off the lights in kitchen, I snagged a chocolate milk pack for Aarav to drink in the car on the way. After quickly looking at the clock, I had a few minutes left, so I decided to make myself some tea, my favorite.

While that heated on the stove, I pulled up my trolley bag, Aarav's bag of clothes for the day, and all of the other assorted essentials, including our travel food. Then, I gently picked up

Aarav, who was still asleep, before leaving the house. I wasn't sure how I was going to manage carrying a child on my shoulder, three bags, and a travel mug of chai tea, but somehow I managed. I always did. I got to the elevator just in time to catch it down to the basement parking lot.

Aarav stirred a bit, waking up in my arms. I gently slid him down my body to the ground, and he rubbed his sleepy face into my skirt until he was finally awake enough to look up at me.

"Hey, baby. Good morning. You want to walk by yourself like a big boy? Mommy has lots of stuff to carry," I cajoled him.

Thankfully, he was on his best behavior. He nodded sleepily, but immediately agreed to walk. My little gentleman even volunteered to open the car door.

After making sure Aarav was buckled in, happily sipping his chocolate milk and eating his sandwich, and had his favorite book to read, I took a moment to refocus on what needed to be done for the day one more time to make sure I wasn't forgetting anything.

Drat the man. Why couldn't my driver have found a moment before eleven-freaking-p.m. last night to tell me he was not going to be able to make it today? Naturally, I didn't want to disturb Wendy, my secretary, for another car service or driver at that late hour, so here I was, driving myself to work.

It's an unwritten code with me that whenever someone ditches me at the last minute or by my own hand, I prefer to do the damage control myself without disturbing others. After all, this was one of the traits (not wasting time or backtracking on commitments) that contributed to my journey towards becoming the Managing Director of the much-respected Castell and Kendall Bank.

Before driving off, I decided to make a quick reminder call to my new colleague, Rohan, knowing full well he might not be ready. Reminding him was hugely important. If there was something I was truly paranoid about, it was timing and commitment. It didn't matter if it was one minute or thirty minutes, late meant late.

It was about a year ago when I met Rohan Rana—Rohan for short—for the first time.

Actually, our first encounter occurred on a very strange note.

It was one of those difficult days where nothing seemed to go right. As a routine, my car was stuck in the gridlock after the Kherwadi traffic signal on the Western Express Highway. I was trying to relax with my eyes closed and listened to the soft music in the car. However, my over-enthusiastic mind wouldn't keep quiet or still. Every couple of minutes or so, my mind would return to my office work and my "to do" list, which was comprised of planning the next day's strategy. We had a morning meeting scheduled at one of the leading banks that we wanted to partner with for rolling out joint services. Although policies are mainly defined by the central bank, each bank chooses their process of implementing them. I had prepared for the presentation and related strategy, knowing their top management's preference and comfort that would gel well with our strength in rolling out the services. Also, I was overthinking in my mind to see if any example could be replaced with something better to convince the bank more easily.

My thoughts were interrupted when my driver began muttering. Bheem, my driver, usually only did that when someone got in his way, fully letting his frustration and anger out for me to hear. I had learned to ignore him for the most part.

After a couple of minutes, though, his mutterings started to get too loud to ignore. I couldn't bear any more, as it was breaking my thought process.

"What is the matter, Bheem?" I finally asked him.

"Ma'am, those two boys on red bikes are troubling me..." He pointed over to the right side.

"What trouble?" I asked him.

He ignored my question and continued, "I will teach them now."

"Bheem, don't act like a real Bheem," I snapped angrily. Once in a while, I needed to remind him that he was not the superhero character depicted in the epic *Mahabharata*.

He didn't reply.

One of the bike riders was wearing a helmet, so I couldn't see his face properly, but I could make out that he was a young, office-going man in glasses who was shouting something at us. He brought his bike closer to the car and tried to make an attempt to talk. And now, Bheem also gained some courage and started replying back.

The person sitting on the back seat of the bike was a tall and breathtakingly handsome man, if I do say so. It was unusual for me to remember what someone was wearing on a first meeting, but I still see it clear as day when it comes to him. He was dressed in a blue formal shirt and dark grey trousers that hugged him in all the right places. His sleeves were rolled up to the elbow. There was a matching tie popping out of his shirt pocket at the left side.

He was leaning towards the front guy and saying something. His companion was getting charged up and increasing his attack.

I rolled down my windows, waved to them, and asked them to talk to me. "What's the matter?" I asked.

"Your driver cut us off in the lane and my bike almost got trapped with the car coming from the other side," he said, finishing in one quick sentence.

Just to end the matter, I asked Bheem to apologize to them.

Now, Bheem was reluctant. "I will not."

Again, I insisted.

He hung his head and said, "Sorry."

The two men didn't hear him.

Again, the person in front was getting louder.

I told him, "He said he was sorry; now, enough!"

"Hey, lady, what is your problem? We're dealing directly with this arrogant driver!" the young man who was in the back said.

Without thinking, I shouted, "Yes, it is my problem. My five-year-old son is waiting for me at home and I need to reach him as soon as I can. I do wish not to spend my time or energy here, arguing over this petty issue," I said all in one go.

He paused, leaned forward, and said, "Whatever. We will take this driver to the police and teach him a lesson," he replied.

Now I knew that he was on an ego trip. He wouldn't back down.

"By all means, please take down my car number and report it to whomever you wish," I said angrily and rolled up my window.

I picked up a magazine from the pocket behind the driver's seat so I could pretend to read and avoid his face. I could see from the corner of my eyes that the young man in the back seat was turning red.

I tried to look at my magazine, but my mind was thinking of him. I wondered what that attractive guy was doing in the corporate world. He should have been in the entertainment business, up on the silver screen, on the pages of a magazine. Anywhere but in a glass office confined to nine to five corporate jobs.

After a few moments, I glanced outside. He was looking at me. Our eyes met for a second, and then I quickly went back to my magazine.

I could see from the corner of my eye that the young man in the back seat had started moving more into his position. He pulled at the bike driver by holding his shoulder. The driver removed his helmet and listened in silence to what the man seated behind him told him in his ear. I could see their faces change and they were silent for some moments. The driver changed the angle of the bike and shifted into another lane.

I was wondering what must have happened. Why didn't they say anything as they simply moved away? Anyway, I shook off the incident and returned to my magazine.

I was determined not to lift my head and meet his eyes again. I picked up an unfinished romance novel from my bag to read.

***

The next day, as we passed the junction where the previous day's incident took place, the whole ordeal ran through my mind like a movie scene. I recollected the handsome man who was in the back seat and his piercing eyes that seemed to see right through me and touch me deeply.

When I entered my client's office, I saw a red bike in the parking lot.

A thought crossed my mind and the very next moment, I brushed aside as one of those silly daydreams.

Although I had come across many good-looking guys in the course of my career, he was the only one who had registered so indelibly in my memory bank.

I reached my client's place in time. After we had all settled down in the conference room, I started my presentation.

I had barely finished my first slide when a young man hurriedly entered into the conference room, muttering, "Sorry."

He took his place and turned toward me.

My heart felt as though it had stopped beating and I had to force my eyes to blink at the sight before me. It was the same handsome young man who had been on the bike last evening. Our gazes met and locked for seconds.

Oh gosh! I was thinking of this devil the whole morning and he is here, I thought to myself.

He looked surprised, but waved and smiled.

I said to myself, *So he is now part of the new client's team.*

I wasn't sure how he would take my arrogance from the previous evening. I wasn't sure of either his position or of his influence on the deal.

I pulled myself together and smiled back at him, restarting my presentation.

"Good morning. Before I continue, let's introduce ourselves briefly."

After I finished, he gave a friendly smile and said, "Morning, ma'am. Rohan Rana, working on research and design activity in this team and working with you in this project," he said, finishing.

I let out a sigh of relief, seeing there were no bad vibes between us.

During our tea break, Rohan came to me with his coffee cup. I was the first to speak.

"So, Rohan, did you file a report with the police last evening?" I asked playfully.

His eyes widened. "Of course not! You know it was said in a fit of anger." He looked straight into my eyes and rewarded me with a playful smile of his own. "You know…" He paused for a moment and then continued. "When you mentioned your little son yesterday, I remembered when I was that age, how eagerly I would wait for my mother to return from the college where she was teaching. I would finish my school at one p.m. and she would finish by three p.m. Those two hours were very long for me when I was a boy." He waited a moment, and then added, "I asked my friend to let go of the incident."

One thing I liked about Rohan, apart from his good looks and friendly nature, was his audacity. I loved men who challenged me intellectually. He was a rare one who didn't worry about speaking his mind, even when it didn't please the opposite sex. The best part was he had either logic or data to back up his arguments. I enjoyed holding small or big talks with him. When he was defeated, he made a silly face that reminded me of the innocence of Aarav.

Just before finishing his coffee, Rohan had made an impromptu remark.

"Avantika, hmmm? Rare name," he softly said while sipping his tea.

He looked at my face for a reaction and, when he found none, he continued his analysis. He came closer to me and watched the expression in my eyes while whispering words to me.

"You know, in Sanskrit, it means 'unknown.' It also means 'first flower to blossom of the season.'"

He was smooth. I smiled at his daring and attempted not to roll my eyes, but for the sake of politeness, I said, "Wow, no one has ever told me that before." I tried not to sound condescending, but I wasn't sure if I succeeded. "Thanks for the information."

He simply flashed his perfectly straight, white smile at me, and we went about our workday. He was filling in for his senior who had just left, and whose replacement would take about a month. In spite of my intrigue, I was determined to keep things purely about business.

However, late one night when I was working in my office, I heard a slight knock at the door. I was a bit startled, having thought I was the only one around. I looked up, and there stood Rohan, leaning against the doorway. He was working at our office with my colleagues on that deal. In the dim light of the room, I could see that he had a cup of coffee in his hand. He didn't say anything at all. He simply walked over to my desk, put the beverage down in front of me, gave me a small smirk, and left.

It was something so simple: a small gesture of kindness and being taken care of. When I recollected such kindnesses, they were things that made me smile, such as the time he'd take handing over the tea, helping me carry the files, sharing a joke when I was down, sending some data or info that could be useful to me, complimenting me to reassure my thoughts, and being more courteous to remind me that I was in charge.

In some ways, his work culture and outlook were quite aligned to a global working style. Sometimes, he reminded me of Chris, one of my ex-colleagues in U&B, one of the leading investment banks in Manhattan. Chris and I were close buddies. He helped me explore most of the midtown restaurants during our lunch. Friday evenings were special for our entire team, as we would all hang out in one of the pubs. It was a carefree life in NYC and was really great during those days.

The feeling that I felt for Rohan was different from most of my friends or colleagues. He touched me deeper with his additional care when we were alone. This type of care was one with which I was quite unfamiliar. It was unsettling and exciting all at once. I shook my head then, and I told myself that I was being ridiculous. I barely knew the man, and all he did was—bring me a cup of coffee. Still, I couldn't help but let my mind wander a bit.

The initial business deal we were working on together was almost complete; however, a small part of the deal was yet to be finished. We were waiting for another round of meetings and fresh approvals as a couple of specifications were going to be altered at the last minute.

But then, the incomplete work remained and, strangely enough, neither Rohan nor his company got back to our team. On the contrary, Rohan suddenly vanished from my business circle.

When I continued on the remaining part of the project, I felt his absence with lack of insights from the client, required information to complete the work, or just to share a joke.

In the absence of friends, it bothered me somewhat, as I could not find anyone to share personal or business talk. It wasn't all that inner feeling, but just someone to share routine hassles to vent to when frustrated. I had been beginning to enjoy Rohan's presence in the office, but it was just as well, I told myself. I was busy with my work and my personal life; or rather, what was left of it.

On the family front, my life was on autopilot. My daily routine was simple— work and only work, seven days a week. Unknowingly or knowingly, I filled up the many empty spaces in my life—such as the lack of enthusiasm, nothing to look forward to, and the absence of laughter—with work. For all practical purposes, my precious Aarav was the only man in my life. He commanded all my personal time or whatever was left of it, at any rate.

I guess love has a tendency to go out of the window when promises go awry, reality sets in, and responsibilities take over. Aarav's father was a former colleague and friend that I had imagined myself to be affectionate enough with to consider him to be my life-partner. Obviously, it did not work out between us. Everything fell apart just before we were set to get married. I had the baby, and I raised and loved him on my own, absolving his father of all responsibility. I moved on. I was a confident woman

—capable enough to raise a baby on my own.

But then, I blinked, and before I knew it, I was in my late thirties. Should any of that matter to me? No! My personal life was no one's business. My time was consumed with working around the clock and I hardly met anyone with whom I felt a real spark.

My professional world spanned an impressive one-and-a-half decades working with various investment banks in a myriad of positions of authority, moving from one strength to another. I seemed to be doing better and better work with each passing day.

My colleagues and juniors admired or, at any rate, envied what they saw. They viewed me as a hard-working girl who grew up in Mumbai and went on to an Ivy League college, followed by a lucrative investment-banking career - professional, committed, gifted, shrewd, business-like, authoritative, forward thinking— were some of the words that had been variously used to describe me.

But was that person really me?

Whatever the truth of it was, the fact remained that I was doing vastly better at work. I was happy and passionate about what I did for a living. I took over as the Managing Director of the bank division that specialized in handling large accounts for corporate clients around a year and half ago. It took me all of three months to settle down.

My work, new colleagues, and professional life kept me absorbed. Joining new associations, conjuring up catchy media bytes, handling press conferences, socializing, traveling extensively, and other top-management-related work kept me on my toes.

***

And then, just as suddenly as Rohan did the disappearing act, he was back in my life again.

Wendy, my secretary, told me Rohan had asked for an appointment. What a pleasant surprise. How could I resist it? In fact, the very thought of meeting Mr. Cute was making me happy, and, of course, elevated. But I was even more surprised at the force of my feelings. I mean, what we had shared was just an uplifting friendship or maybe merely a meeting of minds.

It was one of those rare, lazy afternoons at work when he came over. He looked different. The aura and shine of our last meeting was just not there. It seemed to have faded a bit. But I soon figured out why.

He was out of a job. His position at the investment bank, which had contributed much to his impressive approach and personality, was really gone. A year ago, he seemed so happy, confident, and full of life.

I wondered what had happened to him. But I refrained from asking personal questions and came to the point. Even if the query seemed rhetorical, I asked, "So, what are you doing these days?"

His reply was short and succinct. "I am not working currently. Actually, I wasn't too well for a couple of months, so I went over to my parents'. I couldn't come back on time." He quickly scanned my face for a reaction. Reassured that I was not judging him, he continued. "I have come back now. I have given myself a month to get a job."

I didn't know how to react to that, so I tried to continue the conversation. "No worries," I said cheerily. "You have good experience; you will surely get a new position soon."

He was quiet for the next few seconds, as if gathering the courage to put forth his request.

"In the meantime, ma'am, may I help you with some work on a freelance basis?"

It had taken me a while, but I had somehow gotten used to being referred to as "ma'am," ever since I returned to India after all those years abroad.

I wasn't too sure what to do with him; what sort of work I ought to assign him.

One important leadership trait my boss at U&B taught me was that people always have tremendous talent and potential. A good leader is the one who can recognize those aspects and explore them to the fullest potential that would be beneficial to the team member and the organization as well.

Keeping that mantra in my mind, I guessed it wouldn't hurt to give him some market analyses and research work at this initial stage and later think of taking his profile forward. I wanted to see how seriously he would take it.

He returned in three weeks, presenting before me a basic format for data collection from the market, and asked me to fill in my part. I told him that I needed some time, as I was due to travel abroad shortly. He nodded and left some papers for me to review.

***

It was the beginning of spring. The weather had started to get warmer and I could see the changes in the greenery around our housing society along with nature's bright, vivid colors on my regular office route. The fresh green leaves and colorful flowers that surrounded me had acquired a soft, joyful hue. It was as if they were hinting at a new phase in my life in all their exuberant glory. My morning walks were getting warmer, but not unpleasantly so.

However, I wouldn't be here much longer, as I was all set to leave for my annual vacation, a little tradition Aarav and I followed devoutly. It was our time together, our little getaway from the world.

Aarav loved—well, no—he *adored* travel. He didn't mind the location or the itinerary, as long as he got to hop on a plane, nab the window seat, and see new places. He was game for just about everything—travel, different food, and changes in his sleep time. For him, as for every other little boy, small things counted big time: Window shopping and whooping in excitement at the shiny ware on display, beaming at new people, perhaps even shaking hands with them, trying out strange dishes, generally looking forward to a new life every day. With, of course, his mommy in tow twenty-four-seven.

This year, we chose to vacation in Sicily, Italy; famous for its sun, sea, and spring. I had always wanted to explore this area for its rich culture, the ocean, and unique Mediterranean cuisine. We visited the *Valle dei Templi* at Agrigento and the gate to Mount Etna at Catania and Lipari. The remaining part of the vacation we spent on the beach in Gela, visiting nearby villages. We also enjoyed exploring the old Greek city and its archaeological center.

Aarav was too excited with the new experiences of watching the making of salt and wine. Every experience was brand new for both of us.

One of the chefs in a local restaurant actually educated and gave me a demo on Sicilian cooking. He narrated the history of local cuisine that had Spanish and Arabic influence with liberal usage of tomatoes, olive oil, and lard. It all sounded exotic. They used lots of herbs, which he described to me, such as mint, basil, rosemary, jasmine, and spices, as well as culinary additions such as saffron, raisins, nutmeg, cloves, pepper, pine nuts, and cinnamon. The use of nuts like almonds and pistachios in cooking wasn't new to me, but the way they were used in their dishes tasted much different compared to Indian cuisine.

I retained the taste of Marsala, a favorite dessert wine, in my deep memory. I picked one bottle to bring home, as per customs rules. The only other exotic thing I did during the trip was motor boating around the island with Aarav, with the help of one of the local guides.

The flea market was fun. Aarav gleefully picked out toys for himself and for his best friend back home. He also loved to wish every shopkeeper and passerby *"buon giorno"* or *"buona sera"*. On the street, Aarav enjoyed *arancini*, a form of deep-fried rice croquettes.

We had three weeks to live it up on our self-planned trip.

During the vacation, our schedule was fixed. On weekends, we would take trips to explore far-off places by car, the kind that took up an entire day or two, but gave us a flavor of the Greek and Italian culture we would never taste otherwise. On weekdays, we would do the reverse. We would explore the delights of the city's flea markets, posh malls, beautiful churches, delightful roadside cafes, art galleries, gaming zones, or nearby villages; you name it.

Aarav and I set course by 10:00 a.m. every day. He was on his best behavior, be it while taking a shower, eating his meals, or getting ready *sans* a fuss. The "big carrot" meant real motivation lay in going out to explore new things each day. Each day was a delight, even as we sampled a different area of town, bravely trying out local dishes, giggling over the surprises in store for us, and generally returning to our hotel by teatime.

Exhausted and happy, Aarav would take a long nap until late evening. I would fix myself a nice cup of tea and get cracking at my work files for a couple of hours. Then, a movie followed the work. It was my routine to catch up with selected Hollywood and Bollywood movies during my vacation. Before I packed my bags for each vacation, I would consult my friend, who had similar taste in books and movies as I did, to recommend what I should take along on vacation. This way, I could watch movies when there was no work and Aarav was asleep.

One fine day, there was an email from Rohan in my inbox. It was a bit of a surprise. I had expected him to have bagged a job by now at another investment bank and repeat his little disappearing act.

But this was an email with an attachment of the data he had collected for me.

I began to realize he was serious about my little assignment and so I added my own findings to his data. Satisfied, I sent it off.

There was no more email for a week. It didn't register because Sicily and Aarav were foremost on my mind.

Just a day before leaving, I got another email from Rohan with more information on the same data and a perfect summary of the report I was looking for.

At this point, it began to sink in. Rohan needed more help than he was letting on. Perhaps he was too proud to tell me directly that he needed a job. Maybe I intimidated him. Or maybe, I was just too senior for him to speak up. Or possibly, he didn't want to misuse that friendship. Was I now playing a mind-guessing game?

I wrote to him, asking if he was interested in joining us full time in one of our sub-divisions—mergers and acquisitions (M & A). Perhaps he could fill in for the departmental head until a new one joined us and, later, continue to work on the same team.

But it was a risk I had taken, knowing there were others on the team who could complement him well.

Although Rohan came across as a well-educated, smart professional with a definite talent, it dawned on me that I didn't know much about his actual ability or background other than our brief professional encounters.

It was an impromptu decision to offer him a job. I was concerned about him, although I wouldn't admit it to myself.

At my age, at that time and level of success, one tended to fool oneself into believing that one had outgrown the need for admiration and excitement. Those little butterflies in the stomach, the anticipation of talking to someone, wondering when you'd see them again in person—please. These were emotions and reactions strictly for teenagers.

Although I liked to believe I was a mature and clear-headed pragmatic woman of the world, I was not sure of my motive in the case of Rohan's appointment. I felt it was an emotional decision.

On my return to Mumbai, I got a positive reply from Rohan. I asked Wendy to coordinate with the HR team to complete all the necessary paperwork for Rohan's joining process. His start date was fixed based on mutually agreed terms. He was set to join us on Tuesday, May the tenth.

On that day, I had my quarterly meeting with a client. After the meeting, I returned to the office, but there was no sign of either Rohan or a confirmation of his date of joining from him. It appeared to me as if it was an old, notorious habit with him of taking his own sweet time. But why did it matter so much to me?

At the end of the day, I got an email from Rohan, informing me that he would join the office the very next day.

It didn't seem too professional to me. The next day was not far away, after all. Was he unprofessional? Anyway, I tried not to read too much into his absence nor did I feel it important enough to reply to his text message. We—rather, I—welcomed him the next day.

I felt a discernable positive energy in the office with Rohan's presence. I was not sure if it was palpable others to experience it too, but I felt it keenly. Gawd, my stupid feelings!

Rohan, I could see, was used to marching to his own drummer. He had a rhythm of his own. His lack of discipline was the complete opposite of my exacting, finicky methods. I liked order, punctuality, and perfection.

But Rohan liked to do things his own way. He would come and go as he pleased, although he generally got the job done. On the rare occasions he goofed up, he specialized in saying nothing at all. Not a word of apology escaped his lips. Instead, he flashed his best smile and moved on. And, I would realize that I had forgotten to scream at him. That grin of his was his best defense mechanism on almost all occasions.

Looking back, I see myself for the monster I used to be. I had a habit of bullying everyone on the team. I was a complete control freak who insisted on complete obedience. The "no" word had no business existing in my teammates' dictionaries or vocabularies.

Rohan took things lightly, though. It was part of his charm. He had his own logic to bifurcate into the 'not-so-serious' and the… well, 'not-so-serious'.

***

Before I went deeper into my thoughts with Rohan and his memories, I applied an unconscious brake, a mechanical process I used when I saw someone trying to cross the road without a vehicle. This jerk brought me back from the memories I was recollecting to the present state of mind. Now, I was actually focusing on the road ahead. One hand was on the steering wheel and, with the other hand I rubbed Aarav's head, which was popping out of the two front seats. He was also fully awake and standing behind the handbrake. He was a bit frightened.

When I looked at the clock on the dashboard, I realized that it had taken me around fifteen minutes to walk down memory lane with Rohan. His past memories and his interactions to date were neither bad nor good; maybe just nice ones.

***

When I called, he didn't pick up. Sure, it was just past 5:30 a.m., but I was supposed to pick him up on the way to Pune. We were to drive out about forty kilometers from the city before 7:00 a.m. so I could get to the highway without the traffic hassles. The drive was not bad at all.

I had such a single-track mind. When it fixed itself on a single point of focus, I just could not see beyond that. Since, at that time, Rohan was on my mind, I, unknowingly ignored all other details that I needed to take care of before embarking on the entire trip.

I crossed the Sakinaka exit and continued to Jogeshwari-Vikroli Link Road. I was approaching Powai, where I was to pick him up. He was not there. I got Wendy to call him. She could not figure out where he was either. I pulled the car aside, disconnected Wendy's call, and dialed Rohan. Finally, I was able to reach him. He was at the Mulund Checknaka toll station, about twenty minutes away. I called Wendy to ask if I had the correct time. She confirmed in the affirmative. I said, "Wendy, ensure that you explain our work culture to him well." I disconnected the phone without even saying a formal goodbye and threw the phone on the dashboard.

It was an old habit of mine to disconnect the call when I was angry for two reasons: first, for letting the person know that I was angry; and second, for avoiding any unnecessary discussion or talk that I might end up regretting later.

The thud sound when the phone hit the dashboard didn't bother me. Truly, it was madness. I was furious. How irresponsible could he be?

After a couple of minutes, when I felt composed enough to talk, I called Rohan.

I ordered him to rush. I drove on the Eastern Express Highway toward Airoli. After the turn toward the Airoli Bridge, I pulled the car aside with my parking lights on. After almost twenty-five minutes, his cab pulled over and it took him a few more minutes to cab it out and get to my car.

He avoided making eye contact with me, even as he got in the car seat beside me. I had forgotten that Aarav was right behind him. Rohan reacted with a start as the little fingers connected with his neck. He turned and gave Aarav his best smile ever.

"You are late by twenty-five minutes," I bit out.

"No, ma'am," he said smugly. "It's only been eighteen minutes."

Now, I wanted to punch him. First, he was late, and second, he argued instead of apologizing.

Silence ensued. I was furiously concentrating on making up for those precious few minutes we had lost.

When I reached the first toll on Mumbai Pune Highway, I called Prasad, my maternal cousin, to let him know when to pick up Aarav at the entrance of the bungalow. I spoke in Kannada.

Gathering his courage, Rohan asked me timidly, "What language is that?"

"Northern Kannada, which is a dialect different to Southern Kannada."

"Oh, I see. Is there a big difference?"

"Yes and no."

The mood lifted by the time we reached Lonavala, a beautiful vacation town in Western Ghats located approximately one hundred kilometers away from Mumbai to the east.

I was trying to figure out where my cousin's new house was, as I had been there just once before. He usually stayed in a small apartment with my aunt and his father in central Mumbai. This bungalow was used for vacations only.

We managed to locate it eventually. With a heavy heart, I handed over Aarav with his bag to Prasad, who looked pleasantly happy to have my son over for a week. Aarav's expression fell. He knew Mommy had to go. He didn't like it. In fact, he never liked being at someone's home except ours, where he had his toys, his cycle, his TV, and his space. And of course, his Mommy.

Determinedly, I planted a good-bye kiss on Aarav's cheek and turned away quickly to avoid any sort of emotional drama.

Whenever Baku had a plan to visit her home, I needed a Plan B. My maternal aunt, Prasad's mother, had always adored Aarav, her sister's grandchild and first third-generation child in the home. She enjoyed having him around. She was like my second mother and also felt responsible for me after my mom's death.

Once we re-started the journey, we switched on the FM radio and made for Pune silently. We halted at one of those food courts on the way. It was unhygienic and really in bad shape, as the owner was just getting ready to clean up and was clearly not expecting any customers at that time. Rohan went to the counterperson and asked for the breakfast. I didn't say as much as I wanted, in order to keep my displeasure under wraps. Rohan sensed that I hated my surroundings, and he was trying to make it all better without much conversation. That silence gave me a few peaceful minutes to do my mental planning and strategizing for the upcoming meeting.

We reached the hotel right on time. Both of us checked into our respective rooms and hurriedly changed into our professional gear.

I was most particular about the way I dressed. It was just as important as the content of my presentation.

I could see Rohan getting out of the elevator. He looked terrific in his blue business suit and red designer tie.

It was a busy day. The initial session was taken over by Rohan, who introduced the new products and services of the company and its future worth along with a few charts. The client showed interest in buying that company. This was our initial meeting to proceed further. There were some queries on our past deals and this was where I took over from Rohan.

After his presentation, I took over for the details of the exciting deal and issues related to the same. The problem came along with the delivery of products from the ecommerce company they intended to acquire. I presented more options to deal with it. The client had short-listed two options—one to have a tie-up with a local courier company as a partner. Thus, they shared a certain percentage of the profit, thus directly making them responsible for future profit/loss. The second option was working with another ecommerce company to set up a collective delivery system. This would reduce the delivery cost when they shared the responsibilities. It also offered more control over delivery and customer-related issues

Now, the client raised more queries about the intricacies of the delivery network, partnership terms, and other details.

We decided to develop both of the models fully before we chose one of them.

The whole day passed in a blur of questions and answers, endless rounds of coffee, and intense discussions. I kept glancing at Rohan. He was making little reminders for himself—sketches and diagrams only he could comprehend.

Before I knew it, it was 5:00 p.m. Rohan was visibly tired and I realized I hadn't noticed his fatigue—or mine, for that matter—up to now. I smiled wryly. As the saying goes—old habits die-hard. When I was engrossed in work, nothing else around me existed.

I did mention my single-track mind before, didn't I?

In the evening, I was invited to a cocktail dinner by some old clients. The dinner also happened to be in the same hotel where we were staying. I asked Rohan to escort me. He agreed. Of course, he had no choice.

I changed for dinner. I wore a classic, fitted little black dress; knee-length and slightly low in the neck. Like most of womankind, it is my firm belief that a well-cut black dress is a must-have in the travel case. Dress it up or dress it down—either way, it's a winner.

Rohan emerged from his room at about the same time as I. I saw unmistakable admiration in his eyes. My new look had made an impact, though he didn't utter a word. He hadn't changed, but simply removed his tie and jacket.

Someone fixed me a martini. I asked Rohan if he'd like a drink, but he shook his head and said, "I don't drink."

But a few moments later, I saw a mojito in his hand.

I was curious about his mojito and asked him, "I thought you don't drink?"

He replied in all seriousness, "No, I don't. I only drink vodka."

I smiled at his youthful innocence and said nothing.

His innocence, his willingness to change his career path, and his boyish enthusiasm were all working on me slowly, steadily, and unknowingly.

I went back to my company and continued the professional talk. Around 12:00 a.m., I returned to the room, fagged out. It had been a backbreaking day; a four hour drive to Pune, followed by eight hours of work. Every bone in my body seemed to ache and my nerves were frayed, although the martini had helped me unwind earlier in the evening.

It was going to be an even longer day tomorrow. Driving back to Mumbai after the day's business concluded was going to be a killer. The mere thought was exhausting.

But then, my schedules were always like that: jam-packed, relentless. It was one client after another, interspersed with the ubiquitous preparation that preceded every meeting. Planning and attention to detail were vital.

The next day went on in a similar fashion. The client and department meetings continued all day and then it was back to Mumbai.

***

Driving back was relatively fun, as meeting stress and deadlines were not on my mind. Rohan and I were relaxed. Listening to music and having a casual conversation made me feel better.

I narrated some stories from my college days in India and my time in the United States.

"Rohan is cute name," I started the conversation.

"Really, it was actually 'Rohan Pratap Rana.' Boys would tease me, rhyming my name with the great Rajput warrior, Maharana Pratap, although I had a much leaner physique. So, later, it became Rohan P. Rana, and now, finally, it is Rohan Rana. It's actually a very unromantic name. My father named me after his favorite West Indian cricketer, Rohan Kanhai," he finished.

We started talking about his family background and their culture and he related a story about his family for me. "One of my cousins loved a man. But my uncle and aunt—her parents—didn't approve of him as her boyfriend, as he was from a different community. Once they learned about the affair, they somehow searched for a groom for her and got her married off to him within a month."

I was actually wondering if this still happened today in educated families. Then, Rohan continued talking about his college and friends.

I asked him casually, "So, Rohan, as you mentioned, many of your classmates got married within the group. You didn't find anyone? You guys get married early in your community, I guess?"

He looked embarrassed by my intrusion into his privacy. He was silent for a few seconds, as he was a bit uncomfortable with my unexpected attack on his personal life.

Cautiously, he said, "Actually, I tried, but it didn't work out. I wasted four years."

I said, "Oh, sorry to hear about it. Let me tell you, whatever happens, it happens for the best. Think about this: If it didn't work out after you got married, that would have been far worse."

For a few moments, he was silent, but then he grilled me.

"So, what about your husband?" he asked.

"Well, I have no husband," I replied as quickly as I could.

He looked at me, confused.

"Well, I mean, it is a long story and maybe we can talk about it some other time," I said so he would close the topic.

Silence prevailed for the next ten minutes.

He said, "You know why I was late? My friend's wife delivered a baby boy the previous night. I was helping him get her to the hospital and I didn't get home until well after two in the morning. I was concerned whether I could get up on time, so I thought I could remain awake for the entire night. But somehow, I fell asleep."

"Oh, I am so sorry, Rohan," I said genuinely. "Why didn't you mention it then?" I asked him curiously.

"How could I? You were so furious with my being late. Moreover, you didn't speak to me afterwards, so I wasn't sure if I needed to mention it," he said, further explaining his inability.

I touched his arm for a moment to express my apology.

He just smiled. We made peace.

We, like most Indians would love to do, returned to the favorite topic of movies and Bollywood.

He asked me, "Who is your favorite movie star?"

"Salman Khan, undoubtedly. I was in high school when I first saw his *Maine Pyar Kiya*. I was smitten with him," I said.

I was a bit embarrassed when I realized what I had said, and Rohan noticed that. He tried to hide his smile.

He continued further. "I see. So a macho man is your choice?"

I blushed. He deliberately leaned toward me and stared at my face, taking notice of my facial expression. He just wanted to make his action obvious, as he was now in a teasing mode.

After a few seconds, he turned his face away and started laughing. How wicked of him.

The ice started breaking slowly.

Our friendly conversation made the remaining journey pleasant and shorter than we anticipated it would be.

***

The next day at work, Rohan was visibly unwell. He had a high temperature and red eyes. But I scarcely noticed, as I was concentrating on work.

He checked to see if I was available a couple of times. He wanted a few minutes with me.

We didn't have a formal system of meetings for managers and senior managers in our office. I aimed at a friendly and open culture for our division. People should feel free to walk into my corner office if they saw me alone and of course with a simple nod from Wendy.

After an interview with a business magazine, I went to fetch my coffee and relax a bit.

Rohan saw that.

He stood near the cabin door and talked with Wendy to fill in the time while he waited for me to return. I entered my cabin and signaled him to follow me. He had some data and reports to present, but even then, I made him wait a bit as I answered a call.

He was brief and crisp, and deftly presented a summary of his analysis. I asked for some changes; the rest was okay.

I finally noticed his watery eyes and I called him back. "Why don't you go home and rest?"

"It's all right. I'll manage." He finally left at 6:30 p.m.

CHAPTER TWO

Rohan

It was a Saturday evening and Avantika was in her last meeting. I asked her if she could drop me off halfway home. She agreed easily as she said, "No problem. It is on my way home."

I would like to make it clear here that Avantika was neither a very friendly person nor a friendly boss—she was just a bossy boss.

But then, she was full of life. Smart, savvy, sexy—yup, I said it—and sensitive. She was always on the move and getting things done. It was a common sight to see her deftly handle three or four things at the same time. She could be a brand ambassador for multi-tasking.

When I first met her, I was overwhelmed by her. Undoubtedly so.

She came from a humble background and made it to an Ivy League college on her own merit. With her diversified work experience, she had risen to a senior management position. Her work ethic was influenced by plenty of hardship, coupled with global exposure to the assorted work cultures of Manhattan, Mumbai, and London. I never ceased to be amazed by her energy and dedication. She had two personalities that contradicted each other—one when she was dealing with a deadline and one when she was not. When she was not dealing with a deadline, she had a ready laugh and a sharp wit. Many times, I didn't know whether she was joking or serious. She also had a God-given gift of bringing down a conversation with a thud and saying the most outrageous things with a poker face. She taught me to live with a sense of humor, instead of walking about the office with a long face. This was new to me from her initial impression of "Bossy Boss" she engraved on my mind.

My immediate senior was not there, so I was reporting directly to her and learning to survive in a very fast-paced work environment.

However, she wanted me on her team and tried her best to make me feel comfortable with her humor and unique knack for soothing feelings after the turmoil of our team meetings. That was how she was able to leave a long-lasting impact on everyone every time, be it for better or worse.

To be honest, I had never met anyone like her. At thirty-two, I was still struggling to gain a foothold in my profession; quite unlike my other friends, who knew where both their personal and professional lives were headed. I had been hopping from job to job and had yet to create that long-lasting impact in a single job that would help build a solid base for my career. When I met Avantika, she was one of a kind, and I couldn't help but marvel at her.

She was so unlike the ladies I had met so far; so unlike Neha, my college sweetheart, who didn't know if she was coming or going. Right to the end, I failed to see the shallowness that underlined the sweet, vacuous expression that I had once found charming.

To my own peril, I ignored the warning bells that told me ever so clearly that Neha was not the right girl for me. And sure enough, before I knew it, she pulled the carpet out from underneath my feet by announcing her sudden departure over some petty issue, just a few days after our marriage was announced.

She did not have the decency to explain why she did what she did. Moreover, she behaved as if nothing had changed for her and she continued to maintain a relationship with my folks. I was upset, humiliated, and furious with her, as well as myself for not recognizing her personality. Precious years of my life had been wasted.

After that very public humiliation, my parents predictably did what good Indian parents do. They rounded on me and demanded an explanation as to where my life was heading. Of course, it wasn't anything too subtle, and that also added a hint—a veiled threat cum demand—handing over the responsibility of choosing of my bride to them.

It was easier to do that than to argue. My mom was a cardiac patient, and I desperately wanted her to be happy. As the third youngest child of four, and the only boy at that, I had been cosseted and bullied in turn.

I had a happy enough childhood. In fact, it was the quintessential Rajput family upbringing— firm about tradition, but high on togetherness and camaraderie. My two elder sisters were married within our community. The third one was pursuing her MBA, and was dutifully awaiting her turn to marry after I obliged everyone, that was.

So here I was, working for boss-lady Avantika, and impressed as well as confused by her.

It had taken me a couple of months to learn to deal with her, but eventually, we were fairly comfortable with each other. So much so that I could slip into her cabin with ease and get my work done, with a little help of my charm, which I was sure Avantika had noticed.

The entire floor was taken up by our division. Avantika had a big corner office along with an adjoining secretary chamber. A little terrace, attached to her office on the eastern corner, accommodating a small seating arrangement.

The east side of the section had rows of cabins for the sub-divisional heads who worked on Avantika's team. The other side of the office had rows of cubicles for managers. I occupied one of them. In between were the desks for staff and other professionals.

Near the entrance towards the north side, we had a small pantry and a couple of rest rooms. Since I had never seen Avantika using any of these rest rooms, I guessed boss-lady had one all to herself attached to her own cabin.

Her office was equipped with a large L-shaped desk and chair. The cabin was well decorated and synchronized in a classic

European theme. A neat seating arrangement filled one corner. One wall was full of books, the other contained file cabinets, while a third wall showcased pictures of this hugely successful woman posing with global dignitaries of various sorts. The effect was one of understated power. There were some beautifully shot pictures of Avantika and her son. She adored her baby boy; that much was clear. But where was a picture of her with her husband? Something seemed odd and incomplete here.

***

I did enjoy her aggressive, but nevertheless, safe driving skills when we traveled together to Pune. Avantika behind the wheel was an apt metaphor for who she was — a woman in control of her car, her emotions, and her life. She took her risks, but they were on her terms. And she usually landed on her feet, unscathed. In short, she was a control freak.

Her controlling nature initially made me uncomfortable. But I learned quickly enough to get to the other, softer side of this woman by sharing her sense of humor, and even gently making fun of her. Her die-hard love for Bollywood biggie Salman Khan was a huge surprise, and I just loved to tease her about it.

Little things revealed the chinks in her armor. The secrets she hid so ferociously—her vulnerability and her care and commitment to those in her vicinity. But then, a smile here, and a little gesture there to accommodate others gave her away for what she really was—a deeply passionate, caring, and over-sensitive lady.

***

Boss-lady had asked me to arrange a meeting at her residence. It was a common enough practice with her, arranging meetings and working from home once in a while. I guessed it was more to keep an eye on little Aarav without disturbing his schedule. Whenever she had a nanny problem, she brought him to the work. He played quietly in a little corner of the cabin that she had created for him. On such days, all her meetings were arranged in a conference room located to the northeast of our floor.

That time around, though, her meeting plans went well with mine. I had planned on staying overnight at a friend's home. She lived in the same area and meeting at her residence the next morning would fit perfectly with my itinerary.

Unexpectedly, I heard her voice. "Rohan, are you ready?" I came back to the real world from my virtual one, where I was engrossed in taking down some data and planning for my next analysis.

Instantly, I stood at attention, my previous thoughts forgotten. "Yes, ma'am," I said without thinking.

She did have that effect on me.

"Great. Let us walk down to the lobby," she said, picking up her handbag while the office boy handled her laptop and lunch box.

Walking next to her, I smelled her perfume and heard the tick-tock sound of her stilettos on the hard lobby floor. I had no clue what perfume it was—floral, fruity, woody—maybe all three. But it was probably a classic; the kind that lingers in both your nostrils and your memory.

Absent-mindedly, I took the seat next to the driver, thinking she would drive today. To my surprise, the driver was new.

I looked at Avantika, who was arranging her laptop on the backseat.

"I hired a new driver, as the other fellow was taking too many days off and, most of the time, he didn't inform me in advance." She smiled. "You can shift here, if you wish." She pointed to the empty space next to her.

"I am fine," I said.

My refusal was quick, far too quick. I hoped she didn't notice it. But I didn't want anything to give away the turmoil within me.

On our way, we spoke about the clothes and brands we wore. I also told her that I was going to take advantage of my friend, a store manager, who would help me exchange some clothes or pick up new stuff at the employee sale price.

She was smiling, as usual. I wondered why she smiled at me

whenever I explained something to her. Was it an admiring smile or a caring smile? It was a little strange. I was probably talking a bit childishly. I hoped she didn't mistake me for her boy. I didn't like the thought of that. Oh, watch out, boy.

Brushing aside my idiotic thoughts, I pulled out my phone and showed how I was helping my sister pick out a sari. She took the phone carefully and saw my sister, who was posing with a yellow and blue sari.

"Oh, she is pretty. So good looks run in your family?" said Avantika while handing over the phone.

I blushed from her comment and the way she admired my looks.

To ease the situation, Avantika told me stories about her college days in India. I couldn't stop laughing when she was narrating the stories with all the dialogues.

This was a different Avantika, real and natural to herself, shedding her corporate image. I discovered her simplicity and the hidden girl behind that image. She was becoming more comfortable in my company. She was more natural. I started liking this Avantika.

She narrated a girlish story of a dress exchange and a major fight with her cousin with all laughers and tears …So much emotion was associated with those memories.

"My father also does not approve of exchanging dresses among my sisters and cousins, and, of course, the fights that usually follow afterwards. He always tells my sisters not to do so, but you know girls." I smiled as I said this.

Avantika just looked into my eyes and batted her eyelashes. She was a bit mischievous.

She dropped me off at the Andheri Bridge, which connects the east and west parts of the Andheri suburb in Mumbai. She lived in Andheri West on the Yari Road, while my friend lived in Andheri East.

Andheri is one of the largest suburbs of Western Mumbai and much of this area is busier than the rest of the city. In Mumbai

(Bombay), the suburbs extend along the local rail tracks from the south towards the north and the east. The Municipal Corporation has divided the suburb on these rail tracks into the eastern or western part of the station, such as Andheri E & Andheri W, Bandra E & Bandra W, Kandivali E & Kandivali W. Each one of them is the size of a small town itself.

In the eastern part of the Andheri suburb, there was the MIDC industrial area that is now converted into a commercial sector—SPEEZ (software export zone)—and a few residential colonies. The western side of the suburb contained small residential colonies/areas named like Four Bungalows, Seven Bungalows, Lokhandwala, and so on... Varsoa Beach was the western part of Andheri, which was near Avantika's home. Along the beach, some part of the coast was covered by creeks, a patch of mangroves, and marshland.

I took an auto-rickshaw, India's favorite three-wheeler, to my friend's place.

Alok was at work. His wife, Ash, welcomed me at the door. Both husband and wife were my classmates during my management studies in Pune.

The evening was a riot. Alok joined us later and we drank, ate, laughed, and pulled each other's legs in ways only old college buddies could.

Naturally, it was a trip down memory lane as we recollected the good old days and, inevitably, the conversation turned to our favorite topic—girls. Ash rolled her eyes in exasperation at what she protested was guy talk, but gamely joined in.

I got a few updates on what each of our classmates was doing, while Ash and Alok didn't seem to tire of asking me endless questions.

It was a big group we had in college, and a close-knit one. We put together our combined stash of phone numbers and called some old buddies. We were in luck. Some responded and we talked—it was an evening to remember.

It was past 2:00 a.m. when we decided to call it a day. That heady mish-mash of excitement, chatter, and vodka-based cocktails made it real tough to put on the brakes. But I had to. There was no choice. It was going to be a busy day with Avantika and possibly a stressful one as well.

Alok protested that the next day was Sunday; surely boss-lady Avantika would not begrudge me a day off? "No," I explained. "I have to work this Sunday to compensate for the unscheduled day off we had due to *bandh(strike)*. You remember?"

I was always uncomfortable with this unscheduled *bandh* (closer), usually called by the local political party to mark their protest in the city against a ruling government over some issues such as a price war, scams. It was a perceived political issue to mark the score. Although most *"bandh"* are peaceful at times, the violence might erupt, depending on who was involved. Like we all knew, a *bandh* was the accepted way of protest in India. Offices tended to remain closed if the employers sensed a danger to their employees' lives. Of course, the employers expect the employees to make up or compensate for their unscheduled day off.

***

The next day, Sunday, I got up with a start at nine o'clock. There was no time to lose unless I wanted to risk further annoying Avantika by being late. Besides, we had a serious subject to tackle, and I definitely did not want to risk starting off on a negative note.

I put on my clothes in a jiffy, even though I did linger a while over the absolutely delicious *chhole* and *paratha* brunch complete with *ghee*, white butter, homemade pickle, and creamy curds laid-out by Ash. Like any true-blue northern Indian would tell you, there was just no way you turn down a *paratha* and *ghee* meal, especially when it's home-cooked and served up hot. Besides, I had been living in my rented guest digs for the last seven years, and *ghar ka khana*, home-cooked food, was rarer than a blue moon.

I ended up pigging out, but now I absolutely had to run.

It was going to take me over half an hour to get to her place, although, strictly speaking, the distance between east and west is not much. But the Mumbai traffic has a will of its own and I hoped and prayed it didn't give me a hard time; not that day, at least.

***

Around 10:45 a.m., I called Avantika, but there was no reply. Next, I sent her a text message to tell her when to expect me. Still, no reply. That was so not like her.

I sent another text to inform her of my arrival time. No reply. Now I was annoyed.

Close to 11:00 a.m., I reached her building complex. It was an impressive residential complex with seven luxury high-rise buildings with around thirty-five stories each.

The security checks were stringent. A call to her apartment confirmed that she was indeed expecting me.

Bemused, I compared that strict policy on entry/exit to other housing societies; it was unlike most of the housing societies in Mumbai. Very few high-profile housing complexes had such restricted and inflexible security systems. That was the state of India's financial capital; a big, bustling city with a rising crime graph too, but then Mumbai is Mumbai.

The lift transported me to the twenty-fifth floor. I marveled at the neat precision of the building layout. Trust Avantika to inhabit a neatly manicured environment.

I found her apartment door ajar; yup, the number was correct. It was her home indeed.

Inside, amidst a higgledy-piggledy heap of toys was little Aarav. Only half his attention was on the toys, as he was closely following the antics of Tom and Jerry on TV. Jerry was hammering Tom with a saucepan to a background score of cymbals and drums, something that sent Aarav into peals of laughter. Like most little boys, he found violence hysterical. Madam Avantika would probably frown at that stereotyping, but hey, I was a little boy myself, once upon a time.

Aarav glanced up to look at me and then ignored me royally.

He had enough on his plate—watching cartoons and building a bridge with blocks. I couldn't help but smile. It seemed that multi-tasking was infectious, and inherited.

I sensed quickly enough that Aarav was not about to call out to his mommy, so I rang the doorbell in hopes of being received.

A maid materialized in a few seconds with a polite "*Namaste.*" She asked my name and pointed me to the sofa. I settled myself on it and looked around.

It was a beautiful home; spacious and sea facing. The furniture was expensive, but otherwise, the interior was Spartan. I loved the view. I stood on the balcony. I got an eyeful of the picturesque mangrove forest to the north, even as a cool breeze from the sea assailed me.

I re-entered into living room. Although her apartment was elegant, the walls told a different story. They were, after all, integral parts of Aarav's creativity. I traced his artistic journey from the post-toddler years' squidgy lines, to present-day images of trees, clouds, a little boy, and slices of pizza.

I looked outside the balcony. Although the sky looked largely empty of clouds that day, that is, no sign of rain, which was unexpected of a Monsoon day. There was a morning breeze that kept me cool. The sea was reaching its high tide and water breaking on the shore was making a faint noise. I thought the seashore would be smelly during monsoons, with fish and sea mess. But this was not the case. On the contrary, the breeze was a refreshing one.

I knew for a fact that Avantika had many visitors on a regular basis. A lot of people were staying with her. She loved the buzz of a messy, happy home, and the laughter of loved ones. That vital bit of information came from who else but good old Wendy.

It gave me a deeper insight into the lady who was now my boss, *en route* to becoming a friend. Long before she metamorphosed into her present role of a single mom and boss-lady, Avantika was part of a large, bustling household, with the security and friendship of many.

Quite a contrast to the life she led now; one with little room for encroachments on time and space.

My reverie was broken by Avantika's booming tones. "Baku, has someone arrived from office?" she demanded of her maid.

Presently, she emerged from one of her rooms and found me seated on her sofa. She seemed happy to see me. I told myself to get a grip. She was just being polite and professional.

Her avatar or demeanor was far from official. Clad in casual three-quarter-length capris and a loose, sleeveless top in a soft, girlie peach, she was a far cry from the intriguing boss-lady who occupied so much of my mind-space these days.

Her shoulders were bare—oh lordy, that was a sight never seen before—casual, relaxed, and feminine. I was so used to her sharply tailored business suits at work that her new look had me stumped.

She made herself comfortable on a sofa opposite me. Casual pleasantries over, she turned a firm eye on Aarav. On a center table rested a cup of milk that Aarav had no intention of finishing.

She pulled the little boy into her lap and, in a gentle, but no-nonsense tone, told him to finish the milk. All the while, she was talking.

That was such a new setting and a whole new facet to her. Had I not seen it myself, it would have been hard for me to imagine the tough taskmaster in this mild, mothering role. She teased her son after he finished the milk. "Now, show us your muscles. I bet they have become strong and big just like Chota Bheem's (a popular Indian cartoon character; the name inspired from a mighty superhero in Mahabharata, a Hindu epic) after drinking your milk." She gave his muscles a gentle squeeze and Aarav preened for a minute, then suddenly remembering a stranger's presence, shyly hid his face in her bosom.

She gently tugged at Aarav and asked him to look up and greet me. But he was as willful as he was reluctant, and firmly refused to engage with me.

Wow, I thought. *Here's someone who doesn't listen to*

Avantika led me to her home office, the same room from where she had emerged. But as soon as she showed me this little home office, she excused herself.

It was a neat little space. There were two workstations in the corner, a low Indian-style seating arrangement, a Lazy Boy chair, and a smart little sofa. Behind the workstation was a shelf that contained books ranging from western classics to modern fiction and non-fiction as well. Like I mentioned before, it was a day full of surprises. So many spiritual titles from Hindu culture—from Kundalini to Brahmavidya to the *Seven Secrets of Shiva*, to an unabridged copy of the epic *Mahabharata*. I couldn't imagine Avantika being interested in such matters. Clearly, the collection indicated a much developed taste and passion for reading. And there I was, thinking that only business, profit, and branding mattered to her.

Aarav came hopping in with his blocks and showed them to me. Now, my next task was to build a castle for him.

Recently, I'd done it for my friend's kid, so I quickly assembled it while Aarav helped me with handing out blocks.

I instructed him to fix the remaining block and its position before getting up.

Next, I spied several photos featuring Avantika in her younger days. She looked so very pretty, relaxed, and soft. I especially loved one of her posing with her hair down, and a smile that was mirrored in her eyes so deeply, it was as if she was in love with the photographer.

Unexpectedly, I felt her presence. It was her perfume again. She was standing right behind me, watching at me staring at her photo. For some reason, she was tense and breathing heavily from rushing around.

I was a little embarrassed at being caught gazing at her pictures so blatantly, but she seemed to be unconcerned. Not too much, anyway.

To ease the tension, I asked, "When were these pictures

taken?"

She replied easily, "Almost fifteen years ago. Let me show you some more pictures," and left the room.

Before she left, she asked Aarav to tidy up the place and leave the room.

She returned, armed with a couple of albums. Some were taken in her college days, some during her work-life, and a few with Aarav. She was way prettier in those days, although she still looked much younger than her age. Perhaps it was the expression in those pictures that arrested my attention.

She kept up a steady stream of conversation, explaining the backdrop of the pictures, the people, and situation associated with of each of them.

In one of the pictures, I saw Avantika teaching a class. She looked very engrossed talking with one of the students. In the background, there was writing all over the board. It seemed like some university in the United States with students who had all colored skins. Avantika smiled at me and explained that she had a teaching assistantship during her university days where she taught a couple of undergrad classes for two years.

She mentioned to me, "I love teaching and that is one of the reasons why I give so many presentations all the time..." She smiled and said, "Of course, overlooking those yawns and hidden smiles at times..." As usual, she was her best when being humorous, especially when she involved herself.

After learning about her family through the photo albums, we settled down to work.

But it was as if a barrier had been broken. Perhaps we knew each other a little better that day.

Avantika sat on the low seat, while I chose the Lazy Boy chair. I could just visualize her reading in her free time on this sinfully comfy chair.

It was difficult to concentrate on the work at hand, as my mind wandered again and again to her low neckline, which was ever so visible from my angle. Man. That was just so bloody distracting.

And of course, disruptive to my peace of mind. Why on earth did women wear such clothes?

After a few minutes, Avantika moved to her office chair, as if she could sense my discomfort.

I just hated her being able to read my mind with such ease. She knew I could read hers as well.

We both knew what the hell was happening, that strange connection that was hard to define—chemistry.

Thinking alike is no fun at times. It just complicates everything.

She took the discussion forward, moving smoothly from one topic to the other. It was as if we were desperately clinging on to something to avoid the obvious.

I asked her to print the agenda. She indicated that I could use her laptop to do so while she double-checked the facts in a recently printed newspaper article. I bent over to give the print command. There it was: a sharp, clear whiff of that utterly delectable Victoria's Secret body lotion (I figured that out and its smell later when I helped her choose her dress for PR work). It drove me crazy for a few seconds.

Luckily, Avantika did not notice my reaction, engrossed as she was, circling the important points in the business article with a pencil.

Soon, she handed me the print out. We resumed our discussion. It was a focused negotiation on target and goal. She was tough, uncompromising, and demanding. I was soft and persistent. No, I told her; it was my way, not her way.

Suddenly, Baku, her maid, entered the room with a tray of coffee and snacks. Time for a little break. Aarav took the cue to come bouncing in. Otherwise, he had been busy. There was just so much to tell Mommy and, like all little boys do, he started meddling with the food.

I smiled. By that time, I was used to all that. We had two kids at home: a niece and a nephew. My two older sisters had one brat each. They were the joy of my life, although a couple of years ago, I was extremely uncomfortable in their loud presence. Today, I was used to them. After all, most of my vacations in the last few years had been spent playing with my sisters' kids.

But to Avantika, it did not seem to matter much; Aarav jumping around and demanding to be heard. He came closer to me. I took the cue and picked him up and made him sit next to me. He felt safer with me in that situation; otherwise, Avantika would have shooed him away. I put my arms around him. He smiled at me. I looked at Avantika. She was turning her face toward the laptop screen to hide her smile. She was used to getting her work done in this din.

We finally concluded the discussion. I had managed to convince her of my course of action on my terms and conditions with a smile and a joke.

I took a final sip of coffee and got up to leave. Avantika's so-far grim expression eased into a grin. "Rohan, you are one sweet negotiator. I mean, you have managed everything your way."

We laughed together.

It was time to leave, and we both got up from our chairs.

Outside, in the dining area, there were three elderly people sitting around the table. I figured out that the elderly gentleman was her father, but it was difficult to place the other two ladies.

So they had been at home all the while.

Avantika asked me to join them for lunch. It was a formal invitation, issued without much thought or will.

I would have loved to have joined her, had she and Aarav been by themselves. But not in that setting, no.

I declined politely and walked to the door.

Even as I waited for the elevator, I heard Avantika issuing her standard instructions, although they were in her native tongue. I could make a wild guess what she was saying. She was just demanding some food and I heard a couple of names—*appam* (rice bread from southern India)   and *gobi* (cabbage).

It was the boss-lady as usual. Even at home.

***

The next day, Avantika didn't come to the office, as she was traveling on business.

I found this out from Wendy, who had now become a good friend of mine ever since she had sensed my growing closeness to the boss. She seemed very happy with that development, as Avantika was known to be an aloof person; very quiet and keeping to herself.

That had helped create an aura of mystery around her, but it seemed Wendy could see past it.

I glanced through my email. Wendy had sent me a message about a possible business trip to Hyderabad with Avantika, tentatively scheduled for the next week.

I called out loudly to Wendy, "Hey, can you not find someone else to go with MB?" Monster Boss was our secret short code for Avantika.

"Of course not. It was sweet revenge, since you forgot to get my candy."

"Well, just wait; I will see you," I mock threatened her as we both laughed.

"Sure; see me with a box. Well, no, make it two boxes now," she demanded.

Wendy D'Souza was a sweet colleague—easy going, reasonable, and well suited to her role as secretary to the division head. She had been with the organization for over two decades now and was well versed in its culture. She understood its structure and knew the pulse, especially that of our department. Moreover, she had been with Avantika ever since she took over.

Wendy had worked briefly in New York City when her husband was transferred there for couple of years and understood the global business culture that went with Avantika's work style. With two grown-up kids and a well-settled life, Wendy did not have higher career aspirations and looked to retire from the same department.

She had managed to create a comfort zone for all in this fast-paced, ever-demanding set-up. She played shock absorber when things went wrong from either side.

I went over the travel itinerary mentioned in the email.

"Horrible, horrible," was all I could mutter under my breath.

A flight out at 6:00 a.m. meant almost no sleep the previous night. I was so nervous about angering Madam again that I could barely sleep. After a stressful flight, we reached Hyderabad at the unearthly hour of 7:30 a.m. and headed straight to the hotel. There was no time to change clothes, as we had to go straight to the business conference, where we worked maniacally throughout the day.

We spent the whole day standing, working, and talking mindlessly to promote the business and our product. It had not been an easy task.

I cursed Avantika for that kind of schedule. She was busy in a meeting the previous day, so it was her idea to travel together the next day. She worked like a maniac and expected the same from everyone else.

CHAPTER THREE

Avantika

Wonder of wonders. Rohan had reached the airport way before I did—at 4:30 a.m., at that. He called to ask if he could go ahead and check in. Umm, no. I didn't want him to do that because we would not be able to sit together. I was hoping to spend time with him to chat a bit.

I asked him to hang on until I got to the airport. All I needed to do was rush down the stairs, as the blessed elevator had chosen that hour to give up on me. Luckily, I managed to get into a cab that was waiting on the podium as quickly as I could and reached the airport with time to spare.

He was anxiously waiting for me. Clearly, he had not forgotten how mad I was when he delayed the trip to Pune. I smiled. It was nice of him to pick up on my respect for time. We would gel even better as a team.

Courteous and polite as ever, he brought a cart for me and helped me with my baggage.

There was a flurry of frenzied activity, as I had to reschedule my return ticket at the airline counter. We both boarded the plane exhausted, amidst the hassles of security and other unfathomable issues.

Despite my temper, I noticed, he managed to hang onto his cheeriness. It was as if such things happen every day, so why should he or I be mad?

As I spotted my reflection in one of the mirrors of the plane, I realized what a bloody mess I was. It seemed ages since my hair saw a comb, as I couldn't find mine. It wasn't in my handbag or in the other luggage. I wondered if I should ask him for his comb, but then abandoned the idea. What would he think? For the first time, I was nervous around him, experiencing strong feminine feelings for him.

Luckily, a further search through my purse yielded results. I found a tiny little comb, not perfect, but it would do. And to make things even better, I managed to locate my perfume.

Rohan had been asleep all the time that I had been busy with my little circus. I was a little disappointed at first, as I would have liked to talk. But, oh well, it was still nice to be in his company.

I fished out my Blackberry and started playing my favorite game, Word Mole. For some reason, I could not get the words right. My mind couldn't figure out the word, as I was getting distracted with the touch from Rohan's left arm. That "touch" drove my mind away from getting the words. Due to the nature of the work, we were working and spending time together. In between, we also shared lunch or tea breaks during our client visits. We were laughing, talking, or sometimes just traveling together, which made me feel that he was obviously part of my life, and I had started living in his company. Unknowingly.

Ah, destination Hyderabad, on the dot, 7:30 a.m.

Although it was the beginning of winter, the October heat did not catch on. I guessed a lot of it had to do with the cushioning provided by air-conditioning. If only the same cover could be extended to life's myriad problems, what fun it would be!

Just before we got into the airline's car, Rohan pointed to a girl who was getting into the airport bus to reach to the terminal. She was wearing six-inch stilettos. I observed Rohan turning back a couple of times to watch the girl.

"You know she is Diya, the famous television actress," said Rohan.

"I see." I hardly followed television and did not recognize her. But I saw Rohan and other passengers on the bus looking at her and making her feel like a diva. I looked at his face a couple of times. As the car turned, Rohan seemed a bit disappointed not to be able to see the diva anymore. When he could no longer see her, I felt good in some strange way.

The car dropped us off. We picked up our luggage and headed

out of the terminal. Rohan was pushing the trolley and I was trying to figure out where the cab booth was located in order to book a cab.

Ever the gentleman (and boy, did I have a soft spot for men with good manners, as they were such a rarity), Rohan pushed the trolley all the way to the cab booth. Finding a cab was not easy for some reason. But finally, we got lucky.

Or so we thought, until the cabbie started displaying his driving skills, erratic and over the top just like his enthusiasm for chatting with me, since he discovered I spoke his tongue. However, instead of fretting over his driving, I found myself letting go.

Evidently, Rohan was having far more of an influence over me than I was ready to concede.

The cabbie was friendly and eager to share his views with me on a range of subjects, from the in-fighting between local political factions, to the conditions of the road, and how tough it was to be a cabbie in Hyderabad.

We both enjoyed the conversation, reveling in the safety of knowing we were never likely to meet again.

This was the basic joy of dealing with strangers. Since they don't know us, they have no way of judging us, one way or the other. You could have the most soulful or mindless talk and the best part is, either way, it's good fun.

Closer human relationships, on the other hand, are so much more complicated.

My mind was thankfully diverted from Rohan. But he was observing us closely, even if he didn't quite understand the tongue.

I wondered what he was thinking. Actually, why was I so curious as to what he was thinking?

I wasn't comfortable with my hair. I thought I would make it look better later after reaching the hotel. I took out a hair clip from my purse. I held my hair with my left hand and adjusted my clip with my right hand.

At the very same time, the cabbie took a sharp turn and, in the next moment, I fell into Rohan's lap. He held my head with one hand and pulled me into his arms with his other hand. He just managed to stop me from getting hurt or falling into a gap between the front and back seats.

I held him tightly within the unexpected situation. I inhaled his musky smell. It was mixed with his deodorant. I loved his touch, his fragrance… and more than anything, just being in his arms.

Time seemed to stand still and I was completely unaware of how long I was actually in this position.

When the cabbie asked, "Sir, can we take an alternate route to reach the hotel?" I regained my senses. I looked at Rohan to see that he was watching my facial expression. My eyes met his.

I immediately withdrew myself from his arms and I sat in my seat as far away as I could from Rohan. To avoid him and the cabbie, I looked outside of the window for the rest of the journey.

We reached the hotel a little behind schedule.

The hotel staff was nowhere as friendly as I thought they would be. They were curt and a little abrasive, as much as it was possible to be in the environs of a plush five-star establishment.

I did not carry much cash and I had forgotten to pay for our breakfast at the coffee shop as it was not included in our package. I realized it as I reached our conference; but then I found out the bill had been paid by Rohan.

Ouch! What an embarrassment for a woman so particular about payments.

After breakfast, he walked toward me. He smiled as he handed over my hair clip, which I had forgotten in cab, as it had fallen somewhere on the floor. I smiled as I avoided his gaze due to the strange memory linked with that clip.

But it was so very nice of him. He had a way of filling in the empty spaces of my life in his gentle, unassuming, and yes, sophisticated manner.

I had become an introvert when it came to my personal life. I did not like to speak about personal issues: The man I thought I loved, the letdown that followed, the end of my girlish dreams, single parenthood, my secret love of people, to say nothing of wistful dreams of a large family (that clearly didn't go with my image).

After my mother's untimely death when I was ten years old, my father, as a single parent, raised me. He filled in both roles well.

He taught me to be competitive, focused, and ambitious, and how to cut through the competition without losing the "self." He was influenced by the ancient management guru, Chanakya. He also inculcated the value of business ethics into me.

What he forgot to teach me was about being a girl in love and how to deal with a man you love. He probably did not realize that his little girl would grow up and fall in love one day.

But then, I gradually opened up to Rohan. I didn't remember how and when it started, but it did.

Little by little, professional discussions started leading to personal ones.

Nothing too profound or earth shattering at first. Just this, that, and the other. Small nuggets of information and shared laughter. His love for his parents. My description of Aarav's little habits. He smiled at the unabashed, maternal pride that I had in my little boy.

All through the trip, Rohan was always around, making things just a bit easier for me, be it retrieving my cell phone from where I had forgotten it, reminding me to open the button of my jacket before I put it on, or pulling my scarf in a way that prevented it from getting stuck.

Such small things — yet so personal. And yes, he was my official cell-phone guard. "It is a job that is as addictive as it is rewarding, ma'am," he said with a grin.

His smile was sweet, almost child-like, and innocent, as was his glee in the little things. I had forgotten what it was like to be that way; to live in the moment, not to fret about the past or the future.

The official meeting droned on as usual—meeting new professionals for networking, attending conferences, and coming back for tea, coffee, and lunch with the attendees.

Rohan and I made every effort to reach out to people. "The crux of our business is understanding people, trying to understand what they are saying, and yet not saying it, Rohan," I had said to him in the initial days of his employment.

As I observed him today, it was clear he had taken the advice to heart. I found myself smiling with pride, even as I watched the trouble he underwent explaining products and services to bemused clients with the dedication and sincerity of a schoolboy. It didn't hurt that he looked good too.

By now, I had realized that his good looks were more than skin deep. They arose from a decent nature, a kind heart, and a basic innocence that people like me had lost along the way.

Our eyes met, and I hastily looked away.

It was a long day, and he was tired out by the end of it. His face was red and his cold was visibly bothering him. It seemed to have resurfaced again. He needed the rest very badly.

But, check-in was a long process there, as I was demanding additional service and the best room. Finally, the receptionist gave in and provided additional services and the best rooms reserved for the loyal customer even when I was not the one.

As we went along filling in the check-in forms, I watched him sign his copy. Meanwhile, the receptionist called one of the staff to help Rohan collect the medicine from another counter in the opposite direction.

I collected Rohan's form and waited for the receptionist to take both of ours from me. Meanwhile, I went through both forms to ensure all the details were filled in.

"It is a distinct signature," I said, almost to myself. "Clear, authoritative, and very progressive looking."

"So you read signatures?" asked Rohan.

I was caught unaware. Wasn't he taking some medicine from the hotel staff? Instead, he was standing behind me. I saw the staff was approaching him with medicine.

I regained my composure. "Not much. But I used to read palms for a fun, once upon a time." I shrugged.

"Really? Oh my god, what was your accuracy rate?" he asked with twinkle in his eyes.

I evaded the question and, instead, I just smiled.

***

Our paperwork was ready. The porter picked up our luggage and headed toward the elevators. The manager insisted he had given us the best rooms available. My room number was 901; Rohan's was 903, with just one room between us, contrary to odd numbered given to the rooms on one side and even numbers to opposite sides of the hallway.

My room was opened. Rohan waited, hovering uncertainly outside my room. I signaled to him to enter. The hotel staff member took it as his cue to explain in one go the working of the shower, switches, and other facilities. There was an implied unity in that mundane act. It kind of suggested that Rohan and I were a team.

Was he thinking the same thing too? Rohan smiled inscrutably, wished me a restful night, and left.

I prepared for bed. It had been a crazy day, and I was just dead. My toes were finally registering their protest at being confined to pumps for many long hours.

I picked up the phone to speak to Rohan. "Do you intend on going to the chemist?"

The concern in his voice was unmistakable. "Is everything all right with you?" he asked.

"Ah, nothing much; my toes are hurting like hell. I could do with a painkiller and a muscle relaxant."

"No issue. I am expecting a visitor, my classmate. We intend to go out, so I'll pick up the stuff for you."

I settled comfortably into the pillows and went off to sleep.

I was suddenly awakened by a call from Prasad, my cousin. I wasn't surprised by his call, since Aarav was staying with them, and he connected the call for Aarav to talk to me.

I spent a lovely ten minutes laughing and cooing in turn over Aarav's antics. He had so much to tell me that he didn't quite know where to start.

My eyes were a little misty. I so missed my little boy and, like all working moms, was doomed to live with the guilt of leaving him alone for a long time with different families while I was away. How did I forget to call him today?

Try as I might, I could not wish away my guilty conscience. I longed for my baby's effusive bear hugs and grand declarations of love—"I lufff you, Mommy"— simple words that were guaranteed to make putty out of me.

Before closing my eyes again, I checked the phone and saw on the call log that I had spoken to Rohan twenty minutes back. I could not recall that.

I called Rohan back. He mentioned that I did reply to his call and was blabbering something in my sleep that he couldn't figure out. I asked for the medicine again and he told me he would bring it to me.

The doorbell rang. I supposed it must be Rohan with the medicine.

I got out of bed and then halted. I was in my floral print pajamas and peach-colored top and I wasn't wearing anything underneath the nightshirt. I had a dilemma: should I put something on over my top? My pastel nightshirt was not see-through, but it did not provide the best cover. .

I proceeded to do what I never would have done otherwise and opened the door in that state. In retrospect, I wonder why I did that.

Was it a Freudian slip? A need to tease that I didn't quite acknowledge in that moment?

Rohan stood outside the door. He said nothing at all, but stared at me in silence, at the nightshirt, pajamas, the undone, messy hair.

He stretched his hand out with my medicine. I grabbed it, and then looked at him for a while. He seemed different in his three-quarter-length casual khaki pants and black t-shirt. The black, round-neck t-shirt went well with his fair skin. Very boyish and very handsome.

We stared at each other. I couldn't say any words. My heart was pounding. I swiftly shut the door before my feelings got out of control. Now, why did that moment happen?

I stood behind the closed door, holding my head.

I had spent years battling my needs and desires; I wanted Rohan at that moment. But my pride and feminine dignity wouldn't let me make "that" first move. After all, I was an "old-school-valued" person who believed in dignity more than anything else in life.

After about a good twenty minutes, when I calmed down, I tried to avoid Rohan, but still couldn't resist texting a thank you.

Strangely, there was no reply. Should there be? It was, after all, only a rhetorical message; so why was I so upset?

And why was I constantly trying to analyze his behavior? Sometimes, his interest in me seemed way more than professional. Sometimes, he was to the point and brief. Sometimes, he was overly courteous; at other times, distant.

It is a myth that women are the more complicated sex. Men, too, have their moods and whims. They, too, respond to every gauntlet that is thrown at them, either overtly or covertly.

This struggle between the sexes is as timeless as it is natural. Hey, wait a minute! Struggle between the sexes? Why was I even thinking in this strange direction?

But that night, my mind did not seem to be listening to me.

In numerology, we were both number fives. Mercurial, temperamental, and intellectual, dictated by our ruling planet Mercury.

Yup, I thought, smiling to myself. *It is Mercury that is responsible for the strange connection between us.* Sometimes, I saw my younger self in him.

With this nice little logic in place, I dozed off finally at 3:00 a.m.

The next day was as hectic as the previous one and left us both with little time for interaction.

He was doing his thing, and I did mine.

But a little before lunch, I realized his health was worsening. "Go to your room and rest, Rohan," I said to him quietly.

He did not protest like I expected him to. After lunch, he quietly slipped into the elevator and went to his room.

Looking at his retreating figure, I felt guiltier still. Why did I not realize how badly off he had been all this while? I would be more considerate in the future, I promised myself.

The afternoon passed restfully enough. I went through my long pending files, while he grabbed some sleep.

At five, he emerged into the conference hall. It didn't take much to locate me. He was holding two mugs of coffee. He knew that both of us enjoyed our coffee in the evening.

He settled next to me, looking at the laptop screen. .

"So, the performance grading is good. Does that guy get the promotion now?" he said mischievously.

I smiled.

"I better know your parameters to rate, so I can focus on them and quickly move to the next level." He laughed.

I punched his arm softly.

"Well, Rohan, the parameters are different for different positions. You better focus in all the areas of your responsibilities, as one never knows when it will be useful in future." I just gave all peppy talks and smartly avoided what he wanted to know. And I knew he didn't like peppy talks.

Around 6:00 p.m., we all were closing the conference activities for the day.

I asked Rohan to pack up for us and I left.

I was to attend a dinner with my friends and had already informed Rohan. I also asked him to join me. But he just plainly refused. He wasn't keen on any such boring family dinner sort of engagements.

He informed me that he would be joining his friends in the pub in the same hotel at the lobby level.

Wow, I thought silently in my mind. *These boys have a fun life.*

After an hour, when I was waiting for the car to arrive to pick me up, I got a call from Sanjeev, my school days friend, informing that they had to make an emergency visit to the dentist for their seven-year-old daughter and requested if we could postpone the dinner to tomorrow evening. I agreed without any choice. His wife apologized at least ten times.

It was already 8:30 p.m., and I had no place to go. I felt blank with the sudden time and vacuum in my schedule.

I decided to see what Rohan was doing and see if his plan had gotten canceled as well… that was unlikely, but I just wanted to take a chance.

I dialed his number. It kept ringing. After almost the last ring, he picked up the call.

"Hey, how are you doing?" Rohan screamed into his phone. There was huge noise in the pub. Rohan did sound a little drunk, as I didn't find him very friendly.

"You know something? My grand plan got canceled at the last moment. So I was thinking if you are around, I could probably join you for dinner."

"You want to come over to the pub? We, I mean, my two friends and I are here," he said hastily. "We can just grab some grub with drinks."

I was silent.

"You think this suits you? Or would you like something more elaborate?" He was checking my comfort level.

"Yeah… that sounds great! At least let us live it up for a change. I am at the lobby, if it's not too much for you to come and fetch me?" I asked him.

"No, no… Not at all. I will be there in two minutes," he said.

I went back to my room to change. I kept my jeans and just removed the casual jacket. I was wearing a nice black tank top. I used my colorful business scarf and covered some of my bare shoulders and added color to the outfit. I looked at myself in the mirror. It looked fine, just fine for the pub.

Before leaving, I didn't forget to pop a last dose of my medicine and close the room door behind me.

Within less than ten minutes, I was back in the lobby. I saw Rohan was standing and waiting for me.

He smiled and took my arm. We started walking towards the pub.

After almost six years, I was entering into a pub. The last time I visited a pub was before Aarav was born. After I had him, I was so absorbed by him that I completely forgot this part of life.

Inside, the environment was a bit strange - smoky, noisy, and high on energy.

Rohan introduced me to his two friends. They maintained some distance from me. We talked and enjoyed dancing to Bollywood, fusion, and some western club music.

We had our drinks. We danced for about forty minutes or so. It was about 10:30 p.m. His friends wished to leave, as they had to work the next day. A hangover would get them into trouble.

Finally, after his friends left, Rohan suggested we order some food. He went over to the counter to order food.

After that, I was not sure if I remembered anything. Vaguely, I remembered Rohan carrying or dragging me and putting me in my bed. But I thought it was a dream.

When I woke up the next morning, I saw myself in my bed. I was wearing the same clothing that I had left the room in last night when I went to the pub. Everything was there except the scarf.

It was strange.

I looked around the room.

I saw Rohan was sleeping on the couch with great discomfort. *Oh man, what happened?* Something strange. I hoped I didn't make a mistake. After all, he was my colleague and these things surely would make work life more complicated.

After an hour, I saw Rohan get up with the most discomforting noise I had ever heard. . He opened his eyes. He suddenly sensed my presence and sat properly. He was in jeans and a t-shirt. His hair was messy and his eyes were red. That indicated that he had a rough night.

"Good morning, ma'am. How are you feeling?" he asked; a very straight question.

"What's happening to me? Why are you here? Anything happened? I hope not…" I expressed all in one go—my questions, my worries, and my future troubles.

He smiled and then glanced at me. He was trying to judge me. Was he trying to tell me the truth?

"Nothing serious happened. You passed out when I returned with the food from the counter." He again looked at me to check my reaction. My eyes were almost popping out as he mentioned this. I was in total disbelief. "I somehow dragged you here; sorry, I couldn't carry you properly," he said with a laugh. "I think there was some reaction of medicine and drink on your empty stomach that created this trouble. But I called the doctor on duty in the hotel. He confirmed that it was nothing to worry about, as it would subside after eight to ten hours."

He continued, "I wasn't sure if you needed me or anything in the night. So I decided to spend the night on that couch. I was just trying to ensure that you were safe. But it was a very uncomfortable one… Actually, you were talking some nonsense after I put you in the bed. You were also holding my neck and not letting me go." He was just talking without thinking.

"Oh no! I hope I didn't say anything silly." Unexpectedly, words came out of my mouth as I was thinking about my image.

He didn't comment on my vague statement. He just looked at me.

In the next few seconds, I gained better sense and continued. "I truly appreciate your taking care of me. I never knew I would even land into this situation. Thanks, Rohan. I don't know how to express my gratitude." It was unfamiliar to me to be taken care of by other than immediate family members such as my aunt, cousin Prasad, and my father.

He got up to leave. He came back, put his hand on my shoulder, and gave a gentle squeeze. He looked at me, then simply said, "Take care of yourself."

He turned back, walked to the door, opened it, and stepped out.

I yelled, "Rohan, you go back to your room and take a rest until the afternoon."

"How can you manage alone?" he expressed as a concern.

"I will manage by myself. Don't worry. The hangover is now all gone," I said with a laugh and I picked the brochure. While glancing over the schedule I said, "Moreover, we have a passive day as there is nothing stressful at the conference today except listening to the presentations made by executives from other banks. The last one is from a chairmen of one of the financial regulatory bodies."

He smiled and nodded and left the room.

I was thinking of what I could have said the previous night. I was not sure what I was doing. What was I saying? What secret had I blurted out?

With confused thoughts, I got up from the bed and headed for the shower—a much-needed shower to wake up my mind from that deep meditation called—Rohan-mania.

***

I worked until 1:00 p.m. Rohan joined me and finished the remaining work. We wound up for the day.

At 5:00 p.m., it was time to leave. It had been decided that I would extend my stay at another hotel, while he proceeded to the airport.

He was dropping me *en route*. During that time, we chatted, as in really, truly chatting.

I shocked myself by telling him all about my love life. About Aarav's father. "Why did you let him off the hook?" he asked quietly.

"I was happy to. I am more than capable of bringing up my child myself. Honestly speaking, even though I was hurt, terribly so, I realized that there was nothing very much to lose in the first place. He was not the man I thought him to be. That creature existed only in my head," I said. "Besides, I was looking forward to my baby. It didn't matter whether or not he stayed. There was no 'spark.'"

"You are a very extraordinary lady," he said. "But it is not just women who get hurt in relationships. I had a friend who was a single dad to his daughter."

So on and so forth. His take on life and love were more mature than I expected them to be. He had a depth, he had an understanding, and he didn't judge readily.

I liked him all the more for it.

For his part, he seemed to be as relaxed talking about such sticky subjects as he was talking about the stock market and Forex.

Unlike a lot of other men I knew.

My toes were still hurting and I bent down to adjust my shoe. I did not realize until that moment just how low-cut my blouse was. But even as I caught him staring, I straightened up. What I saw in his eyes was desire—a very rare and much unexpected expression from Rohan.

The easy moments were over. I was now a little cautious.

We arrived at my hotel and it was time for me to leave him. We shook hands, but it was an awkward handshake.

And oddly disappointing. Was I expecting a hug, of all the things in the world?

The rest of the day was far from fun. That hotel was even worse than the previous one with messy rooms and messy arrangements. I guessed I was so used to well-served five-star hotels that hardly messed up reservations or room allocations or cleanliness. It was a strangely annoying experience. Much more than it should have been.

I found myself yelling at the bellboy. "Why the hell does this room stink? Where is this smell from? Ever heard of a bloody thing called air freshener?"

It was a gross overreaction, when a simple request to clean up the room would have sufficed.

Was there something else that was bothering me?

The room was cleaned. I changed into my nightdress.

I glanced at the clock. Only 8:00 p.m. It was going to be a long and lonely night ahead.

I finally nailed down the problem; it was Rohan. I missed him, like a sixteen-year-old would miss her boyfriend for the first time.

Ugh, what was wrong with me? I was too old for that nonsense, or was I really? I wanted his presence so badly that nothing else would make me happy.

The cell phone beeped. There was a message from Rohan. *"Take care of yourself. Don't work yourself too hard."*

Nothing earth shattering. But, oh God, it made me so happy. I read and re-read it. *Yes, Avantika,* I told myself. *You are attracted to him.*

A cheap little potboiler was playing on TV. It was so delightfully tacky; just the distraction I needed. Thank God for some of the Bollywood no-brainers. They were so relaxing. I finally drifted off to sleep after midnight.

***

After a couple of days, I traveled back to Mumbai at 10:30 p.m. It was way too late to call Rohan to ask about his health. I wished I could. He was as careless with his health as Aarav was. *Get a grip on yourself, girl. Don't do this. Not now.*

To my disappointment, I didn't see him in the office the next day. He messaged that he was down with a bad case of flu, to say nothing of diminished immunity. Not to worry, though. He was going to the doctor and all would be well.

My heart gave a little flip. I so wanted to pop over to his place and see how he was doing. Was he eating healthy? A well-balanced diet was so essential with the medicine.

Of course, I didn't go. When did bosses start visiting juniors for a mundane case of flu? I was shocked at myself for even considering it.

He messaged me once again that he was better. That put an end to my tension and my wild thoughts. Few people knew this about me, but when I got emotionally attached to someone, I tended to worry about them. Endlessly. Irrationally.

***

He came back to work pale and drawn from all the antibiotics. But his humor was there, despite his weakness. I couldn't do much. I had to work and visit Bangalore for yet another earth-shattering meeting on the state of the economy and our expected response to it.

CHAPTER FOUR

Rohan

A sense of disconnect, I suppose, was only natural. I was joining work after five days of being home sick, after all. Avantika had been monitoring my health closely. It felt strange, but good.

Over the last few days, I realized I had been getting used to Avantika and her subtle desperation to reach me. It was so apparent, even as I left for the Hyderabad airport. She had been trying to reach me, just to talk.

Something told me that she missed me too.

We traveled together, worked together, ate together, went to the pub together, and laughed together. Everything about her was charming. Her smiles, her humor — even the odd sniping every now and then had a sense of companionship to it. Familiarity, in this case, did not breed contempt. Even her unpredictability, which could hurt at times, did not have an unpleasant feel to it.

But, there was an invisible line that you could never cross with her and, because of it, I realized that perhaps getting close to the boss was not a great idea.

That night, when I brought her to her room in her drunken state, she was almost hanging on my neck with her powerful grip. The hotel staff was looking at us strangely, but in a dignified way, they ignored it when my eyes met any of theirs.

When I put her down in her bed, she pulled me towards her. She whispered or blabbered—I was not sure—"Rohan, I love you. I need you. Please don't go… Please hold me."

She was holding my arm. It was so tight. She planted a kiss on my palm. She fell asleep holding my hand. She was not in her right mind, as I could never imagine that a person like her could ever do this. She was always in control; emotionally and professionally.

"Hold me," "Don't go," and "I love you, Rohan." Those words were piercing my heart. I never realized Avantika would ever fall for me. I knew she liked me, but in an almost semi-conscious state, she revealed the thoughts that were hidden somewhere in a deeper chamber of her heart. They just surfaced with the effect of medication and drink.

I loved her too. I loved every bit of her and every moment I spent with her. She was nothing less than a cherub in my life that brought tons of laughter, who inspired me and who gave me some sense of purpose in my life.

I was confused by her: she was unconventional and I was a totally opposite person. It would be better if I would avoid her. The last thing I wanted to do was to hurt her in any way.

All the fun and games had a stressful undertone, but every time I tried to avoid her, it just didn't work out the way I wanted. I ended up missing her.

We were like a cat and a mouse—a natural team. Well, they are just supposed to play games with each other, aren't they?

I didn't tell Avantika that I was at home and not at my friend's during my sick leave. Despite my closeness with her, I just wasn't ready for her to drop in.

***

"Hey, handsome, what's going on?" Wendy greeted me with a wink. I smiled back. No point in going red. This was just the way she was.

"Well, nothing much." Then I decided to tease her back. "By the way, I missed you, Wendy."

"There is the consummate lie, buddy. It's not me who haunts you night and day; it's Avantika, right?" she said dramatically.

I had no choice but to smile back, although I could have happily strangled her. But I was sure that she would keep this "secret" well.

"By the way, madam is off to Bangalore today."

"Oh, when will she be back?" The words were out before I knew it.

"Well, sir, if you like, I can message her to come back soon," Wendy continued playfully.

"No, thank you, Wendy. I wouldn't like that." I gave her a light tap on the back with a sheaf of papers. "But now, I can breathe easy. I can do some of my own work for a change. I have heaps to do." *Really? Who am I trying to kid?* I said to myself.

"Well, handsome, is there anything more I can do for you?" she purred.

Right. This was my cue to leave her desk—ASAP.

"Bye, Wendy," I said decisively as I made for the door.

On the way out, I could not help but glance at Avantika's empty corner office, which was looking lifeless.

***

With my hectic schedule, I didn't realize how quickly six months had passed. I had no further time to dwell on my complex and fascinating boss, as I was busy updating my reports. It was well beyond lunchtime and my growling tummy told me it was time to head to the canteen before it closed for the day. Not that it was exactly what anyone would term gourmet cuisine, but it was food, and I had to have some.

I ordered my lunch.

It came, piping hot and, for a change, freshly prepared. I settled down to enjoy my repast. Ah, bliss. The canteen was empty, except for one other person.

There was a pretty girl eating daintily all by herself, conscious about how and what she was eating. I hadn't seen her before. Clearly, a new joiner -

I decided to be sociable. "Hey, eating alone?"

She visibly brightened at the chance to have someone to talk to. "Yeah, I just joined yesterday, you see, so I don't know anyone yet."

"Well, now you do."

She smiled politely before launching into an introduction of herself. She was good-looking, all right. And yes, she had a few grey cells in the ol' cranium. Normally, I would have asked for her number before we parted ways. But this time, I forgot to.

Forgot to, or didn't want to?

Madam Wendy had to choose that precise moment to enter into the canteen. She saw my lunch partner getting up from my table and broke into her cheeky smile.

There. Now I had given her something to harass me about the whole week.

But the way Wendy was, one didn't mind her teasing. There was a native goodness and dignity about her that gave her a lot of leeway.

She made a beeline for me. "Hey, handsome, I have some news for you. Dunno, if it is good."

"What is it, Wendy?"

"Well," she said briskly, "MB wants to arrange a meeting at her home tomorrow evening, as she is unwell and wishes to work from there." She paused for dramatic effect. "So, what is a good time for you?"

My mind was already working overtime. So, Madam was gonna be back home. It would be nice to see her in familiar surroundings. Perhaps I'd get to see her in something sexy, like the last time. I firmly pushed the thought out of my head. This was work we were talking about, nothing else.

"Well, evening would do, maybe around 5:00 p.m., so I can finish by 6:30 p.m.," I said.

***

All of the next morning, I was so excited at the idea of meeting Avantika that I could not concentrate on work. I told myself it was a good idea to stick to a corner desk, lest my nervous energy became visible. Nevertheless, I hadn't accomplished much for the day. What on earth was happening to me?

I had carefully selected my best shirt and trousers for the day. The shirt was all crumpled, but I went to the laundry and got it ironed immediately.

My phone rang around 4:00 p.m. It was Avantika; who else?

But why was she calling me ahead of our meeting? I hoped like hell she wasn't cancelling.

"Good evening, ma'am," I greeted her.

"Very good evening, Rohan," she replied, but her voice was strained.

I realized she wasn't well. "How are you feeling?"

"Well, not too good, frankly," she replied. She sounded weak and I could hear her labored breathing. "Rohan, there won't be anyone else at my home when you arrive."

I just laughed it off. No idea why.

"That's fine. No issues," I said.

My heart was now pounding. What would it be like being alone with her in her apartment? Would something untoward take place?

Calm down, Rohan, I told myself. *You are behaving like a silly teenager.*

Even so, I left only after a good dekko at myself in the washroom mirror.

CHAPTER FIVE

Avantika

After calling up Rohan, I called Baku to get me a glass of much needed orange juice. I sure needed the dose of vitamin C right then.

I had been unwell since the previous day—a heavy period coupled with fever and overwhelming exhaustion. I had just come home and crashed. My aunts were busy with their activities, and I did not feel like interrupting them.

It had been a hectic trip and I had little time to pay attention to myself. But now, the neglect had caught up with me. However, it had been a successful stint, and all Rohan and I needed to do was submit the report by the end of the week to clinch the deal.

Rohan. The very thought of meeting him made me feel better.

Baku brought me the juice and hastily packed up Aarav for playtime at the park, lest I ask her to stay behind. I smiled to myself. Like all working women, Baku clung to her time fiercely. This was the time of day that she had completed most of her work so that she could catch her breath and share a bit of gossip with the other maids—it was her way of enjoying life.

After the juice and a hot shower, I felt a little better.

What should I wear now? It had better be decent, or he might start getting ideas. Rohan was from a conservative background, and I had to be sure that whatever I wore didn't embarrass him, especially when no one would be home except the two of us.

I carefully chose a black Ann Taylor tank top and black Reebok tracks. Classy and chic, yet non-threatening.

As the doorbell rang, I quickly pulled a DKNY black and white animal print shrug over my shoulders.

He was early, by at least twenty minutes.

I took in the sight of him with pleasure. He looked great, as usual, and what he was wearing suited him well. It was one of the many things I appreciated about him. He took care of himself.

I directed him to a sofa.

He sank in.

I sat down opposite him on the other sofa. Frankly, I did not possess the strength to make small talk. But his mere presence was reassuring. There was a bond between us that made words unnecessary.

I told him to help himself to whatever refreshments he might like from the kitchen counter—which he did not. He thanked me with a smile. No stifling formalities for him. He was a guy who was holding back a bit.

While he was shifting and making uncomfortable gestures, we discussed his work. Rohan was clued in and enthusiastic about the report and analysis. The deal was very much ours, he assured me.

In just over thirty minutes, we had wrapped up the work and moved on to other topics, like his career.

He told me all about his future growth trajectory, the way he saw it. He was spot on for the most part.

I explained a couple of finer points to him and told him not to forget the bigger picture. I knew him well enough by now to be confident about his inherent abilities. In fact, I would be more than happy to groom him for bigger and better things, possibly even as my successor. And why not? Despite my soft corner for him, I was enough of a realist to assess his potential. He was intelligent, smart, and mature for his age and capable of handling the work.

One story led to another. His family, the Rajasthani way of life, their food, their outlook, their interpersonal relationships, their big fat weddings, and their larger than life celebrations. As the only brother, he was bullied and pampered in turn. Clearly, he had enjoyed a happy childhood, with much warmth and camaraderie. It explained his general air of self-belief and easy, relaxed attitude towards life.

He was very close to his three sisters—little wonder that he understood so much about women.

Once again, the conversation steered toward his career.

He talked about his role, his job, and mainly his salary. He was the sweetest negotiator. He managed to get everything he wanted with ease.

And he had a mind of his own. Despite my promises, he was unconvinced about his future in the organization and had his doubts. I noticed he was continuously fidgeting with his phone—as if being alone with me was disturbing him.

As for me, I was more emotional than usual, thanks to my medical condition. Before I knew what I was doing, I signaled him to come and sit next to me, which he did, albeit with some hesitation.

I took his right hand in my own and put an arm over his shoulder. By my gesture, I tried to tell him what I couldn't express in words. I wanted him to trust me implicitly. I began to rub his arm gently, just to give him the assurance of my commitment to building his career.

"Trust me, Rohan; I will be there to help build your career in whatever way I can. This is my commitment to you."

It was at this very moment that I realized my unconditional love for him. The physical attraction was melting away—just the feeling of watching out for him made me happy. The spark of Rohan remained unchanged. But the silly thought of constantly wanting him around or possessing him was giving way to new feelings of love. This love I could realize was more profound, much deeper than the physical attraction. It just meant to see him happy. In this process, I could sense that his need, his feeling, and his comfort were overshadowing my feelings; maybe letting go of my own feelings and sacrificing my happiness over his needs. This was again the old school thought of his priorities over my needs.

Something very profound had changed within me. I was never this free with the opposite sex. Even with Aarav's dad, it hadn't been me who had taken the initiative.

I didn't realize just how long we sat that way. In silence. But when I realized that I was still holding his hand, I woke up with a start and hastily moved away. What message he got, or what he made of my behavior, I didn't know. But he went back to his own seat.

An awkward moment or two passed before Rohan suggested that we call it a day. "I think you need some rest. You can lie down and I will leave now," he said.

Like a zombie, I made for my bedroom, and as he walked toward the door, he asked me about putting off the lights in the living room.

I turned to the other side and picked up my novel to read.

A few minutes later, I heard, "Should I go now?" Rohan was standing at my bedroom door and asking this silly question.

To ease the tension, I made a clumsy attempt at humor. "And should I refuse permission, will you stay?"

Oops. The silence was deafening. And then he gave me a confused smile as he entered the bedroom.

He walked all the way in the middle of the bedroom and stood in front of the mirror that was placed on the side of the bed. I got up and sat on the edge of the bed, facing Rohan. He stared at me. I was confused.

'*Why he entered into my bedroom*?' I asked myself.

To ease the tension, I spread my arms. We hugged. It was a bit awkward, but it felt so good, like this was just how it was meant to be.

He left immediately after.

I couldn't analyze as Aarav and Baku returned a few minutes later. My little one was full of energy. He had enjoyed a lovely match with his buddies in the park, and wanted to tell me all about it.

For once, my mind was not on Aarav. I was thinking of another man. But Aarav wasn't having any of this. "Mommy, you haven't heard a word I said," he said accusingly.

"Sorry, baby. Yes, so who was it you said won the last match?" I asked.

Aarav started his narration all over again, after giving me a scolding. *My little boy*, I thought fondly. *How articulate he is. How well he is beginning to express himself.*

I wondered how Rohan was as a little boy. Had he practiced his charm on others a child? Was he a good little boy—no, he couldn't have been one. Something told me he was very determined to have his own way. But he must have been so very pleasant in getting things down, that no one would ever have minded.

Aarav gave me a furious pinch. "I hate you, Mommeee; you are not paying attention!"

Oh, God. Now I had really done it. There was no one like Aarav for sulks and prolonged tempers. *Good; you deserve it*, I told myself. *Now, at least, you won't think of Rohan.*

"Baby, you know what is there for *khana*… for food today? Roast chicken with mashed potatoes."

"Yay!" screamed Aarav, his anger forgotten.

No sooner had Aarav and I sat down at the table, than the door opened to reveal my entourage of oldies. They were back from yet another golden/diamond/platinum wedding anniversary celebration of their never-ending circle of friends. "Hey, Avi ," they said, "you will never guess what the Banerjee's son presented them with."

Soon, the noise was all-encompassing; laughter and chatter abounded. Thank God for normalcy. Thank God for family.

I didn't really need anyone else, did I?

The next morning, I woke up anxious and confused. Whatever had transpired between Rohan and me—should it have happened at all? I tried to justify his awkwardness to myself. Hugging friends was routine enough for me; it was simply that Rohan hailed from a conservative background and was not quite used to it.

Who are you kidding, Avantika? said that nagging little voice in my head. It was attraction at its most elemental that had motivated the hug.

Now I was truly worried. Whatever there was between us, he was not the right person, nor was it an appropriate situation for a woman of my experience to find herself in. If I had learned anything about men, especially Indian men, it was that it didn't take much for them to presume a lady was theirs for the taking. Whereas I, despite all the trappings of being a modern, independent woman of the world, had always been restrained and cautious in my relationships. So, why this change of behavior for Rohan? Why this unconditional acceptance that overrode my sense of survival? Had he misunderstood me?

Either way, this would prove to be the turning point in our relationship. Something had changed between us. Unacknowledged and unspoken, but real all the same.

It was with some hesitation that I rang him up for an update on another client.

"Avi—Avantika," he began.

Well, this was new. He never referred to me by my first name.

Unusual in more ways than one, I thought, bemused. Indian culture, like most, is formal, structured, and hierarchical. You refer to older people as sir or ma'am. This new-fangled corporate practice of referring to seniors by their first name was yet another instance of mindlessly aping the west, something that I have honestly never been comfortable with. Despite their apparent friendliness and easy-going ways, people in the west are fully aware that frankness does not equal familiarity. Each person has a role to play—personally and professionally—and there is a line never to be crossed. And each one is expected to behave accordingly with a sense of responsibility missing out here. It is precisely the absence of this corollary that makes it laughable to adopt this approach in our work environment.

Perhaps Rohan remembered my views on the subject. Hence the immediate revival of a professional tone. "Good afternoon, ma'am," he said briskly.

True to his nature, he was confused and unsure of what he wanted for himself. But I could sense that he was not quite okay.

I barely listened to the details of the latest deal, even as he signed off with a formal "Have a good day."

In the coming week, I would not see much of Rohan, as he was traveling to Pune to meet a client.

I would miss him for sure, but the doubts would not let up. Perhaps this distance was just as well. It would give both of us time to think.

Just a day before his coming back from his office trip, he sent me a text message telling me he had to help out a friend on an urgent matter. *Typical,* I thought to myself. He was always like this, on-and-off.

As things turned out, yet again, Wendy arranged for another meeting between us at home. I had no choice. Aarav had just been vaccinated and he was cranky and feverish. I had to stay back with him.

Damn Wendy, but then, how was she to know?

I decided to play it cool and formal.

This time, I deliberately ensured that Aarav and my band of oldies were around, in addition to a public relations executive who had some files to show me. Additionally, she had arranged a photo shoot for an upcoming business magazine.

I carefully selected a formal *salwar-kameez* to wear. All the better to put everyone at ease.

Aarav was sleeping with his vaccination trouble. My two aunts were with him in his room to comfort him.

When Rohan arrived, he found the door ajar, and me in deep discussion with the PR lady.

I went to my room to change clothes for the photographer, who had just arrived.

When I returned, I saw distinct disapproval in Rohan's eyes. I motioned for him to follow me. He suggested that I try a different outfit. I was confused as to what to wear, so I called to Rohan and pointed toward my wardrobe.

He looked at it in disbelief and said abruptly, "Oh. You have so many options."

I murmured, "Yes, I do, but there is none to go out with."

I came out with the new dress he helped me select.

I picked up pearl earrings and started struggling to put them on, but just couldn't. Rohan came forward and took the earrings from my hand. I closed my eyes and felt his fingers on my sensitive ear lobes as he put on the earrings.

After that, he immediately left the room and went to living room and started thumping a magazine. I guessed he was embarrassed and he avoided my gaze.

Finally, the photographer with the PR lady finished their photo shoot after he gave me couple of options to present myself.

Luckily, this started the day on the right note. Rohan, who didn't have any role in the shoot, offered his views on how it was important to revamp an image with time, and the conversation that followed was comfortable and animated. Both the PR lady and the photographer happily confirmed that view. That made me comfortable with the shoot and photo selection. Now I didn't have to go through this process for at least a year.

Once the shooting was done, the PR lady and the photographer packed up. Before leaving, both assured me they would send their respective work to review.

When they reached the door, Rohan and I went to see them off. I mentioned, "It would be a good idea if you keep Rohan cc'd in the mail."

"Sure," both replied at the same time. We smiled and left with a goodbye handshake.

Now another task was reviewing Rohan's presentation on the acquisition strategy of "Mix-n-Match," a renowned upcoming online retail firm for Rohan's Pune-based client.

It was almost 1.00 p.m. I was hungry. It was a good idea to work on a happy stomach.

Great! Perhaps he would join us for lunch? He agreed with a grin.

A sense of relief filled my heart as I served him my trademark *dal*, fried rice and other Indian dishes. Thank God, we were laughing together again. I teased him for his radical views on revamping our brand image. He smiled back and helped himself to some Bengali-style veggies cooked with poppy seed paste. "The salad is great. Did you add *'tadaka'* to the diced cucumbers and tomatoes?" he queried to my delight. "I love the salad seasoning made of crackling mustard seeds, curry leaves, and green chili in hot cooking oil."

"Yea, it is called *koshimbiri, a* kind of salad in Kannada," I said demurely.

I tasted the salad from my dish and it had no salt. I looked at him in disbelief. I asked Rohan, "You didn't notice that there was no salt?"

"Well, no. It was tasty otherwise. I didn't know it required salt," he said sweetly.

I gave him a punch on his arm and fetched the salt shaker to add it to his salad.

"Wow! You mean you can actually cook?"

"Yes, Rohan. In fact, I am a very keen cook. I love trying out new recipes whenever I get the time."

"Seriously?" He gaped at me.

I saw him relishing the simple homemade food. I just loved watching him eating, or rather, enjoying it.

It was a quiet lunch, but his presence made all the difference to me. All in all, a fun lunch.

Lunch done, we put our heads together for a presentation that he was supposed to make the following week.

I listened to him with rapt attention. This guy, he sure had done his homework, unlike others his age who just did so much and no more. But Rohan had made note of the client's feedback with meticulous care. I was impressed.

We went out to visit a client at 3:00 p.m. and the meeting lasted for a couple of hours. When we walked out of their office, it was almost six o'clock in the evening.

"That was great, Rohan," I said with a smile. "You have your finger on the client's pulse."

"Thanks, ma'am. I aim to please." He bowed with a dramatic flourish.

We burst out laughing. Before I could stop them, the words were out of my mouth.

"All work and no play make Jack a dull boy. Why don't I take you out for dinner and drinks at Indyaki? I hear they do some great sizzlers."

Rohan looked me straight in the eye. I could see clearly he wasn't displeased; far from it. But he refused all the same. "That would be lovely," he said with sincere regret. "But I have to meet my old buddy who is leaving for another place. It's important." I could see it was a sheer fib.

"So important that you would forego dinner with me?" I said playfully.

The hooded look that I had come to dread came back. He was uncomfortable, and I could have kicked myself for it.

CHAPTER SIX

Rohan

It was a Friday evening in October and I was already in a weekend mood. I thought of leaving early to catch up with a few friends at the pub. As I prepared to pack up, my phone rang. It was Wendy. Boss-lady requested my presence. Immediately!

Ugh. All my dreams of a drink with the boys went up in smoke.

Is it every boss' specialty that they can sense their employee's plan and figure out how to blow it up?

I reached Avantika's chamber. She was in a conference that she excused herself from as soon as she saw me.

"Rohan, there is an emergency, and I need your help," she said apologetically.

"Sure, ma'am; tell me."

"I need to attend a business party directly. Actually, I forgot about it, and I, ummmm..." She stared at her business suit.

"You need me to pick up some appropriate eveningwear from your home?" I smiled.

"Yes, that's it. Whatever you can get my aunt to pack. She knows my style," she said, throwing her keys to me.

"Do you have anything particular in mind?" I asked.

"My mind isn't working in that direction. Please bring whatever you and Aunty think is all right," she said. "I need to go back in and complete my presentation."

I quickly ran out of the office building to the main gate and saw Avantika's car was waiting for me.

I got in. The driver started the car. It was about fifteen kilometers, but traffic was unpredictable at 4:00 p.m.

There was nothing to do but soak in the smell of Avantika's signature perfume that seemed to emanate from the cushions.

There were magazines in the back seat. I was curious about her taste. There were a few business magazines, a few fashion ones, and wow! Some romantic novels from Nora Roberts. Bodice Rippers, sensational stuff. I told to myself, "Rohan, oh boy, remember how you had read your sister's stash of those forbidden books during your high school days?"

I grinned. So MB was not as cut and dry as she made herself out to be. Who would have thought that the steely exterior hid a romantic bent of mind?

That was Avantika for you, I mused. What you saw was what you got, sure. That was a major part of her attraction. But she was a woman of many layers and hidden facets, I thought, running my fingers over the well-leafed Nora Roberts novels.

I reached her home quickly enough. Luckily, the traffic from the office hadn't been too bad.

No one answered the doorbell, so I used the key.

There was no one at home. A note on the dining table informed Avantika that her aunties had made a plan to enjoy *kulfi* at Carter Road in Bandra and had taken Aarav with them.

Gawd. I panicked. This meant I would have to open her wardrobe myself. The very thought was petrifying. Opening a woman's cupboard, a woman who just happened to be my boss, scared me. If I survived this, I could take on anything.

Taking a deep breath, I unlocked Avantika's bedroom. This wasn't the first time I was entering it.

Most of the room was taken up by the king-sized bed draped in a regal maroon and gold quilt, offset by contrasting off-white cushions. An expensive painting hung over the headboard. On one wall was a window with matching drapes, overlooking the sea. Another wall was covered by the wardrobe.

The room was hers, all right; feminine, yet dignified. Restrained, yet pleasant.

I unlocked the wardrobe. It contained her business suits, pants, skirts, scarves, blouses, and some Indian office-wear. The top section of the wardrobe was covered with perfumes, handbags, and other accessories.

Then, I looked at another section of the wardrobe. I unlocked it. To my surprise, there was a huge collection of party wear—skirts, dresses, blouses, evening gowns, trendy tops, and saris. A corresponding section contained jewelry, handbags, make-up, and shoes.

Oh my Gawd, what an awesome collection, but what a waste of money.

Obviously, a woman wouldn't share my opinion on the subject of having too many clothes.

A careful search revealed what I was looking for: a formal cocktail dress in an understated coral. To contrast that, I picked up a beige stole with matching shoes and clutch. A delicate set of pearls and rubies would go beautifully with the stuff, I told myself. Thank the good Lord for having grown up with sisters.

I left her home after locking her wardrobe and bedroom carefully.

I reached Taj Lands' End where the party was scheduled to start around 7:30 p.m.

Avantika met me in the lobby. She was carrying a parcel in her left hand.

"Oh, Rohan, that is soooo sweet of you." She gave me a hug. It made me a little self-conscious. She laughed at me and handed over the packet to me.

I was confused.

"Well, you need to dress up as well, Mr. Rana, as you are escorting me to the party."

"Really, no, yes, maybe next time." I had no words to acknowledge the unexpected invitation.

"Nothing doing! Just go and change. Meanwhile, I will take a look at what you have selected for me," she said.

The packet revealed a pleasant surprise. It was a smart dark blue Hugo Boss shirt that fit me like a second skin. It seemed to me as if it had been purchased with great thought. How very generous of Avantika, and how like her. Just as you were left fuming at her bossiness, she would do something that was so thoughtful and considerate.

I got ready with whatever resources I had in hand, and slicked my hair back with gel that someone had left behind in the men's common room.

When I stepped out of the rest room, I almost banged into Avantika. She was looking very different from her regular self. The coral dress was just gorgeous on her and lent her complexion a gentle glow. The lipstick suited her, and thankfully, her hair had been left down.

I complimented myself on my selection. Apart from being elegant, the outfit would stand out in a sea of black and set her apart from the crowd.

She smiled. "So, Mr. Rana, are we ready to rock and roll?"

"Umm, can I have the keys to your car? I need to put my stuff in there."

She looked a little put out. "Alright. But be sure to come back real soon," she warned, even as a group of suited and booted types made a beeline for her. Naturally. Avantika Desai was quite the woman about town; admired, feared, envied, and dissected for her professional achievements.

By the time I entered the ballroom, the party was in full swing. Everyone was talking to everyone, drinks in hand, pretending to be amused. A couple of Page 3 types had managed to find their way there, although this type of party was not the muaah-muaah air kissing type of shindig. Far from it. It was the kind of event that saw deals finalized by dinner and new alliances forged before dessert. The corporate czars were on the prowl. And there was Avantika, talking to one of them.

He leaned towards her and whispered something in her ear, and they both laughed. He sidled up to her and put an arm on her shoulder.

The sight displeased me immensely. The bugger looked old

enough to be her pop, but he was flirting with her.

"Rohan, there you are! Let me introduce you to Mr. Dinshaw."

And so we began the business of networking. I was amazed at Avantika's ability to look so relaxed and interested in all that was happening around her. After a hard day at the office, I was so bored and there she was, a dazzling smile in place, as if she could not have found a better way of enjoying herself.

No wonder she had achieved what she had.

"How come this shirt?" I asked shortly.

"Well, I had planned to gift it to you on your birthday next week, but this was the perfect opportunity to inaugurate it." She smiled up at me. "Don't worry; I'll get you something else for your birthday."

"Hey, no. I didn't mean that. Please don't buy me anything more. I feel awkward with so many gifts." I meant what I said.

Avantika seemed ready with yet another sparkling retort. Before she could say anything, some joker swept her up in a bear hug. She almost lost her balance, but I managed to save her drink from spilling onto her dress. "Amit, you rascal! Where the hell have you been all this time?" she shouted.

And so on and so forth. I hated the evening. Hated all those men trying to get touchy-feely with her. Why couldn't Avantika see through their intentions? If we were here to talk business, why weren't we doing just that? Why this great show of familiarity? I was surprised at the ferocity of my own feelings.

Jealousy, red-hot and searing, coursed through my veins. It was as if someone was encroaching upon my turf. My Avantika. Wait a minute. When had I started thinking of her as "my" anything? Surely I wasn't falling for her? Huh? How could I? She was my boss.

I excused myself abruptly and left before she could protest.

I reached home and quickly changed out of the shirt. *Time to rest, Rohan*, I told myself firmly. *You are losing it.*

I lay on the bed, wide awake. Sleep wouldn't touch me. Only thoughts of Avantika would.

Why was I missing her? When had I started caring for her? Why should the thought of anyone getting close to her bother me so much? She wasn't answerable to me for her actions.

Why did I enjoy hugging her so much? Why did I feel so like a winner when she smiled at me? Why did I enjoy arguing with her? Was this that much-glamourized emotion called love? Or was it mere infatuation? Or a thwarted urge to possess her sexually? Yes, that was all.

No, it wasn't just that. I respected and liked Avantika. But what good would it do me or her?

She was years older than me, and worlds apart. And as the saying goes - without a doubt, "Never the twain shall meet." We were never meant for each other. I would do better to keep myself away. I mustn't mislead Avantika further.

There was no future for us together. It was plain as a dot on my nose. Why was I allowing these silly emotions to overpower my rationality and logic? Not to mention my dislike of emotional entanglements.

After my earlier relationship went kaput, I had been careful not to get involved with any other girl. I was scared of getting hurt again. As far as my ex had been concerned, ours was not a relationship; merely a pleasant way of passing the time. In Avantika's case, the relationship had no goal, no direction, no meaning, and no value. But it had feelings, deep emotions, and strange sensations that I couldn't measure.

Get off my case, boss-lady, I begged her silently. *Anyway, who knows whether or not you have a lover stashed away somewhere? I only know that you are a single mom. Even that bit of information about your personal life is precarious. So just leave me alone, will you!*

I heard Avantika in my head and her laughter seemed to be getting louder by the minute. I could just imagine her sitting on the corner of my bed, grinning at me, as if my falling for her was a great joke.

What are you laughing at? I asked her in my mind's eye. *You have a miserable personal life, if you can call it that.*

A son and a couple of aging aunts for company. Don't you need a partner? Someone to hold your hand and talk to you at the end of the day? But someone as lovely as you, surely you have a man in your life. Why am I hoping against hope that you don't? That I would be the one to love and cherish you the way you deserve?

I know for a fact that you are lonely. I have seen the sadness carefully hidden behind your energetic, radiant persona. The vulnerability in your eyes, when you think no one is looking. You surround yourself with people, Avantika, so the din can make up for the deafening silence in your world. I have understood all this over time.

My eyes were wet by now. Why, I couldn't pin-point exactly.

Was I crying for Avantika or myself? The fact that I could never have her? That my family for one would never even entertain such a prospect? That there was not one single person in the world who would understand?

I got myself a cup of warm milk with a dash of cinnamon, a tip helpfully provided by Avantika. Sleep finally washed over me like a gentle blanket, putting an end to my thoughts. For the moment.

Just as well. There was no way to swim against the stream. I decided to keep myself away from Avantika, since I couldn't offer her a future and didn't want to waste her present. With this resolution, I fell asleep.

CHAPTER SEVEN

Avantika

What was wrong with Rohan? He had behaved so strangely at the party, making a brusque exit as if he was annoyed with me and the whole wide world. It was quite unlike him. Perhaps it was because most of the people in that crowd were much older than he, besides being absolute strangers, I reasoned.

Maybe he would cheer up the next morning. Turned out, no such luck. He looked as grumpy as he was the night before. Even so, there was a definite change in his approach. His body language was different, the "ma'am's" seemed to be on their way out, and his stance was that of a longtime friend who was upset about something and had decided to get his own back by deliberately being hurtful.

"Did you count all the jewelry pieces in your box?" he asked curtly.

"Huh? Now why would I do that?" I was genuinely puzzled.

"No, I mean, I opened your wardrobe and jewelry section, so just checking."

I could feel my temper rising. Rohan could be cruel at times and, obviously, today was one of those moments. "No need for that," I said evenly, resisting the urge to shake him and ask him why he was acting that way.

For starters, I did not go around giving my wardrobe keys to members of my staff. With Rohan, it was a first, and one would have thought that the gesture should have told him volumes about the trust and faith I invested in him. It sure as hell is not easy for a woman to allow anyone such access to personal turf, but I had done so with Rohan. Spontaneously. Did he not realize that the depths of my feelings for him were unfathomable? And that his superciliousness had no place in our relationship?

Sure, he had done well at work, largely on his own merit, and not because of my mentoring. He had that potential and I was sure I would be able to harness it to the optimum. He was involved, professional, and hardworking, so I could think of training him for a senior position, sooner rather than later.

And his mere presence made my day. His being there imparted a strange sort of strength to me, a feeling words would not articulate. This, despite my age and experience with men and life. He made me want to lean on him. And that was risky. Whenever you lean on anyone, you put yourself in their power.

"Bye, Avantika," he said, slamming the door shut. Really now. Men do preserve their trait of childishness, so Rohan's outburst, for whatever his reasons, should not have upset me. *He and Aarav could well be contemporaries*, I thought to myself.

Perhaps a gap of four days and a client visit to Hyderabad would cool him off. Just as well. We had a client visit on Friday at Worli, in the central part of Mumbai City, and it would help to have him in a better mood. Wendy assured me that she had told him about the impending meeting. He intended to join me at the client directly.

Come Friday, at 3:00 p.m., as I waited in the client's reception area, there was no sign of Rohan. I was absolutely livid by now. This was no time to treat me to his sporadic show of tardiness. *Just you wait, Mr. Rana,* I muttered under my breath. *You better have a credible excuse for this.*

"Hi. I am ever so sorry," came a familiar, cheery voice. *About time*, I thought furiously. One look at the million-dollar, thousand-wattage smile and my steely resolve to give him the cold shoulder flew out the window. *Rohan, oh, Rohan, how on earth can I be mad at you for long?* I thought.

The meeting went off smoothly enough. Rohan listened in rapt attention and took down a couple of notes. Even though this particular interaction had not much to do with his area of expertise, I felt it would be a good idea to get him introduced to other aspects of business as well.

As I shook hands with the client and walked toward the elevator, Rohan followed me and turned to whisper to me, "You were great, just great. You spoke to them in their language, and correctly gauged their requirements. No wonder you convinced them," he said.

He was always like this and made me feel good in a very dignified way. But hey, I wasn't quite ready to forgive him for his mean behavior the last few days.

While we waited for an elevator, I deliberately and pointedly handed my purse to him and, with quiet satisfaction, watched him turn red. *Let me play boss-lady for a change; it's fun*, I thought wickedly. Rank and seniority have their privileges.

Poor Rohan. There was little he could do apart from smiling politely. But his eyes seemed to pop out of their sockets, even as I slowly took off my business jacket to reveal a chic black and white animal print 'Armani' top, teamed with a formal A-line skirt.

Well, I said defiantly to myself as we made for the parking lot, *let him look*.

We had planned to go out for dinner, but it was early, so he suggested a tea center in town. Huh? I really didn't like tea, and I was in the mood to spend time talking to him quietly. But I was just so eager to spend time with him after a gap of almost a week, that I agreed.

Although the tea-palace was a good and classy option on any day during late afternoon, it wasn't an appropriate choice for a long discussion. But he seemed to like it well enough. I excused myself to use the rest room.

He was just about to place the order, even as I returned. "Hey, wait, Rohan. Let's go somewhere else, shall we?" I employed my most persuasive tone. *How naïve he is*, I thought. Relaxing over drinks was what he had in mind, but he couldn't tell me so directly.

He got up with a grimace. "Those people must have thought that we were there to use their rest room." I guessed he was embarrassed.

"Now, where can we find an ATM?" I said.

"Let's walk towards the Churchgate Station," he said. "We are sure to find one there. Besides, I quite like the energy of the place." He smiled.

I had not entered the station for over twenty years now, and the smell and clutter were cloying. I didn't want to appear snobby, and it sure wasn't as if I had been born into the elite class or any such thing. It was just that I had lost touch with the concept of public transportation completely.

Unfortunately, none of the ATMs (Automated Teller Machines) at the station was in working order, so we waded through the sea of vendors and jostling passengers and made our way to EROS cinema. Sensing my discomfort, Rohan smiled and confidently took my hand in his. "Just so you don't get lost." He grinned.

I liked it when he took charge like this. It felt so reassuring.

The search for a working ATM continued for some time before I finally managed to withdraw a respectable amount. This was another issue with me. I hated going to dinner without a comfortable sum on me. Not every place accepts credit cards or there could be technical issues with their card line, and I dreaded the embarrassment of not having enough to pay.

He smiled knowingly at me, as if he understood this aspect of his control-freak boss only too well.

"*Chalo*. Let's go to Caprice, near Churchgate," I said.

"How come?" he teased. "I thought you would take me some place swankier."

"And I thought you enjoyed good, wholesome food," I said. "Sure, I can take you to any posh restaurant you want, but none can compete with the Caprice for sheer quality."

"Lead on, Madam! I am right behind you," he cheered.

While walking toward the restaurant, I told him all about Aarav, preppies, and their preferences. Absolutely the wrong things to discuss with a man, let alone someone as young as

Rohan. Had I lost it?

When we reached the Caprice, I found out that the inside section of the restaurant was not open, as we were early by forty minutes. Only the outside part of the restaurant was open. To pass the time, we sat outside and ordered cold drinks. As we drank, we discussed different things; a bit business and a bit personal.

So I steered the conversation back to the professional. Immediately, he perked up, confiding to me the problems he had experienced due to the cultural differences. "I wish I could understand some of the jokes and repartee that are tossed around in Marathi," he said. "It would help me get the vibe better."

Despite his seeming confidence, I realized he continued to harbor doubts about his ability to deliver.

So I described to him the training I intended to put him through in some detail. "Don't let the stress get to you; just enjoy your work," I said soothingly.

Just then, a waiter came up to tell us our table was ready. Well, it sure was a relief to enter the air-conditioned interior after all the heat and dust we had encountered.

We ordered our drinks, and the conversation steered from professional toward the personal.

"Women," I mused, stirring my drink, "are emotional and proud creatures. They need to be respected and cherished in a relationship or else things don't work out. That's why I left my fiancé."

On an empty stomach, the drink started working on my mind faster than I thought. I told Rohan about Ajay, Aarav's dad, and his departure. I spoke of the emotional turmoil I experienced when I had to choose the baby in my womb over my fiancé. "Not a day passed without a glimpse of Ajay's abusive, temperamental behavior. He would hit me and say the nastiest things. I just hadn't seen the violent aspect of his behavior in the early days of courtship. He was charming and thoughtful, and I thought of setting up a home with him. By the time I decided to leave him, I realized I was pregnant and he did a *volte-face*. It was as if he felt

I had no choice but to stick with him, regardless of his treatment of me. Well, I refused to put up with it and showed him the door. It wasn't easy. He created a scene after couple of months. I called the cops. With the warning from cops in a foreign land, he left me in peace. I would bring up my kid alone," I recounted.

It felt so good to unburden myself after all these years.

He listened in silence. It was one of his best qualities, the ability to listen whether or not he was interested.

Could I sense a faint discomfort in his body language? Men, especially the unmarried ones, are uncomfortable with intimate talk. Such talk, a wise woman would reserve for her girlfriends. But today, I wanted to let my guard down. I needed him to know me better, as if a hell of a lot depended on it.

To ease the conversation, Rohan asked me, "Can I taste your drink?" and pulled my glass from my hand without waiting for a reply. I retaliated similarly, but I hated his choice of drink. A mojito, sans sugar or mint.

"Yuck!" I said while he laughed.

"But Sex on the Beach is just fab!" He smiled with a wink.

This should have been my cue to leave serious issues strictly alone. But I couldn't help myself.

I rambled further on mindlessly, under the influence of too much drink and emotion. "It would be nice to share a rewarding companionship with someone. But if I don't find it, I guess I will have to find solace in the spiritual world."

Oh, my gosh. What an idiot I was. Why did I say that to him?

Casually, he changed the topic to his friend and his meddlesome, do-good wife who were conspiring with his folks to search for a suitable bride for him. And to that end, he was fixing himself a meeting or planning for a trip. I wasn't sure what he was doing. But, it seemed to me that he had a great plan ahead.

As far as hints go, it was quite a thunderbolt. A none-too-subtle warning to leave him alone.

He would have seen the anguish on my face had he not been too busy texting her. "We are supposed to meet up for coffee late tonight after dinner. That's when she gets off from work." He smiled.

I wished my innate pride hadn't chosen that very moment to abandon me. "Are you two going out alone?" I asked.

He replied cautiously, "Oh no. It's not what you think. We have other three friends to accompany us."

Now, I very much doubted that, but I could hardly say so. My heart was sinking. I was visualizing his next meeting with a girl, maybe his potential bride. He would fall for that beautiful girl. Soon, he would have no time left for me. I could see the lonely road ahead of me.

I had fallen in love with this man, and he had no idea. I had never felt so much for anyone, ever, and he did not value it a bit. And no, it wasn't just a case of physical attraction either. I was into it much deeper.

Had I misinterpreted the signals from his side? Had I confused respect for affection or professional awe for admiration? The blatant sexual looks he shot at me from time to time; were they just that and no more? I was feeling dizzy and needed fresh air badly. I paid the bill, and asked him if we could take a short walk.

He said politely, "Yes, we will take a short walk and make a U-turn and go back to your car." Was he in such a tearing hurry to reach this woman he didn't even know? While walking toward the car, I was feeling a bit weak. I held his right arm. He didn't protest. It seemed that he was comfortable.

To hide the pain, I feigned humor. "Will you join the business party at the Marriott next week without throwing up at the sight of so many oldies?"

"I didn't throw up last time, did I?" he countered.

"No, but you were pretty much frothing at the mouth," I shot back.

I was concerned about revealing my personal life, which was different from the image created by the bank for professional reasons.

I simply said, "Rohan, I am not sure where our paths will take us in future. I just request that you keep our talk to yourself."

He didn't say anything.

After seeing us walking towards the car, the driver brought the car to us. Rohan hurriedly gave him directions to where he could take a fast train to reach her.

As he got off, I handed him a gift, a popular best seller he had been planning to buy for some time. I had thought the book would be the perfect finishing touch to a memorable evening that would bring us closer. But that was not to be.

He took the book with a cool thank you, and left without a backward glance. I went home feeling rejected, dejected, and depressed.

Aarav came to me with hands open in a bear hug. He had been waiting for me, to kiss me goodnight. "Why are you so late today, Mommy?" he complained.

I gave him a tight hug. My precious little one, the best and most beautiful part of my life. Today, I needed his unconditional acceptance more than ever.

***

I tossed and turned the whole night and finally gave up the fight and fixed myself some coffee. That was far from unusual for me; in fact, it had been years since I had perfectly uninterrupted sleep. The effect of the alcohol had diminished and I could think more clearly. Why the devil had I drunk so much? The details of all that I had said to him had blurred, but not enough for me not to remember what a fool I had made of myself in discussing personal stuff. I hoped against hope that Rohan wouldn't misunderstand and feel pressured in any way. If he didn't love me, well, hard cheese. I would just have to live with it.

Avi, girl, you have handled much worse; you will get over this as well, I told myself grimly. Just to make sure that Rohan did not feel crowded in any way, I thought it would be a good idea to write him a nice, long email, clarifying my stand.

After all, he was a valued colleague and he must know that.

From: Avantika   Desai   <Avantika.desai@castell-kendall.com>
Subject: Professional Concern
Date: 25 April, 2004 1:29:33 AM GMT+05:00
To: Rohan Rana <Rohan.rana@castell-kendall.com>

Dear Rohan,

Referring to the discussion yesterday.

I do value all your sincere feedback and the visible difference you have made to improving the current situation at work and elevating it to an acceptable level. As a cherished member of the team, you will appreciate that the task ahead in terms of building the division with the new clientele and creating a better work culture is a daunting task and will take time and patience from your end. Irrespective of friction, market fluctuations, and new challenges, you will have to take on more responsible roles.

Here's to a new beginning with better understanding and more maturity.

With best regards,

Avantika

I ended the message with a quote.

"When all the illusion breaks down, the turmoil created starts leading to a path of pursuit of the 'self.'"

No reply as usual. That was Rohan for you, the only team member who neither returned my calls nor replied to emails on time. At times like this, I felt—I was being taken for a ride. And he had disappeared once again. What was it this time? Sick leave or casual leave?

The much-awaited reply finally came as I was checking the phone in the course of a shopping trip at the mall.

I wished I had waited to get home before I read it. It was hurtful and humiliating. Schooling my features into a hard expression, I got into the car before reading it again.

Hi,

Thanks for the email and also for the patience while listening to my concerns on Friday. I deeply value the trust you place in me and, God willing, I will do justice to it.

The reason I am replying to your email late is because I wanted to think again.

I am more than a hundred percent sure that we can work on the concerns we discussed that day. Moreover, you have given me more confidence in terms of your support.

I respect you as an individual, as a senior, and as a mentor. And you have been a great boss.

Saying that, I wish to confine myself to a professional relationship, as I am not used to something so comfortable. I am also apprehensive that things will become complicated in the future. I had contemplated quitting. If you feel, even after sharing all these things honestly, that we can work as a team, please let me know.

I can be back in the office tomorrow. Like you put it so well yourself, here's to a new beginning with better understanding and more maturity.

Regards,
Rohan

Come again? What the hell is that?

In which direction were his thoughts headed exactly? Did he imagine I was looking for some sort of a fly-by-night affair with him? Clearly, he had neither the maturity nor the depth to understand my feelings for him. He had, in fact, reduced our relationship to the lowest denominator.

I felt nauseated, used, heart-broken, and humiliated. Never before had this happened to me; not even with Aarav's dad had I experienced such a complete letdown. What made it worse was that it was my own vulnerability that had brought me to this.

I called him. He was having his lunch. So I asked him to call back.

He called, but this time, I didn't hear the call.

This hide-and-seek continued for a bit until I managed to speak to him at last. Politely, I asked him to explain his email.

A long silence at the other end. I could practically hear him struggling with words. He said carefully, "I just meant to say that our relationship has reached a different level and that it makes me uncomfortable."

Indeed!

***

The years of ironclad discipline came to my rescue.

Choking back the tears, I replied in as steady a tone I could muster, "I will talk to you later." *Click.*

I was not angry. I was deeply hurt. I was at a loss for words. I was not sure what to say. I wanted to scream, yell, and scratch the stupid man's eyes out.

Rohan, oh Rohan, why did you write all that? How will I ever look into your eyes again? That email was beyond hurtful. No one before you had ever succeeded in making me feel so cheap, so tacky. I really care about you, in spite of what you did to me. I told myself a hundred times that it wasn't right, but my heart refused to pay any heed.

I am so sorry. I have no idea how it happened. Who exactly was I apologizing to? To Rohan? Or my own beleaguered female pride?

Why have you done this to yourself, Avi girl? Allowing someone to compromise your dignity and self-respect, after all that you have learned from life.

That practical thought brought a semblance of sanity. I

reached for my Blackberry and slowly typed out a message to him. *"I will reply to you tomorrow, as I have some preparations to make for the meeting."*

Even as I pressed the send button, tears started flowing fast, furiously, and relentlessly in their intensity. I could hear the front door click. Aarav was back from school. I didn't want him to see me in that condition.

Luckily, Aarav was distracted today and didn't ask for Mommy immediately. Instead, he was more interested in showing off the new picture he had made in the art class to Baku, and demanded to know whether or not it was a better effort than her own son's (who was just a little older).

"Hey, that's enough of your shining, baba," said Baku cheerily. "How about a *paratha?* I made you a cheese *paratha.* Want some?"

"Only if I can have some jam with it," replied Aarav, stomping behind her to the dining room.

Numb with pain, I lost track of time. The dusk hour gave way to darkness and the blackness was all-encompassing. I did not even hear Aarav opening my bedroom door.

At last, the clear, childish voice brought me to my senses. "Mommy, why are you crying? Did someone hurt you?"

I hastily brushed back the tears. "No, baby. Just a bit tired; that's all."

One thing about my son: he was not a stupid child. Far from it.

He clambered onto the bed. "No, Mommy, you are telling lies. Someone has hurt you; shouted at you," he said firmly. "Just tell me who it is. I will punch them so hard, I will break everything. I will beat them up and make them cry."

I smiled at the dark revenge he had planned for the guilty party. Obviously, he got all his ideas from the Cartoon Network and his own rambunctious little pals. *Dear, dear Aarav. You never fail to make me see the sunshine in my life.* I pulled him towards me, breathing in the smell of his body lotion and the freshly laundered pajama suit he was wearing.

"No, *bachcha*, my sonny; everything is all right. Not to worry. I will feel better when you show me the picture you made in class today," I said brightly.

"Oh, you will love it," he assured me. "It's much, much nicer than the one Rishi, my friend, made."

Atta boy, Aarav. Competitive and confident, just the way you should be.

Even as I rocked him to sleep, I forced myself to think of all the pending work emails I had to attend to.

No use. I couldn't concentrate on work. I tried to sleep and failed.

This is just not working, Avi. You have something on your mind. So go ahead and spit it out.

I composed my reply to Rohan.

Dear Rohan,

This mail is difficult for me to write. Nevertheless, I am keeping aside my ego, self-respect and dignity to try and clear the air between us.

Without a doubt, there has been a huge disconnect between my intentions and your understanding. I am not sure you will understand, even now, but I am trying anyhow.

Rohan, I care about everyone in our team without exception. I am particular about surrounding myself with people I can relate to and work with. That's why you are a part of the organization. Sure, I have a soft corner for you—and I'm not sure why. Perhaps it's because some personalities complement our own so well. But please note I have no expectations beyond the work-related from you.

My caring for you does not have a selfish motive; indeed, at times, it is similar to what I feel for Aarav.

I am not sure how we started talking about our personal lives. Had I understood your discomfort, I would not have done so. But then, you too shared your personal life with me and this is where I am lost.

Your inconsistent behavior leaves me confused at times.

I went out with you just to relax after a hard week at work, and hoped that you would be able to tell me frankly about the pressures you experience at work.

But I guess I failed miserably to create that confidence and positive impact.

If you read my email carefully, you will realize that I was merely touching upon the professional aspects of our life and hoping we could improve matters there. That's all.

At the end of the email, there was a quote on spiritualism that implied that I would be walking on that path, even as I sought to ensure a good environment in the company.

And then came your reply that just left me astounded. For the life of me, I failed to understand why you had written what you did.

I sincerely hope the picture is clearer now and that you would be able to understand my mind and the situation better.

If not, just move on.

Whatever is the case, here's wishing you luck and loads of blessings for your future.

With best regards,

Avantika

I meant every word. I was determined to walk on that path. I felt spiritualism was the only way to save my life for another few years for my son.

In broad daylight, though, the email did not seem like such a good idea. In fact, it would be downright idiotic to send it.

It was my usual habit not to send emails immediately and to rewrite them if necessary after a gap of a day or two.

I did the same this time.

The next morning, when I read the email, I felt that it was not a good idea to send that, as it was an emotional one. With that thought, I deleted the email.

With the morning tea, I drafted a new email, a much more

formal and shorter one.

Dear Rohan,

I will ensure that there will be no discomfort for you in any form. This is my commitment to you. My interaction hereon with you will be restricted to the professional and bare minimum, that too, only if the occasion demands it.

If you feel my email gives you enough confidence and you will be happy here, you can come back. Although I am hoping for a positive answer, please note that I will not bear you any ill-will should you decide to move on.

Lastly, please forgive me if I have hurt you in any way.

Regards,

Avantika

That evening, a client called me to arrange a visit for a prospective investor. I refused. I just wasn't feeling up to it. I did not want my emotional turmoil to color my professional interactions. It was best to lay low until I felt better.

The next morning, it was raining heavily. I said my prayers with a heavy heart, hiding nothing from God. He knew what was happening to me and he would help me. Sooner or later. Despite all, I found myself praying for happiness and prosperity for Rohan. I just couldn't help myself.

Weeping softly, I asked God for strength and positivity to carry on. The situation was getting out of hand and I needed some sort of divine intervention to restore my sense of balance.

My chain of thought was suddenly broken by a BBM (BlackBerry Messenger) alert. I checked the message. It was my client, who was asking again if I had changed my mind and re-organized my schedule to accommodate the investor. I gave in; time to get back to work. After all, I hadn't climbed this high without the ability to separate my personal life from the professional.

For some reason, though, this time, I felt I was being an escapist. Instead of allowing myself to live the hurt, I was covering it up with work.

Someone loves you and you can't love him back. You love someone and he can't love you back. Life is a chasing game. That's why we say there is usually a spark from one side only and the other person compromises and settles for it, thinking it was best for him or her. It is very rare to see the spark from both ends.

***

It had been a week since that disastrous email. I had accepted life without him, though I missed him terribly.

What I liked was his honesty of letting me know the state of his mind, all mixed up and confused. He didn't know what he wanted. One time, he said that he loved my company, my presence. His actions were all puzzling—smile, flirty looks, over-courteous behavior, his struggle to impress. Another time, he said, "The best thing in this office is you." I had been over the moon, like a silly teenager.

And then came the email that had left me wounded and broken.

How had it all come to this? Where had the bond, the camaraderie disappeared?

But my innate sense of justice wouldn't allow me to kid myself. Rohan had been up front about his stance. He had not minced words. Nor had he attempted to take advantage of the situation. God knows, women in love can be unbelievably dumb. But he had not aimed to deceive me, not for a minute. This sincerity made me feel worse.

In my heart of hearts, I could not help wishing for a miracle. A miracle that would make him see the light and return to my life. It was selfish of me, but I just couldn't help myself. I was behaving like the giddy teenager I had never been. That girl had been focused on career, exams, and responsibilities. Rational and pragmatic, that Avantika had been respected by young and old alike.

Whereas Avantika today was a person in quest of a mirage, a fruitless search that would only make her lose her bearings.

I had not yet received a response from my second email to Rohan. I told myself it didn't matter; I would accept any decision he made.

Finally, the suspense came to an end.

Hi, Ma' am,

I have thought over the matter and now feel confident enough to join back. If you so wish, I could resume my duties tomorrow.

Regards,

Rohan

Two words from my Blackberry completed my reply. *"Welcome back!"*

On a realistic note, I told myself that it was best to think of Rohan as a temporary option until I found someone suitable. I would be on the lookout for a fill-in, in case Rohan continued with his mercurial ways.

I kept away from work for some time. I just pressed Wendy for all the updates.

All was well with the world, she reported. Rohan and the others were performing their duties well enough. In fact, everyone's status report was ready and she would send them shortly. And by the way, our new project had received an enthusiastic response from all parties concerned.

Things couldn't get better than this, could they?

***

The next six months crawled by, albeit uneventfully. I kept my distance as promised, in the larger interests of the organization. To be honest, I have never approved of emotional entanglements at work. They usually result in a mess, in a loss of productivity, tarnished professional reputations, and sometimes even expensive lawsuits. I had lived abroad long enough to witness this first hand, and yet, I was all set to commit the same mistake with Rohan, a man a few years my junior. It was best I killed my feelings for him.

And so, for the time being, my feelings were in deep freeze. Maybe I'd get lucky. A relationship that is not actively nurtured dies out eventually, I told myself. Or does it?

For his part, as I directed, Rohan stuck to communicating through Wendy mostly. If that good woman found something odd, she never mentioned it. On a few occasions, he and I spoke, but it was all about marketing strategies and targets.

As to his personal life, I had no clue. At last count, he had told me that his family was looking for a suitable bride for him. But so far, he had not applied for marriage leave, nor had he invited any of us to his wedding. Perhaps the search was on in full sway. Sometimes these things take time.

And then came the night of the office party.

We had all worked towards the successful completion of a tough assignment. It had taken time and much trouble, not to mention getting past the obstacles created by a cranky client. However, we were finally able to deliver to his satisfaction. Our accomplishment called for nothing less than a celebration.

I really did not want to attend, but Wendy and my team wouldn't take no for an answer. They would take care of all the arrangements. "Boss Lady, you just come to unwind," said Wendy.

Unwind? Relax? With Rohan around? Ha!

I stood quietly in a corner, hanging on to my virgin drink for dear life. I felt so out of place. Work was all right, but partying with these kids?

As for our man, he was busy dancing with all the girls. Was it any wonder that they liked him so much?

It felt good to see the team happy and enjoying themselves. The next day being a holiday, no one was watching the clock.

I felt a familiar breath over my shoulder. Rohan.

"Hey, come and dance with us," he yelled over the loud music. Without waiting for a response, he dragged me onto the dance floor.

Huh? What was wrong with him? Perhaps he was drunk or something.

"Look, Rohan; I can't dance, meaning I don't want to," I spluttered.

"Nothing doing. You are gonna rock the dance floor tonight," he replied.

With a sigh, I resigned myself to my fate. I would dance a couple of minutes and quietly slither away.

But that did not happen. I slowly began to relax and enjoy myself. Rohan's unabashed joy in my company was definitely good for my bruised self-esteem. *Careful, girl,* I told myself. *You are crossing into treacherous territory again.*

After an hour or so, I coolly extracted myself from the dance floor and left without a backward glance.

What was that all about anyway?

Over the next few days, Rohan's attitude towards me became visibly friendlier. He'd greet me with an overly bright "hi" each time we crossed paths. He would try to share a joke with me and get past Wendy to talk directly to me.

I noticed he didn't call me "ma'am" anymore.

But I was not ready for this shift in position; far from it. I kept my guard up and refused to respond to his friendly overtures.

From the corner of my eye, I could note with grim satisfaction the hurt he tried to conceal, the subtle desperation as I resisted every attempt to get closer.

What exactly was he looking for? Did he really want to renew our bond, or was he just trying to ease up the tension at work?

Yeah, I told myself crushingly. *That's it. He just wants a happier atmosphere at work. Nothing less, nothing more.*

On the backdrop of this uneasy guessing game, another couple of weeks slipped by.

***

"Oh, Wendy, must I?" I asked pleadingly.

"Yes, ma'am. You must! No one else will do. Rohan needs to be accompanied by no less a person than his big boss to make an impression on this client. You know how these Delhi-ites are; they just love the importance they get from senior management personnel. Actually, why am I telling you this? You know I'm right. And Gulati's not the only one. You could fix up a meet with Chhabra as well. He has been leading us a merry dance for some months now!"

I gave in. Wendy, for all her affability, was a war-horse when it came to work and I had no desire whatsoever to prolong the argument with her.

So there we were, Rohan and I, booked into facing rooms at one of the five-star hotels in New Delhi.

Our first meeting was at 9:30 a.m. in Cyber City, Gurgaon, so we reached New Delhi the night before. Even as the hotel staff greeted us with a welcome drink, I looked at Rohan. He looked like he wanted to talk to me, perhaps even have dinner together.

Not a chance, mister, I vowed to myself. I put down my juice glass and vamoosed.

I could hear him calling out to me, but I pretended not to hear. The last few months had been very bad for me and I had no intentions of walking down that path again just because the great man had had a change of heart.

I slept soundly, worn out by exhaustion.

I was up at the first ring of the alarm clock. Seven a.m. *I better give a wakeup call to Mr. Rana just to be sure he isn't late.*

What I heard over the phone didn't sound too promising to me. His voice was slurred with sleep. Would he take my wakeup call seriously enough?

Well, I couldn't afford to take any chances with a client as imperious and demanding as Mr. Harsh Gulati. I would just have to make doubly sure that Rohan Rana toed the line.

By 7.30 a.m., I had on my business suit, but I couldn't be bothered with hair or make-up before waking up Rohan. I walked over to his door and banged loudly on it. It was a rude thing to do, I know. But he had let me down several times in the past.

The door swung upon and a shocked Rohan stared at me. Folded arms, pursed-up mouth, and messy hair held up by a clumsy hair clip. "So sorry, Rohan," I said in clipped tones, "but it's getting late and we need to make a move—now!"

Jolted out of his reverie, he made a grab for a T-shirt before pulling it over his head. His embarrassment at facing me without a shirt was acute.

Well, just too bad.

I once again pointed to my wristwatch. "Fifteen minutes, Rohan—that's all you have," I said, making my way to my own room.

Wonder of wonders. A smart rap on my door in less than twelve minutes.

There stood Mr. Rohan Rana, freshly showered and neatly turned out, with a huge smile on his face. The smile seemed to say, "See, see; I said I would be on time, didn't I?"

So much like Aarav, who needed to have every childish accomplishment applauded. I gave him a cool smile and pressed the elevator button.

The client meet went off like a breeze. Gulati liked our presentation and the services we intended to offer. "Just send me the new proposal with the changes I asked for, will you?" he said. "I guess that will be all."

We agreed and promised to do just that.

We could have left Delhi the very same day, had it not been for the troublesome Mr. Chhabra.

Rohan called his secretary to check to see if we could meet a couple of hours early. If they agreed, it would help save our time.

No such luck. Several calls later, his secretary called to say that the meeting had been cancelled, as Chhabra had to fly to

Sydney on urgent business. "We are so sorry. I had sent an email to you last evening. Apologies once again for inconvenience," she said with practiced ease.

I gritted my teeth. Clearly, Rohan didn't notice the mail when he went out last night.

It was 11:30 a.m. We had the whole day ahead of us. Our checkout was not planned. If we intended to leave, we would have to reschedule our flight to the 6:00 p.m., as the earlier ones were too expensive for our budget.

"Well," I said, "there's nothing more to be done but to prepare for the meeting in Hyderabad next week. It promises to be complicated, and a bit of homework won't hurt us."

Rohan's face fell. I had just rewarded a good job with more work. Unfair, I know. But I was in that kind of a mood.

On our return to the hotel, we saw the staff busy with preparations for an art exhibition. "Why don't you check it out?" suggested the manager. "Satyasheel Jagtap's works are always a treat to the eye. He may not be a maestro yet, but he's getting there. Besides, he captures women and their moods so well."

Rohan looked at me wistfully. "Half an hour. No more," I conceded reluctantly.

We strolled in. The manager had been right. The artist was extremely gifted. And he sure had an eye for women in both urban and rural settings.

I noticed Rohan lingering over a particular picture. I decided to join him and instantly regretted it.

It was a sensual image of a woman in a wet, diaphanous sari, blouse half-open, hair disheveled. Her almond eyes and bow-like lips were united in an expression of desire and longing for her lover. At any other time, I would have appreciated the observational skills of the artist. He had beautifully captured the awakening of a woman in the first flush of youth, the shyness interspersed with the knowledge of the power she could yield over a man if she chose to, the wistfulness juxtaposed against passion.

Rohan was now looking at me with an inscrutable expression.

I hastily moved past him.

The moment passed, thankfully. Rohan caught up with me in a bit, suggesting we get down to work.

"Will my room do?" he asked hesitantly.

I shrugged. It hardly mattered to me. After all, we had practically been strangers for almost eight months now.

He opened the door, and I made myself comfortable on the sofa. Even as he set up the laptop, I helped myself to a soft drink and some cashews from the bar.

"This is what I have completed so far," he said, pushing the laptop over to me.

I frowned at the data. Sure, he'd gotten the synopsis right. But were the figures up to date?

"I got them from the latest issue of *Biz Wiz*," he assured me.

I nodded and turned my attention to the laptop again.

Hmm…Let me see now. Yeah, most of the figures were okay, but we'd have to elaborate on the bullet points in the synopsis.

Lost in the work, I kept narrating my part for ten to twelve minutes or so. When I finished, I lifted my face to see his reaction. I noticed the myriad expressions on his face. He looked like a man under torture.

I was ready to leave the room. I tried to get up with my eyes still fixed on the laptop screen. Unknowing, while reading the summary, I put my entire body load on the right arm of the chair. I lost my balance in the process and was about to hit the ground.

Before I could think and come to my senses, I found myself in Rohan's arms. He held me firmly.

After a few seconds of silence, finally he whispered, "Avi."

I startled as I watched him. This was the first time he had used that intimacy with me. Only my closest friends ever called me that and, in the space of a few moments, he had dispensed with both ma'am and Avantika.

He put his arms around my neck, encircling me in a close embrace. The blood rushed to my head. I was frozen with shock. Pleasant shock; joyous, explosive, unbridled.

My resolve never to do anything with this man flew out the window. I had done an excellent job of kidding myself, but the charade could not continue.

I looked into his eyes and saw the same naked emotion in them that I had only dreamed of all these days.

I tried to pull away, but he was having none of it, encircling my waist with a firm hand. I closed my eyes and gave in to the moment. He brushed my hair back and gently stroked my arms, and neck.

He whispered into my ear, "Avi, I love you."

I pushed him away firmly. But not for long. In an instant, he had me backed up against a wall while he blocked my escape with both hands.

He moved his mouth, trying to capture mine. I turned my face away. He took my chin in his left hand while still holding my waist firmly by his right; he kissed me softly on my cheek. I held my breath as he held me tight. I closed my eyes, knowing I couldn't face his gaze.

He softly whispered, "Avi, look at me… please."

I slowly opened my eyes.

"Trust me. I have always loved you, since the first time I saw you in the car on the highway. Please trust me. I love you. I do," he urged. I saw some strange honesty in his eyes. They looked different from the serious, angry, playful, desiring gaze. This was the first time ever that I could see some sincerity.

I hugged him with all my might.

He pulled my head back softly and brought his face closer to mine.

Our first kiss was like I'd died and gone to heaven. His lips were demanding yet gentle, aggressive yet strangely reverential, like he had a precious treasure in his arms that he would never let go.

Petite and delicately built, I was completely overshadowed by his tall, strapping physique.

In a few seconds, he had managed to pull the blouse over my

head. I tried to protest, but he crushed me against his chest. Skin to skin. No barriers. No secrets.

Time stood still, even as we made love. Desperately. Furiously. Gently. Wistfully. So many moods of love to savor; the only thought in my mind was why had we wasted so much time?

For me, the rest of the world simply ceased to exist as I lay wrapped in the security of Rohan's arms.

I felt overwhelmed, exhausted, strange, and emptied. My spirit felt released from months of bondage. All my burdens seemed to have miraculously lifted in the space of a few moments.

I fell asleep, overcome with exhaustion and relief.

CHAPTER EIGHT

Rohan

I came to my senses around 4:00 in the afternoon. My arm felt heavy. Avantika lay fast asleep on it. She looked worn out, but relaxed and content. The expression on her face was oddly vulnerable and child-like. I tried to push away the hairs on her face, but they kept falling back. I enjoyed her soft breathing. It was a new experience for me. *What a lovely way to spend the day*, I mused.

Deep in slumber, her face was a study in contrast to her general air of serious preoccupation. I observed her features carefully; a slightly round face framed by well-shaped eyebrows, long black lashes, an uncompromising, aquiline nose, and a small but firm jaw line. A very pretty woman by most standards. Desire coursed through my veins again. I just could not have enough of her, and her bare body against mine felt warm and soft.

***

It was one of those humid mid-August late afternoons in New Delhi. Far from pleasant weather. I wasn't sure what to do. Should I wake her up or should I let her enjoy her sleep? But I loved taking her in my arms.

I smiled. In a matter of a few seconds, Avi would transform from the giving lover of the day before to the all-too-familiar Monster Boss (yup, I said it again) persona. *Aaargh*!

But then, that was part of her charm. The relentless energy and uncompromising passion. Sure, she made me nervous, just like she did everyone else. There was something about her professional energy and unpredictable temper that made you want to do your best. Being in her company was nothing short of a roller-coaster ride. You were up and down in a matter of a few seconds. She was an acquired taste, far from everyone's cup of tea. My fondness for her had built up, bit by bit.

Thanks to my considerable experience with the opposite sex, I was sure that she had fallen for me during our Hyderabad trip. She tried her best to keep it from me, but I could see through the façade of the taskmaster. It gave me the strength to deal with her. Everyone in the office kept a safe distance from her, but I loved to play wicked with her. Subtle mind games that no one but she and I could interpret; bringing her to her knees every now and then gave me a high. Not a nice thing to say, I know, but then, the power struggle is an inevitable aspect of the man-woman relationship.

The day before, I had been far from happy when she suggested we prepare for our next presentation instead of taking the rest of the day off. But I knew better than to say so outright. She had been very cold towards me these last few months—justifiably so. However, I missed her every day and was desperate to restore our connection. It hadn't been easy, though. She had fought me every step of the way.

The art gallery visit was uncomfortable for her, busy as she was tottering around in her four-inch stilettos. Sure, they looked good, but I wondered why on earth women put up with such torture just for vanity's sake? She looked visibly in pain, but oh so hot.

The business suit was softly tailored and very feminine. The light blue silk blouse gave me a closer look at her expensive knitted bra. She was well endowed in the right places, I thought to myself wickedly.

Taking pity on her, I had suggested she sit for a little while. But even as she bent to adjust her shoe, I got a generous eyeful. The blood gushed to my face.

Sure, Avantika was around six years older than I was. But she was fit and attractive with an appealing persona and sense of assurance that most other women seemed to lack. And I had fallen for her.

As she straightened up, I turned away. I had no wish to let her know of her power over me.

However, as we had proceeded to my room, it had all spiraled out of control.

Months of repression and denial had taken their toll.

Fortunately, she had reciprocated my need and urgency.

What a beautiful moment it had been! One I would treasure as long as I lived. All my fears and nervousness had just seemed to melt away.

Surprisingly, she had been submissive and giving, as opposed to demanding. This side of her was new to me, and positively endearing. And I loved her even more. How I wished I could take care of her forever.

But then, like Julia Roberts' character in *Pretty Woman*, I pushed away all thoughts of tomorrow and decided to live simply "moment to moment" and to the fullest. It was, after all, the only sensible way to live.

Life comes with no guarantees. Who knows whether the next day's sun will dawn at all? Best to savor everything right now.

I wanted to read something until Avantika got up. While doing so, I wanted to keep her close, in my arms, as I didn't wish to lose the warmth of her body. I could sense Avi reaching out for my arm when I picked up the magazine that was lying on the side table. Still asleep, she buried her face in my chest. Her vulnerability was touching, and it made me feel terrific to be able to comfort her and make her feel a bit secure.

This was a woman who had been through a lot in life and had seen things that I could not even imagine.

So why on earth had she fallen for me? Her business circle was vast, and she could have had her pick of powerful men; individuals far more suited to her position in life than I. There was no way that some of them had not tried to flirt with her. She was too engaging a woman to lack male company.

So, why me? What is it that women want, really? What makes them tick? Well, never mind. Greater minds than mine have pondered the question and drawn a blank.

On a pragmatic note, I wondered how Avantika would behave

with me today. Would she recoil from me? Or would she acknowledge me? Scary thoughts crossed the mind. I had no choice but to wait and watch. The thought of losing her was simply inconceivable.

***

Avantika was still asleep. It seemed she wouldn't wake up for another few hours. *Let her sleep*, I thought fondly. *Poor girl; she works so hard. She sure needs a rest.*

The soft ring of my mobile phone indicated the arrival of a new text message. I stretched my right arm over the side table, grabbing the cell phone quickly so as not to disturb Avi.

It was Khushi, my kid sister. Bubbly at any given time; today, she seemed positively effervescent. "Bhaiya*(elder brother), congrats!*" She was overjoyed and I could actually feel it in her text message. "*You are hooked, booked, and will be soon cooked. I mean to say your engagement is fixed for this Sunday. Shreya's parents approve of you heartily and are hoping for a prompt engagement followed by an early* shaadi*(wedding). Come home soon; today, if possible. Mom, especially, is on top of the world.*"

With the shock, the cell phone slipped from my hand and it fell onto the carpet noiselessly.

Sure, my family had been looking for a suitable match for over two years now. It had seemed easy enough to give in, rather than contest their wishes. I had met this Shreya over six months ago and, in fact, had forgotten all about her. Oh my Gawd! What a thing to happen just as Avantika and I had picked up the threads of our relationship again.

Terminating the wedding engagement a second time would have killed both my parents. It would be too much of a shock for the folks to live with it.

I hailed from a typical conservative Rajasthani Indian home, the kind of set up where it is *de rigeur* to marry by age twenty-five, the golden cut-off for all decent boys and girls to settle down. My ex-girlfriend had belonged to the same clan as I did, and thus, my family had been willing to accept her.

But Avantika?! Never in a million years would my folks give their blessings to a wife older to me by six years, with a son to boot. My ma would die of a heart attack, and my papa would cut me off completely.

I had approached the matrimonial match fixing with cold practicality. There was little emotion involved at either end. You saw a boy or a girl, examined such essentials as family background, skin color, and financial stability; carefully scrutinized the surface for prospective scandals and annoying relations, and decided whether or not it was a viable deal.

Foreigners may balk at the very notion. But for a good Indian middle-class boy long brought up to do his duty, this was hardly new ground. On the other hand, if I were to choose my own partner, well, that would be truly unacceptable.

As the saying goes, many centuries co-exist in the Indian reality. This love-marriage business may be tolerated in the cities, but for small-town India, romance before the sacred nuptials is nothing more than self-indulgent nonsense; another unwelcome, suspicious import from the wicked, wicked west.

He bhagwan(Oh God), how would I look Avi in the eye and tell her all this?

Knowing her, there was no way she would let me walk out on her. She was an intense, committed woman, and would fight for her love; for our future together. The very idea of Avi arguing with Ma and Papa had me sweating.

My parents and Avi belonged to different planets. They would never be able to understand her, in several lifetimes. A single mother? Such a woman could only be a fallen creature; one who had her claws into their son. They would not be polite to her for an hour, let alone accept her as a prospective *bahu*(daughter-in-law).

Somehow, the very idea of her being humiliated was an anathema to me. And I couldn't let down my aging parents either. The controversy our relationship would generate would be too much to fight at any level.

My community had a long memory for errant marital

arrangements. It would not only affect my sisters' marriages, but also those of the next generation of Ranas.

Talk about ties that gag. But I owed my life to my family. Avi was only a newcomer. There was no contest; there never could be.

I would have to do as Ma and Papa wished. There was just too much at stake.

Heaven help me! What kind of a cad was I? How could I tell this lovely woman I adored with every fiber of my being that she and I had no future together? That I was to get engaged to a stranger by the end of the week, and possibly married by month's end? It would simply break her. Avi was too committed a woman to survive such a betrayal.

Why, oh why had my base desire gotten the better of my good sense? In my heart of hearts, I had always known that I would only set up my home with a girl selected by Ma and Papa, so why had I led Avi to this?

I had behaved deplorably and given in to every sort of weakness I despised. My punishment? Well, I would simply have to live with my conscience for the rest of my life. And the knowledge that Avi hated me.

I couldn't possibly wait for her to get up. I would have to sneak away. Right now. Like the coward I was.

Tears flowing, I gently got out of the bed. *Forgive me, sweetheart. Forgive me,* I begged silently, even as I replaced myself with a pillow.

I quickly rose from the bed and scribbled a note for Avantika. A clumsily worded good-bye, the best I could come up with in my present state of mind.

To make doubly sure that Avi was left with no doubt as to my worthlessness, I placed her beautiful gold timepiece over the paper. The irony of it. The very same Titan Nebula timepiece that had been witness to our union would now herald our separation.

I hastily stuffed my bags with my belongings and put on my clothes. I slowly lifted my trolley bag and opened the door to let it out. But I couldn't leave without a final look at her.

She looked so heartbreakingly beautiful, so trusting. *God forgive me,* I muttered under my breath. The tears just wouldn't stop. I prayed for her well-being and prosperity. Lord, let her get over this with her sanity and trust intact. Let it not affect Aarav.

A pair of dark glasses concealed my raw-red eyes as I headed for the elevator.

I informed the receptionist that the room would be paid for by the company and fled, without even waiting for the hotel attendant to bring me a cab. Instead, I walked over to the main road and hailed a cab that would take me to the private bus station.

I was in luck. A luxury private bus was about to leave for my hometown, which was about five-hundred kilometers from Delhi. It would be an overnight journey, and I would have plenty of time to torture myself in air-conditioned comfort.

Who would have thought that the happiest moment of my life was simply preceding the worst? Papa would often say to us kids that the worst fate that can ever befall you is to fall in your own eyes. How could I tell him that I, the son he was so proud of, had already achieved the most unbearable self-loathing that could be imagined?

What if someone had done this to one of my sisters? My inner voice just wouldn't let up. *Avi, forgive me if you can, 'coz I never will.*

It wasn't just Avantika's dreams I had murdered. A part of me died that day, something fundamental and precious, never to be recovered again.

CHAPTER NINE

Avantika

When I got up, it was early evening. An eerie silence reigned supreme. Slowly, it occurred to me that I was in Rohan's room, in his bed, with only a sheet covering me.

I put a hand over my head. What had I done?

My mind was crowded with a thousand questions. Where was Rohan? How would he view me today? He could be very unpredictable in his responses. How would this impact our professional relationship? My throat was parched. I urgently needed a glass of water. Gathering the folds of the sheet protectively, I headed for the jug of water kept on the table. No sign of Rohan. He wasn't in the bathroom. Perhaps he was in the coffee shop.

A handwritten notepad covered by my wristwatch caught my attention.

I took a deep breath and first drank the water.

The note exceeded my worst expectations.

Dear Avantika,

I am terribly sorry for whatever happened in the afternoon. It was a huge mistake, even though my love for you is real. I really should have had more control, knowing that it would be difficult, as our paths would never meet.

But, Avantika, believe it or not, I love you. I respect you. And I have known how you felt about me for a long time when you blurted it out in a drunken state in Hyderabad. I have deliberately tried to keep myself away from you. I never wanted to hurt you in any way. I did succeed until today. But trust me, that love and attraction for you was uncontrollable. I just got carried away into that powerful tide.

This morning, I had courage and was thinking of talking about our relationship and future, and let your love overpower me.

Strange coincidence or God's will; just now, I received a message from my sister.

The timing is appalling, and even I couldn't have imagined telling you this right now. I am getting engaged this coming Sunday.

I have little to say in my defense apart from this - I really did not know about it myself until this moment. But in my community, this is how things work, and I am no exception.

We are completely different people, inhabitants of parallel worlds, and they will not meet. Not to our advantage, in any case. In fact, if I were to drag you into my life, there would be little in it for you apart from humiliation and insecurity. And you, Avi, deserve much better.

I know nothing that I say will lessen the burden of my actions, and you would not be wrong to say that I took advantage of you, ravished you.

Avantika, at this stage of my life, I have nothing to offer a special lady like you.

Thus proving life rarely works out the way we want it to. The best I can do for you, and me, is to end this here and now. Before the fires of destruction consume us all—you, me, our professional reputations, and worst of all, our loving families.

I cannot express myself any further. And there's nothing more I have to say other than that I hate myself more than anyone else possibly could. I can never forgive myself for this.

Take care of yourself.

Love –

He may as well have flung a hand grenade at me and finished the job of killing me. *A drink,* I thought to myself in panic. I needed a stiff drink, or the pain would kill me.

I hadn't so much as touched a drop of alcohol since that dinner at Caprice's, but today, my survival depended on it.

I ordered a vodka and Sprite over the phone. Wait. That would take some time to arrive. And I needed something right now. I couldn't find anything better.

The waiter arrived in about fifteen minutes, and despite his best efforts, could not keep his thoughts to himself.

He knew this wasn't my room, that the last he had seen me, I had been the epitome of chic dignity, asking him to get additional water.

Could he make out what had happened? Did I imagine the pity in his eyes, the surprise at seeing me in Rohan's room, the empty bottles lying by my side at 7:00 p.m., for God's sake? Silently, he left the room after carefully positioning the vodka and Sprite bottles and a tray of snacks in the middle of the table.

But I couldn't bear the sight of food. Not today.

Five, or was it six, drinks in quick succession knocked me out. I slept through dinner, surfacing only at 10:00 a.m. the next day.

The hangover was killing, even as I fixed myself some coffee and ordered a cheese omelet with garlic bread from room service. I ate ravenously and felt a little more human.

I went back to my room. I couldn't stay in this hotel that smelled of Rohan for a moment longer. And to think, I had felt so fulfilled just a few hours back.

I packed my bags and left for the airport, even though boarding for my flight wouldn't commence for at least four hours.

Time enough for me to figure out my own decisions. In fact, I thought with black humor, I could be a poster girl for a book titled *Smart Women, Dumb Choices.*

In my life, I had enjoyed the attention of several men who valued my presence, and would have loved to get closer. They were smart, successful men themselves and appreciated me for my achievements, both professional and personal. Without being immodest, I knew that I was perceived as an achiever; a fairly attractive woman who could talk well, hold an intelligent conversation, and say the right things at the right time. I dressed well, and could fit into any world, from the traditional to the corporate. My value-based upbringing gave me the strength to withstand the quicksand of the business circles I moved in; a point that wasn't lost on my male friends.

I could have chosen to be with any of them, possibly even committed to one of them. But I hadn't wanted to. Not for one moment had I experienced the all-important spark vital to sustaining a relationship. Nor had they extended the quiet support that Rohan had over the last few months. They had just been friends. Nothing more.

Most of them knew me much before Rohan, yet none of them had been able to touch my heart, and break it, the way he had.

I reached home around midnight. It had been the most memorable trip of my life, for the very worst reasons.

I burst into tears again. I needed to talk to someone right now. I called my father.

"What is the matter, Gubbi, my pet?" he asked, startled. It was wrong of me to do such a thing to him at his age. But who else could I turn to apart from the man who still referred to me as *Gubbi*—little sparrow—in Kannada?

To him, I would always be his little girl, no matter the march of time.

It was my grandfather who had given me this name as a fond reference to my chattering ways. And Dad had loved it. How uncomplicated those days had been. In that time, there were people like my mother and father to solve all my problems.

Today I could do with some of that tender loving care.

"What is wrong with you, my child? You don't sound right," said my father, deeply concerned.

"Could you keep Aarav with you for a week?"

"Yes, of course, Gubbi. But first tell me what is the matter?" he persisted.

"Nothing," I sighed. "Just with work pressures and insane hours, it would help me if you could keep him with you for a bit."

My father knew better than to force the matter. "You send him over with the driver and the maid. I will wait for them. A little child around the house is therapeutic," he said comfortingly.

As is their way, children, however, choose the most inconvenient moments to assert themselves. It was with great difficulty that I managed to send Aarav away.

He held on to my pajamas for dear life. "Mommy, don't make me go. I want to be with you. I will not trouble you. I will be a good boy for you," he howled.

But I steeled my heart, like I had a thousand times before and firmly handed him over to the maid. "Now, come on. How silly of you not to want to go to grandpa. Remember all the fun you had last time? The stories he told you, the play zone he took you to? You are going to do all of that and more and, in just a little while, mommy will be over to pick up her baby," I said.

His teary eyes and incessant sobbing added to my existing misery. It was a heartbreaking moment. But I was a single parent, and there was just so much I could do. I did not want him to observe me in this state of devastation.

***

The next week went by in a haze of incessant crying, sleeping, and trying to watch stupid movies on television. Work suffered, but for just this once, it could take a back seat.

But all the junk food and bad movies could not make me feel better. I felt used, abused and abandoned.

How long would this need for love continue to pull me down? How much pain was I supposed to endure? How many heartbreaks were enough?

It would be so easy to just throw in the towel had it not been for Aarav. My little boy needed me more than anyone else in this world.

At this moment, however, I needed someone to talk to. Someone who went back a long way and understood what made me tick: my college pal, Sanjeev. I knew for a fact that he once had a soft corner for me; perhaps we would have been a couple if only I had reciprocated. But in those days, romance didn't hold much interest for an ambitious girl like me. In fact, I had been too busy to even go out with him. Ever the gentleman, Sanjeev had accepted my decision with grace and moved on without disturbing our friendship.

He was now married and settled with his family in Hyderabad. But then, an old friend definitely had the right to disturb him now and then.

"Hey there," I said softly.

He did not need any prodding. "Avi, oh my Gawd! Where the hell are you?" he yelled joyfully into the receiver.

"Mumbai, where else?" I said wryly. "How have you been?"

"I am fine; you tell me," he demanded with the authority of someone who had been my partner in crime over long years.

"I need some time to talk. Are you free now?"

He sensed something serious. He said, "Let me call you back in couple of minutes."

After five minutes, my phone rang.

"*Bolo*(say)," he said.

"Hey, you loved me during college?" I said flatly, without preamble.

There was silence.

"Tell me, Sanju (Like all friends in our group, I fondly shortened his name in our college days)," I pleaded.

"Why are you asking me all this now? If only it had struck you then," he said uncomfortably.

"I know you did. I just want to know what you felt when I moved out of the city," I said.

"Well, I was very sad. But you were so much into your so-called career and ambition. You didn't have any place for me in your life. Moreover, you would scoff—no, laugh at the mention of the word 'love'. In fact, your views on the subject were well known. You called it a waste of time; as per you, there was a lot to be achieved in life without letting romance get into the way and so I did not pursue the subject with you. Sure, I wanted to tell you about my feelings outright, but rejection is not a nice thing at any level," he said. "Nevertheless, I am happy to see that you achieved what you wanted to in life. Actually, I am proud of you."

"You know, Sanju, I didn't want you to waste your life following me, and so I never encouraged you. Today, God is laughing at me because I laughed at everyone when they fell in love. I have fallen in love. At this stage of my life, it is hopeless. I am unable to handle it."

"Hey, Avi, please don't cry. I will come over to see you," said Sanjeev.

"Hey, no; don't bother. I totally deserve whatever has come my way," I sobbed.

But he was having none of it.

The next morning, he was sitting at my dining table, lecturing me over a brunch of Chinese cuisine from our favorite local restaurant. "Now, sit next to me and eat properly. Look at you, all skin and bones," he said in mock anger. Then, more gently, "Avi, just forget him. That fellow, Rohan, he wasn't worthy of you. You have so much to do with your life. Don't throw it away on him."

My dear, dear friend had missed work to catch an early flight to be with me in my hour of need.

We spent a nice day, catching up, talking about college, old mates, dreams, and life in general.

"It took me over three years to get over you, but I did, at last. But you, Avi, should not waste that kind of time on a loser like Rohan. Just what concrete base did your relationship enjoy? It was just a case of him using you," he said.

"Hey, it wasn't like that," I protested.

"Yes, Avi, it was. Please. Now don't justify it. He did use you and taken all advantages when he needed your help. And now disappeared when you needed him. He never loved you. If he ever did, he would have refused to get engaged and married you. He is good for nothing. Selfish bastard!"

I just couldn't bear Sanjeev being so upset with Rohan for hurting me. I could feel his hidden love for me.

Sanjeev sensed my discomfort and softened his tone and continued further.

"You will find someone much better than him; give life a chance," argued Sanjeev. A rational, pragmatic soul, he went on to enumerate the losses I would encounter if I were to throw in my lot with Rohan. "Are you going to spend the rest of your life witnessing hatred from his conservative parents? And what will become of Aarav? Are you crazy, woman? Leave him, forget him now. I know it is not easy. But you can try. Believe in your karma. You have not done anything wrong, so everything will be fine. *Whatever happens, it happens for the best,* says the Gita.

"Just trust me for this. Once you accept this thought, you will feel much better. When you will look back after few years, you will realize it.

"Just let go of him. Just accept the life as it is… Especially when you can't change it. "

His spiritual words had the desired effect on me.

***

Gradually, the sane voice of reason began to speak to me. Quietly and firmly, it made me pick up the books on spirituality that had gathered dust on my bookshelves for years.

Initially, it was difficult to concentrate. My eyes felt droopy after all that crying, but I persisted in my efforts to read a little every day.

It had been a good idea to force myself in that direction. Little by little, the contents began to sink in and a small window of hope opened up.

From M. Scott Peck to a synopsis of the *Bhagavad Gita* to regular helpings of the *Chicken Soup* series, the books began to show me a side of life that I had only glossed over in the past. Life wasn't easy, nor was it fair, but the human spirit was resilient, and one must keep walking despite the obstacles.

The emotional loss was there, but something else took over; a sense of purpose.

Aarav came back home in a fortnight, having extended his stay by another week, none the worse for the wear. He looked visibly happy and plumper; all rosy cheeks and gurgling laughter.

I resumed work with a grim determination; crisply, in a voice that would entertain no further queries, I directed the HR lady to calculate Rohan's dues and send him his termination letter with a note of thanks for the time he had spent with us.

The days went by and, gradually, the mood swings became fewer. I would not presume to say I was happy, but I was willing to concede that life, despite its ups and downs, was worth hanging on to. I scanned online websites for the latest titles on spirituality and experimented with new authors. It definitely helped lessen the grief, but somewhere, I guess his betrayal had taken its toll on my health.

***

One Sunday morning, I woke up with a nagging pain in my chest. I told myself it was just indigestion. I had suffered from a stomach infection for some time now and then it struck me that my annual check-up with the doctor was overdue.

Coincidently, Wendy got a call from my doctor to remind me about my annual checkup. "You are just awful, boss," she scolded over the phone. "All the time, I have to remind you. Now please go. Doctor Vasan is working today and will take you in first."

"But Wendy, it is Sunday," I protested.

"Tough luck," she shot back.

I smiled. Wendy and the doctor were among the few people who could make me do what they wanted. Otherwise, I was notorious for never listening to anyone.

I dragged myself out of bed.

The doctor admitted me to the hospital, where I was subjected me to a battery of tests: sugar, blood pressure, ECG, ultrasound, and so forth. Three days of this nonsense and I was ready to collapse with boredom and impatience. Getting in and out of that hospital gown ten times, do this, do that, don't touch this, drink water now... it was just awful.

Tuesday morning, when I went to collect the test results, I was informed by the receptionist that I would have to get them from Dr. Vasan himself.

"But why?" I asked, truly annoyed now. "I have to leave immediately; please give me the results."

"Not so fast, lady. I need to talk to you first," boomed a voice I recognized well.

I resigned myself to a long lecture. It was much worse. For the first time since our association, Dr. Vasan looked worried. None of my cardiac tests had been good, he said shortly. Besides, I was hypertensive and had a borderline sugar problem.

"I just couldn't believe they were your reports initially," he said. "But the data corresponded with the other reports for sugar, thyroid, etc. All the lab technicians can't go so wrong, can they?

"Now tell me, Avantika madam (that was Vasan at his sarcastic best), what is going on in your life?"

"Well! Nothing, doc. I mean, just routine as usual," I replied.

"I see you have learned to lie to me now." Like most doctors, he was great at putting on the no-nonsense schoolmaster act when it came to dealing with troublesome patients like me; people who refused to accept they had a problem in the first place. How could I share such intimacies with him anyway? Unlike today's twenty-somethings, my personal life was personal and too sacrosanct to share, even with my doctor.

"Now come on, Avantika," he continued. "What is it? Work pressure? Office politics? Your… um… love life; if you have one, that is?"

My tortured expression told him what he needed to know.

"Look, if you can't tell me, no issues. I understand," he said in a softer voice. "But your reports have me worried. You are still young, and your heart has no business to be in this condition. I can only beseech you to cut-off anyone or anything that adds to your stress. I have no magic wand to cure you without your cooperation."

"So is it time to make a will, doc?" My clumsy attempt at humor fell flat.

He looked at me with serious disapproval. He didn't say anything for a few minutes. "Please come back in a week. I wish to redo a couple of these tests," he said.

But I had already decided not to see him ever again. I disliked anyone controlling my life. Sure, he was a committed and decent doctor, but I just wasn't comfortable with this level of intrusion.

***

What doc spelled out was shocking or unexpected, to say the least... I never imagined the bond I thought was severed and buried in the deepest unknown chamber of the ocean with a small letter would now continue until the last breath of my life. Even when we think of controlling our lives, God always has different plan. It was first time that life taught me the lesson that a few things can't be controlled.

The new course of my life was already decided by that unknown/imaginary one who controlled the universe—some call him Bhagwan, some call him Allah, and some call him the Holy Spirit.

***

I realized that I could no longer continue to remain in my job position due to the demanding role that now could not be aligned to my newfound situation. Moreover, I realized that work wasn't giving me the happiness that it used to. Rohan, it seemed, had walked away with all the passion in my life.

Close friends began complaining that I had become too serious, too dry, and too spiritual. "Such philosophy at your age?" they asked incredulously.

Slowly, I came to the conclusion that moving back to the United States would do me a world of good.

I put in a request to the head office for relocation to the US with whatever possible profile I could get; I sure could do without the glamour of meeting people around the clock and answering the media. I loved the anonymity that a mega city brought to my life. Nobody cared who you were or what you did; you were just a speck in the crowd. Far from being put-off, I drew energy from people at crowded places. There was a delicious sense of being lost that made you forget your worries.

In about a month's time, I got a letter from our bank's Global HR informing me about a position in the quiet environs of St. Louis, Missouri, in the United States. The operations were on a much smaller scale, and that suited me well. Sure, Missouri lacked the hustle and bustle of New York and Los Angeles, but then, a stint there would give me a chance to pursue my twin interests of spirituality and teaching.

And when the quiet got to me, I could always take a plane to NYC or LA for my dose of big city crowds.

I was to leave the tag of Head of India behind. No pesky journos watching my every move. Yay!

The news of my departure raised several eyebrows, and I was at the very heart of the office grapevine. Why was I abandoning such a lucrative post with so much potential for growth? I heard the same question in my successor's voice, but he refrained from asking me any questions.

The usual rounds of farewell parties followed; it was comforting to know that despite my reputation for being a taskmaster, a lot of people liked me.

I had so many memories of this place. It had given me so much: fame, money, and respect. And also Rohan, the heady feeling of being in love, the sheer joy of sharing a cup of coffee with him, chatting with him, and the inevitable brush-off that still hurt.

I wished I could delete all his memories from my mind—the same way we format a computer and delete everything from its memory chip. I wondered why human lives are so complex and melodramatic.

I informed my family that I would be leaving forever with Aarav.

They weren't surprised. They knew it was coming.

***

It took about ten days to pack all our belongings and donate the rest to charity. I kept our luggage to the bare minimum: books, papers, and clothing.

My girlfriends and their daughters rejoiced at the colorful party-wear I readily gave away. None of this glam stuff was required in my new role; best someone else enjoyed it. Besides, I wanted no part of anything remotely associated with Rohan. Not the dresses, not the handbags, not the jewelry.

I would just have to replenish my wardrobe at a later date.

My father and aunts, along with the faithful Baku, bid me a tearful goodbye at the airport. For his part, my father made a last-ditch effort to persuade me not to bring on my downfall (his take on where my career was headed) with this ill-advised shift. But I remained firm.

Baku was a lot more considerate; assuring me she would look after my dad and aunties for the rest of their lives, so I was not to worry about anything. "You just take care of *baba*," she said emotionally.

Aarav, on the other hand, was impatient to say goodbye and embark on this fun, exciting journey. Anything new in his world was a welcome adventure and he dove in with gusto.

Today, more than ever, I missed my mother, the distant figure I had lost when I was just ten. How different my life would have turned out had she imparted to me some of her wisdom about love and relationships.

From what the elders in the family told me, she had been a great lady.

I missed her. Sure, my father did his best for me. It was he who taught me the value of hard work, focus, and competition. It was he who harnessed my energy to the yoke of integrity and principles.

But the soft skills that were so necessary to succeed in one's personal life could only have been imparted to me had my mature and wise mother lived just a little longer. Perhaps I would not have loved and lost had I had the benefit of her touch.

PART II

CHAPTER TEN

Avantika

Fall in St. Louis was breathtaking. And it was no different day when Aarav and I walked out of the airport. A profusion of colors of trees, which resembled a canvas painted by a skilled artist in gentle melody of shades—bright red, electric orange and effervescent yellow with hues of gold; it would offset a young romance, a sight to gladden most hearts. Except mine.

A medium-sized city in the Midwestern United States, it could well rival the world's greenest places with its collection of a hundred parks in and around the city. As we cabbed it to the hotel, I mused that this was an appropriate place to bring up Aarav. There was no dearth of good schools and universities here, nor would we fall short of things to do in the evening. There was a well-defined shopping area, ma-pa stores, and a reasonably active cultural scene. It might not have been the most action-packed city, but it would provide me with enough to do.

For the first fifteen days, we were booked into a hotel while I contacted a real estate agent to help me shop for a decent home. It took some effort, but I finally zeroed in on a two-story home with three bedrooms on Cambridge Avenue in the family-oriented neighborhood of Maplewood. There was a metro-link within walking distance; something that suited me well.

After some deliberation, I decided to buy it outright. Chances were high that I would retire here. Luckily, there was enough money saved from my previous tenure in Manhattan that I was able use for the right thing at the right time.

A fence around the house dotted with some tall trees assured me of additional safety as well as some privacy. The house was on a curve and we could watch the incoming and outgoing traffic in this gated community. The view from the porch was great. I could just visualize the two of us sitting and laughing together.

Along with the porch, there was a large patio and a garage that could accommodate two cars. Thanks to this, we had the option to create lots of greenery and a play area for Aarav, something he had missed in Mumbai. "I want a basketball ring, first. Next, I want a cycling track," he spelled out his demands.

The biggest bedroom would serve as my space. It was converted into three sections: one section contained a king-sized bed, second a sitting area, and the third section was a little *devghar*, or worship place, in the corner. In a wave of inspiration, I extended the bedroom into a cozy little home library that would be right next to my little *devghar*. This same place would double up as a space for meditation. Perfect.

This was one decision I would not regret in the days to come. Beautiful trees, colorful spring flowers, and attractive-looking homes alongside small roads. The entire scene seemed to be straight out of a storybook. For some reason, those sweet little homes looked happy to me—the very embodiment of family life. At least, this was the closest I came to it.

Aarav was happy to settle into his space. The attraction was that he had his own study place and a brand new TV that he need not share with anyone. He always had this issue with his nanny in India.

In fact, it had been the perfect time for him to start anew; entering first grade with new friends in a new school. *Good*, I thought. The kids would, in all likelihood, grow up together. In the absence of any siblings, these bonds would serve him well in adulthood. His little world was so full of exciting new adventures that he would draw me into them despite my low moods.

We went to Super Wal-Mart for shopping. Aarav went from counter to counter, choosing his stuff with great care: books, DVDs, games, posters, and other decorative and kiddy stuff, the purpose of which I could not understand. But I suppose he had picked up these ideas from TV. To complete the rest of his shopping, I had to promise to take him to the famous kiddy shop in downtown St. Louis. It was just fascinating, the sheer clarity of thought that accompanied his wants. I thought of myself and my cousins at that age. We sure did not have such a sense of entitlement, I thought, amused. Perhaps it was because of lack of awareness or the availability of choice or both. We were happy to get whatever was available.

In any case, settling down into our new neighborhood and Aarav's new school took up about two months. Like always, I had been bang-on in my decision to move to St. Louis a good time ahead of my work start date. Winter was still here, and I was all set to begin work.

***

I was replacing a person who was about to retire. Evan had been working for the bank for almost thirty years. He was used to this place, and everyone was used to him. He had made a detailed plan for the hand over.

But then a visit to the hospital confirmed that my health troubles that had started in India were not something to be wished away. So I requested Evan to kindly consider delaying his retirement for the next six months or so with an additional note to HR to complete appropriate permissions and paperwork.

He was only too happy to agree, as it would give him time to work out his post-retirement life.

We jointly sought permission from our head office for the same.

***

The six months passed quickly enough in this strange new city. Every day introduced me to more people and new experiences and one would have thought that all this was the perfect antidote to Rohan. That this fresh start would erase hurtful old memories and I could begin over again.

But it didn't quite happen that way.

His memory and part of him would stay with me forever.

For all practical purposes, I started my professional life in the middle of the spring. It was my favorite type of work; therefore, I found it less stressful. All I had to do was manage and guide the research and analysis work of two divisions with a team of twenty-eight members. It was a relatively small operation, with less administration and of course no targets or chasing clients to raise the temperature levels or my blood pressure, for that matter.

The pressing demands on my time were less, unlike in Mumbai; no giving smart sound bites to the media or attending parties post-work to network or work towards expanding contacts or maintaining the relationship. Without any additional frills, this was wonderful job, because being a single mother is not easy at any given point of time. Now, at least, I could linger with Aarav over his little games and listen to his endless stories.

I felt content and peaceful despite the fact that I was no more the mini-celebrity I was back in Mumbai.

I wasn't complaining. My new role also brought more comfort in terms of clothing. No need for branded formal business suits with expensive accessories. On most days, business casual—a simple shirt with trousers or additionally a nice scarf—was good enough. And best of all, there was no daily stressful commute to and from work. In Mumbai, I would spend something like ten hours at work, and almost three hours in travel. By the time I reached home, I would be dead. Even then, I was not free of the files I was forced to cart home.

Here, we were dealing with research data that was confidential, so there was no question of working from home. No one worked for over eight or nine hours and I had a whole lot of time for myself again.

I decided to utilize it better and enrolled in the Ph.D. program at the University of Missouri, St. Louis.

I started by taking six online credit hours the first semester that were available on weekends.

***

My life as a professional and as a part-time research student wasn't much different from the life I had during my university days in my early twenties. During my master's program, I would work twenty hours and spend forty to forty-five hours on campus for studies. Now it was reversed.

So there it was—my life was all set: work, study, books, Aarav, and his activities. My son was quite a popular little person at school and in the neighborhood as well. He was a natural leader and had a lot of kids looking up to him. It was cute to listen in on the words of wisdom he would dole out to other little boys and girls. He was getting more independent by the day and wasn't taking up as much of my time as he used to. Moreover, he was a person with a mind of his own, and a great sense of freedom.

And so life went on in a pleasing rhythm. No fuss, no excitement, and little time to brood.

Autumn came and went, the silver white winter melted into spring, and spring gave way to summer, when we traveled to India and other places for our annual vacation.

Season after season, time just flew. I was not sure how many springs I saw and how many cycles of these seasons passed.

For every new place we visited during the holidays, Aarav would mark it out in green on the world map that hung on the wall in his room. His ambition, I guess, was to cover the whole map with green. He truly enjoyed travel.

Aarav had been doing very well in middle school. His progress was more than satisfactory and, for a single mother, it was a vindication. It had been my decision to bring him into this world, and he must do well in every area of his life. To that end, I would make an effort not just to keep an eye on his academics, but also his hobby classes.

He was growing faster than I could imagine. His thick Missouri accent was a mystery to me, and during every shopping trip, I would be left wondering how he had outgrown his clothes so fast.

His teachers assured me he was growing up fine. He was a well-adjusted fellow; responsible and mature for his age. So what if he kept treating me to slang all the time? My new secretary's daughter, who was his age, helped me decode some of that stuff.

For his part, Aarav's favorite hobby or habit was to correct my pronounced Indian accent.

"Mom, can't you say 'Ms. Natalie'?" He would get irritated with my repeated failure to mimic his accent.

"Why do you have to say 'dot'? You must say 'dat.'" Now he was my new phonetics teacher.

I said to myself, "How can I change at this age? A person gets the correct local accent if he or she starts speaking that language when they are ten years old or younger."

Well, that was a proven theory.

This was life. No matter how far away I went from home, no matter how relentless the march of time, I was still Avantika Desai, proud daughter of a middle-class Kannadiga home.

***

In addition to my professional work, I offered to teach a few classes at the university after completion of my first two semesters.

This new part-time life as an assistant professor started without much trouble. Since I was passionate about teaching at my work place, the university teaching was fun.

Meanwhile, I was persistent in my pursuit of spirituality. I read and wrote about spirituality, and quoted meaningful, relevant philosophies in my novels and research work. The quest to look beyond the obvious became a big part of my life.

Morning prayers were an important aspect of my day. But I was careful never to ask God for Rohan; it would have been selfish of me. He was married, and asking for him would surely disturb his life. I just wanted him to be happy wherever he was.

Loving someone selflessly would mean praying for his or her happiness whether you are part of that happiness or not.

Although I had not much believed in God as a teenager, I had always believed and respected the presence of a supernatural power that controls us and all other living beings.

Eventually, I started experiencing the power of prayer and the power of thought that we would send out and receive in return; a liberating power of the mind. This belief in the supernatural, coupled with my morning prayers, provided me the biggest moral strength in my life. It also helped me to maintain my equanimity as I started unknowingly believing in destiny. It was the new philosophy from the Gita I started believing in - *If something is written in destiny, it would happen. Or else, it just wouldn't.* I consoled myself. Rohan was not part of my destiny, thus, he had gone away. If he was written in my destiny, he would come back whenever the time was right.

***

I was woken up by a strong nudge on my left arm. It was Aarav. He was standing in front of me. He was holding out a glass of water and demanding me to drink. My eyes were teary. Face was pale. Head was heavy.

Aarav had woken me up in the middle of the night.

"Mom, are you dreaming? Are you hurt, Mom?"

"Why?" I asked with surprise and looked at Aarav.

"I heard you crying. You were calling someone named Rohan. Who is he, Mom?" Aarav asked with great inquisitiveness.

"Nothing, honey… Maybe I had a bad dream," I said and took water from him.

As I finished drinking the water, Aarav took the glass back from my hand, gave me a hug, and left the room.

I was trying to recollect the dream.

The dream I saw was—

I was in a hospital bed.

I was crying. I was sobbing. I was just broken down.

I was in Rohan's arms. His arms were strong, comforting, and I felt much better. That was beyond my imagination.

I was in Amarnani, one of the plush hospitals in the western suburb. I sent the driver to fetch Aarav from his picnic drop-off point.

I read all the reports that the nurse brought and were hooked into a notepad hanging at the end my bed. With all the stress, I was unable to lie down in the bed, so I sat; forget about sleeping peacefully.

My mind and body were numb. I was unable to move my hand.

I pulled out my mobile phone from the handbag that was lying next to the side table.

I dialed Rohan's number. I couldn't believe what doctor told me. My condition had become complicated with the physical and emotional stress and the additional data added further stress. How can I handle this?

I was talking to Rohan. Actually, I wasn't talking. I was crying miserably. In between intervals, I was sobbing and trying to convey the message. I just couldn't do it.

He was holding me in his arms and kept saying, "Avi, don't cry."

He just couldn't find words and kept saying, "Please don't cry."

***

Aarav again came back in to check on me.

In the last couple of years, he had suddenly become more mature than his real age.

I said, "It was really a bad dream," and wiped my tears with the paper napkin he offered me.

He hugged me and offered to stay there in the bedroom.

Although I insisted that he go, he didn't move.

He went out and brought his quilt and made a place for himself on other side of the bed.

Before I tried to sleep, I glanced at the clock. It was 2:05 a.m.

CHAPTER ELEVEN

Rohan

"Rohan, what's wrong with you?"

I came to my senses.

It was pitch dark except for the table clock, which displayed the time as 2:05 a.m.

Shreya, my wife, put on the light and tried to read my face, or rather, my dream. She wanted to know what I was blabbering about and, to be precise, she wanted to know about the woman in my dream.

"Who is Avi?" she demanded.

"Avi?" I pretended. "I am not sure I know this name. Maybe one of my school friends named Avinash; we called him Avi." I made up some story.

"Hmm…Wha…te…ver," she said. Clearly, she didn't buy my story. She looked at me in disbelief.

I walked to the side table. I poured water in a glass. My hands were not steady. I was actually shaking.

I managed to drink the water without spilling it on my nightdress or on the floor.

Now, I desperately needed some fresh air.

"You sleep. I will read a novel and try to fall asleep in the living room," I told her before walking out of the bedroom.

The thought of keeping my wife awake with Avantika's memory would further disturb her sleep and my peace. This was one of the rare days when I shared the bedroom with Shreya. I was not keen about talking to anyone about Avantika.

I had just had a dream and Avantika badly wanted me.

I was trying to recollect the dream I just saw.

In my dream, it was actually from the days when I was working with Avantika.

One of those days—

It was around 2:00 p.m. when my phone rang. I was surprised to see that I missed my lunchtime while engrossed in my work.

Avantika's smiling face appeared on my phone. I had downloaded her picture from the company intranet and saved it against her cell number. I loved her peaceful smile.

"Rohan, Rohan." I could hear only these words and sobbing and, subsequently, it turned into a miserable cry.

"Please don't cry," I pleaded with her. I was unable to find any words to say further. I was in a state of disbelief, as I never thought this iron lady would ever sink to this level.

I was trying to think faster to find suitable words.

"What happened? Is everything okay?" I was an idiot to ask such a stupid question when I already knew it was unusual for her to cry and surely everything was not okay.

She was not able to control herself; she was unable to put any sentence in proper order. I was just trying to gather the information from her broken sentences and mismatched words.

"Please don't cry," I said once again. "Everything will be fine," I added.

I took a moment to catch my breath before pressing on.

"You can call me. You can talk to me. You will feel better," I said.

"I just called you. I didn't know who to call at this juncture," she tried to justify herself. She was feeling uncomfortable about disturbing me. She was too proud to take any help.

After few minutes, she calmed down a bit and thanked me before disconnecting the call.

After the call, I thought over and again, Oh, what a stupid man I am. *She needed me during this time and I didn't get it. She was too proud to ask for any help.*

It took almost fifteen minutes to complete my unfinished work.

I walked to Wendy's desk. After analyzing my face, she just smiled at me. I informed her that I would be leaving for the day for an emergency. I was informing her in Avantika's absence, so she could pass the message on to her.

I didn't want to inform her any of my activities after office hours to prevent my professional image from getting affected in any way.

She nodded and focused on her computer screen to pretend that she was busy and I could leave.

Around 4:00 p.m., I reached the Amarnani Hospital in the western suburb. It took a few minutes to gather information from the reception desk and locate her ward.

She was sitting with her head down on her bed, unaware of the world. Her folded hands indicated that she was in her prayer mode.

When I stood in front of her, I saw she was murmuring something, and a few teardrops were flowing, trying to make their way out of her closed eyelids.

After watching her divinely, I wrapped my hand around her folded ones. She opened her eyes in total disbelief.

Before I realized it, she leapt into my arms. No words, no noise; just tears flowing and making my new shirt moist.

I slowly put my arms around her and let her emotions ebb over time.

"Don't cry, Avantika; please don't cry, Avi," I urged her.

She was crying vehemently, embroiled in her own emotions.

I was completely disturbed by Avantika's persona.

I held her tighter and softly said, "Avi, please don't cry."

This was when Shreya woke me up from a deep sleep or from that dream.

And this was end of my dream.

***

After closing the bedroom door behind me, I walked into the living room.

I took the latest Jeffery Archer book and lay down on sofa.

I was on page five, but couldn't remember what was on the previous pages. My thoughts were not with me in that living room.

***

Once again, I started dreaming. This time, I dreamt, or rather, recollected my past about all the things that happened after I left Avantika in the hotel room.

***

It had been five years since I had abandoned Avantika in that hotel room. Five years since I chose duty over love and married Shreya, the girl my parents approved of.

Not a day had gone by without my guilt killing me softly. I kept imagining Avantika's reaction in my mind's eye. It was an obsessive thought, one that wouldn't leave me in peace for a minute. There was just no condoning my behavior. This was one burden that time would not lessen in any way.

Sure, I hailed from a conservative background and had responsibilities toward my parents, but there was no getting away from it; I had behaved like a coward. And for that, life had paid me back in the same coin through marriage to a woman I barely knew, let alone loved.

When I met Shreya for the first time, I felt she was fine. Not much hassle and not much trouble in life. Since there was no love involved, it hardly mattered who I was marrying, as long as she fit the bill. In retrospect, my own behavior at the time is far easier to judge objectively.

Within a month of leaving Avantika, I was engaged, married, and decided to make the shift to Delhi. It was the only way to survive. How else would I get over her and manage to shift her memories to the all-important delete button so necessary for the human brain?

But life is never so cut and dry, and despite my new life and new wife, I never got over her. The busiest schedules couldn't keep me from wondering what Avi was up to, and all the shifting and adjusting in the world wouldn't keep her out of my thoughts. If only it were possible for the human mind just to keep those memories that are good for one's health, how free of misery and sorrow our lives would be. All the psychologists would be jobless, and emotional well-being would cease to be such a hot research topic.

Instead, subconsciously, unknowingly, I compared my wife to Avantika.

No matter how big or small the episode, I would think, what would Avi say? Would she laugh? Or would she make a sarcastic remark? How would she feel?

In all honesty, there were two women who had made an impact on my life: Avantika and Shreya—my past and my present. Sure, Avi had only been around for two years, but she had created a long-lasting impression.

For her part, Shreya had grown up in a small family of three, just she and her parents. With her father being in the defense services, the family moved every three years to a new location. And so, unlike me, her roots with family were never that deep.

She had not experienced life with guests hanging around in her home for months on end, nor was she accustomed to the noise, laughter, and arguments that reigned supreme in a large family. Thus, she had gotten used to her space, her life, and her choices. In absence of any siblings, she was used to getting all the attention, but not giving the same to others.

A determined woman, Shreya ensured that it was her way or highway in our life. Before the end of the first year of our married life, our extended family members had stopped visiting us. By end of the second year, my immediate family members, including my sisters, my brothers-in-law, and my parents, started avoiding us.

The proud owner of a one-track mind, Shreya was a goal-oriented person. And it would be me who would be left dreading its consequences. If it were a realistic one, it was fine, as it would keep her busy until the matter was over. If it was unrealistic or difficult, then it would be sure to give me nightmares.

In addition to this, Shreya, despite being a homemaker, was never willing to visit any of my relatives for any functions or get-togethers. Quietly and firmly, she made sure that all expectations from our end, as far as she was concerned, were pared to the bare minimum.

Slowly but surely, I found myself cutting off from my family. Sure, I had a wife to share my feelings with, but our wavelengths rarely matched, in either joy or sorrow. The "disconnect" between us began to grow, and I began to feel lonelier than ever. The product of a large, bustling home of ten, with *uncles*, aunts, cousins, and nephews dropping in on us regularly, I was just not used to this way of life. But how was I to explain this to a girl who had never known what it was like to be surrounded by so many loved ones? The sheer pleasure of spontaneous card games, *antakshari*, or even homemade ice cream painstakingly made by the whole family— all was lost. The little joys of close-knit family life that made every trouble worthwhile—how could I convince her of their intrinsic value?

On the other hand, Shreya's parents would plan to visit us for one week and extend their stay up to another weekend. Slowly, these stints, especially after her father's retirement, started getting longer and longer each time.

If I was east, she was west; that much was sure.

There was just no matching of minds, no pulling together, no shared values, and no understanding of each other; the perfect recipe for disaster.

Initially, my sisters would hint, but later started complaining outright about our absence in the family social life. The day my mother realized that, she categorically advised them not to do so. She was just concerned about my happiness. She wanted me to have a happy and peaceful married life. It was her part of sacrifice, her understanding, and her unconditional love.

There was only one other person who could have done this and it was Avantika. Not once had she attempted to contact me. She just disappeared from my life, far away to make me happy. But I was sure that she would always love me, keep me in her prayers, and her love for me would always remain the same. Of course, it was my instinct.

****

When it rains, it pours. And problems have a way of coming at you. Not one at a time, but as an army. Similarly, a simple decision to relocate led to fresh misery.

Shreya's father insisted that we use their old house in the Defense Colony, an up-market area in Delhi that was built by her grandfather, who had retired as a brigadier from the Indian Army. In time, most of the bungalows had given way to high-rises, but her bungalow was one of the few left untouched.

The idea of moving into her maternal home did not appeal to me at all, as I was sure it would create more complications between us. But Shreya's father, a retired army major general, wouldn't stop until he had imposed his will on us. It was in his pushy nature to make a proposal and insist it be accepted by the others, a sort of commander-in-charge. To top it off, Madam Shreya had no intentions of giving up a chance to live in the luxurious bungalow, and I had no choice but to give in. At least, I told myself, it would make someone happy.

Of course, we had to redo the home to make it ours. This little enterprise took us over a year and a million-odd rupees budget. Of course, it pinched. After all, I was only a salaried professional.

Although my professional life wasn't extraordinary, I had managed to get a job in a bank with a profile that would concur with my previous experience.

I would work for twelve to fourteen hours, including travel, and at times would bring some work home. Shreya, who led her own sweet life, had nothing much to do. It would hurt me to see her wasting her education, and I would subtly egg her on to take up a job or a serious hobby. No thank you, she would say. She was quite happy with her life and her circle of friends and family.

To my great anguish, she soon signed up with the friendly neighborhood kitty party group —something I had been dreading for some time. Most of the families in our neighborhood were from affluent backgrounds and, apparently, if you wanted to be one of them, you had no choice but to present yourself as a stylish and pleasant member of their gang.

This motley group of ladies who lunched consisted of fifteen young women from the colony. Most of these women had enjoyed a decent education either from top Indian schools or from abroad, but had chosen to stay at home. With servants to do their bidding, the kids at up-market schools, and absent husbands, they had all the time in the world.

It wasn't that we hadn't had stay-at-home moms in the past—just that they neither had so much money to spend nor so many servants to ensure they didn't have to lift a finger. And what's that they say about an idle mind being the devil's workshop?

All these ladies, including Shreya, would fill their days with card sessions, nasty gossip, fashion shows, and so-called social work.

Before we completed our second marriage anniversary, Mohit, our son, was born.

I thought that after the baby was born, Shreya would change for the better; that she would acquire some depth of thought. Some sense of responsibility.

If only wishes were horses.

Shreya was not happy with my career, as it was not good enough for her friends. I was rapidly tiring of her constant demands that on most occasions were difficult to fulfill. Shortage of money was just half the problem. The crux of the matter was the complete lack of chemistry between us—the all-important willingness to go out of your way to make your partner happy. There was little passion or affection between us. Everything had become a duty for me.

There was just no way I could win her over; both my life and wife were miserable in the absence of any spark in our lives. As was her way, Shreya would complain long and loud about it, but I refused to pay any attention. What good would it have done anyway? What was there to fight for in the first place?

I decided I was better off concentrating on my career. At least professional stability would endure, even if marital happiness did not. My long-term goal was to see myself as the head of the Asia-Pacific Region for the bank.

To maintain the peace, I chose to remain silent and passive in most of the decisions involving home life. That silence was misinterpreted as compliance.

***

Like I said, all my hopes of watching Shreya metamorphose into a loving and committed parent came to naught. Life had a way of throwing surprises at you, whether you enjoyed them or not.

To start with, Shreya expressed her inability to take care of our son alone. Initially, I thought that providing her with an extra full-time maid would solve the problem and convince her to spend more quality time with the baby. But she was adamant about bringing her parents to stay with us.

"Shreya, how can you think of this?" I erupted at long last, before I popped a blood vessel. I was a calm man and rarely resorted to verbal violence, but she had pushed me too far.

"What is wrong with it? My mom can help me with the baby and you know my dad can't stay without my mom." In her mind, she had it all neatly worked out. Whether or not I liked it, it was my problem.

"How can you do this? I, being the only son, couldn't take care of my mother. What will my parents and family think when they find out about your folks staying here?" I asked, trying to reason with her.

And so she took off on a tangent. "Well, I can see you don't care about me or the baby," she screamed. "All you can think of is your own family. You have three sisters and they all are capable of taking care of your parents. But my poor parents have no one except me. You knew I was an only child before getting married to me. I will have to take care of them later in the future, so why not start now?"

How could I explain to her that Indians, especially elderly folks from conservative communities, do not live with their married daughters? That such a prospect would never enter my parents' heads?

In the end, she won, like she always did. A peaceful person by nature, there was no way I could stand another bout of her sulking temper. I made it clear I was most unhappy with this, but she wasn't listening.

Finally, without my consent and in complete violation of my wishes, Shreya's parents moved in with us.

A small consolation to my mind was that the two levels arrangement would afford us some privacy. As time passed, I realized that I was assuming the wrong things. Assume. If only I could rearrange the word, it would be an apt description for me. Ass-u-me (making an ass out of you and me).

While I was learning to cope with the new arrangement and adjustments, Shreya's mind, as usual, was working at a much faster pace than mine possibly could, all the better to take away my peace of mind. At least that was how it seemed to me.

CHAPTER TWELVE

Avantika

One spring evening, I was returning from my friend's place after attending her sister-in-law's baby shower. It had been an elaborate affair, and I had been coerced into staying the whole evening.

While driving back home, I was lost in my own thoughts. Thinking of Rohan was almost second nature to me when nothing was on my mind. Besides, US 50 (the interstate highway) was my usual route, so it was just a mechanical progression. The car was on cruise control.

Precipitously, I heard a police siren and I froze. Sure enough, a police car was flashing its lights at me. Automatically, I pulled the car over to the side and switched the parking lights on.

I was worried and confused. To the best of my knowledge, I had not done anything wrong, as the cruise control was set on sixty miles per hour. It was the highway and I didn't have any traffic lights to consider.

I rolled down the window. A tall, well-built policeman was striding purposefully towards my car.

"Good evening, ma'am," said the cop.

"Good evening, officer," I replied. *Calm down*, I told myself. It was imperative to keep maximum control over my nervousness. Although a couple of students I taught at the university were cops and friendly enough to approach if I needed any help, being an alien, it was an overwhelming experience to be stopped by the law. Perhaps the images of cops created by Hollywood were way too strong to overcome.

I handed over my driver's license and other car papers to him for verification.

"Where are you headed tonight, ma' am?" he asked, rifling

through the papers.

"Home, St. Louis," I said and continued when I realized the gap in my answer. "I mean, I am returning from a party in Lee Summit."

It was clear he wanted to engage me in a long enough conversation to figure out if I was drunk.

"Oh… I…" He stopped mid-sentence, looking at me with a quizzical expression. "Are you Ms. Aaaavaaantika Desssai?" he asked with the typical American twang. I didn't exactly enjoy it, but I had managed to get used to their way of pronouncing my name. There was always more stress on "A" and "V" and "tikka."

Now it was my turn to be surprised. Why should my name mean anything to him? Moreover, my role wasn't as glitzy as it was in India, so people hardly recognized me. "I am."

"My sister works at your office. She mentioned you a few times while talking about her work," he said. "Believe me, ma'am, she thinks you are absolutely cool."

I smiled with some relief. "Well, it is just work. With nothing else to do, I keep working all day." Remembering my manners, I added, "But thank you for the compliment."

"Actually, I had to stop you because your car was not in the lane. It was kind of going zigzag," he said simply.

"Oh, I see. I will be careful and drive in the lane," I promised, turning on the engine.

"Oh good!" he replied with a smile. It seemed that he was enjoying the conversation and looking forward to talking some more. However, the buzzing on the radiophone put an end to his plan.

He looked me and said goodbye. "All right, ma'am. Take care."

"Thank you, officer." I drove off.

I drove home with a bit more care.

***

About a week later, I happened to be in the university library after my class. Engrossed in my book and making some notes on my smart phone, I had a busy day ahead. A breezy "Hi there" had me looking up.

A handsome white American was standing next to me with a friendly grin. "Hi," I replied cautiously.

"So how's it going?"

Oops, this was embarrassing. I just couldn't place him, although he did look vaguely familiar. I guessed he read my mind and rescued me from embarrassment. "Hey, it's Officer Steve Miller. We met the other day on the highway."

"Oh, I am sorry. You looked quite different in uniform." I smiled back.

"What do you mean? Did I look good?" he asked with a twinkle in his eyes.

I sighed softly. Men would be men. "Yeah, you did," I said politely.

"So you are… sorry, Ms. Desai; I didn't quite get your first name," said Steve.

"Avantika."

"Aaavanteeka," he imitated. I nodded. "Did I get it right?"

"Yup, you did," I said. Only, I didn't add, the way you say Avanteeka, it rhymes with *paneer tikka* or chicken *tikka*.

Poor chap. The American accent is not easy to overcome.

But he was a sharp one. I suppose one does not become a cop without some basic observational and mind reading skills.

When he caught up with me in the corridors the following day, he demanded the truth. "Be honest. Why do you grin when I call you by your name? What am I doing wrong?"

I assured him it was far from a crime to pronounce my name in his unique way. "Only thing, *tikka* is associated with *paneer tikka* or chicken *tikka* or the red dot we Hindu women put on our foreheads."

"Oh! I got it." He laughed. "Do you go by any other name? I mean, an easy name?"

"Well, you could call me Avi."

"Oh, that is a nice and sweet name," he said.

We chatted a bit before he announced that it was time for him to get back to his class. Steve was taking a few graduate classes in criminal justice. He intended to add those credits towards his master's degree.

***

It was almost six months since I met Steve. We would keep running into each other at the library or sometimes on the way to his department. My department was located next to his building. One set of his classes was on Monday, Wednesday, and Friday for one hour each day, and the other was on Saturday morning for a duration of three hours each. He was trying to finish six credit hours.

My classes were on Tuesday and Thursday in the evening and on Saturday morning for three hours, which meant I would bump into him regularly on Saturdays.

It was fun to talk to him. He was knowledgeable and easy-going, apart from being a good listener.

One Saturday, he accosted me at the library. "It is 12:30 p.m. Aren't you hungry?" he demanded.

"I guess I am," I said easily.

"Well, lead on to the cafeteria, then," he said.

A meat burger for him and a veggie sub for me and we settled down at our table.

"So, how's it going?" he asked, comfortably arranging our food trays.

He had ordered a Double Whopper from Burger King. Not that I am particularly fond of those, but the fried onion rings with sauce are a different story altogether, something I just can't resist. I reached out for one, without so much as a by-your-leave. "Watch out, Steve. I'm gonna eat all of them," I warned.

"Go ahead. That way, I consume a few calories less," he said with a laugh. "So, tell me about your family."

Since he was a cop by profession, I felt comfortable answering personal questions.

"As of now, it's just me and my kiddo."

"I see. Where is your husband? You're married, right?" He immediately tried to adjust his statement.

"Well, no. I am a single mother," I said.

"Wow, that's a tough job," he said. "So, is it a boy or girl?" he probed.

"It's a boy; he's all of ten. He goes to New City School." I gave him the additional information to avoid further questions. "How about you?" I asked him in turn.

"Well, I work as cop, as you know. Apart from that, I am a single parent and a student at the university; both of these are on a part-time basis." He smiled.

"So your ex-wife shares the responsibilities?" I asked.

"Yeah, but it's not that easy, you know. My part-time job as a parent is all dependent on her." He left the sentence hanging. I sensed some issue with his ex-wife.

"I see." And that was that. No point treading on sensitive turf. The rest of the lunch was pleasant enough; we talked about studies and the forthcoming mid-semester exams.

Life in India! Oh lord… how much I missed the hustle and bustle of our home and my folks in Mumbai, a home filled with their chattering, laughing, mocking or sometimes just silent presence. The presence of human life with or without din makes so much difference. The vibes and energy emitted by them create the homey atmosphere.

I did call my aging aunts once a week until each one took a new route and left her share of void in my life. They all were eager to meet my mother somewhere in the "cosmic palace," the new term they coined for afterlife.

My father didn't take my calls after he comprehended the real cause of my departure.

Initially, he was very furious with the development and refused to talk to me over the new development at my side. He detested the way I threw my career away. After two years, the idea of my new life had sunk into him unacceptably. Although he was not at all happy with the choices I made and roadmap I had chosen, he had accepted it unwillingly. On rare occasions, he would mention it and I would avoid it. But today was a different day.

"Gubbi, what is this?" he asked after our formal talks.

I was silent.

"I want to tell you that you have ruined your life. You have thrown away once-in-a-lifetime opportunity," he said excruciatingly.

"Well, I didn't. You have to understand a mother's heart. How she feels? No mother will want 'bad' for her children. And I did what was best.

"Normally, we think the highest professional goal is the ultimate goal in life. But that is not true. There could be other goals. Life can be made more meaningful in various ways. Apart from a professional goal as CEO or President or whatever the tag I could have achieved, I can certainly look beyond that 'goal' to create meaning in life. Why confine myself to that goal?

"Honestly, I am more happy …

"After Mother's death, you didn't marry. You wanted to take care of me. You found your world with me and, similarly, I found mine. It is content. Peaceful. Meaningful."

Now, I was teaching him. Or I was just reminding him.

He took a long breath and just said, "Fine. Do whatever makes you happy. I've got to go for my walk now. Naik Uncle must be waiting for me at the gate."

"Bye, take care." He disconnected. I sounded beaten. None of my philosophical talks could pacify him. He continued to feel guilty for not doing his best in inculcating the right values in me. I accepted his silence and he reciprocated mine on most occasions.

***

CHAPTER THIRTEEN

Rohan

My life changed drastically after Shreya's parents moved in. They settled in quickly; I suppose it was only natural, since it was us living in their house, instead of the other way around. In fact, it was me who was more of the outsider now. The baby was very young and would cry often in the middle of the night. Shreya would get up to feed him, and her mother would enter our bedroom to help out. I hated the very idea, but I had no choice.

So, to avoid inconveniencing both mother and daughter any more, I simply moved my belongings from the bedroom and shifted to our study. This move completed my sense of alienation. Whenever home, I would spend most of my time in the study, unless we had guests, or household chores that required me to chip in.

***

One Sunday morning, Shreya and I had a fight. Her father came up to our bedroom and started interfering in our conversation. He took her side without even knowing my thoughts or feelings. In her parents' eyes, she was always right.

These were the regular scenes at our home. At times, my frustration levels hit the roof. In order to maintain a sense of decorum, I would opt to remain quiet. Unfortunately, my silence was interpreted as weakness.

***

It was almost five years since we had gotten married and settled in Delhi.

It had been on my mind for some time now to take a much-needed holiday to Jaipur and meet up with my parents. I missed them badly. A few days with them would work wonders for my morale. Accordingly, I put in my leave application at work. I told Shreya all about my plans that evening. If possible, both she and the baby could join me.

"Oooo, just hang on." She didn't allow me to continue further.

I was puzzled.

"You know, sweetie," she started. I knew something was coming up and she didn't want me to get angry with her, so she put a spanner in the works.

"What is it?" I asked, dreading the answer.

"See, you won't be angry with me, will you?" she said pleadingly in a put-on, little girl voice. "I just wanted to surprise you." She was struggling to come to the point. "I had this terrific offer I just couldn't refuse. So I booked us on a ten-day holiday package to China…" She trailed off.

"You should have asked me before you did that," I said furiously. "Anyway, I want to see my folks, as it has been quite a while."

"You always have these boring plans of going to meet someone in your family. When can we learn to enjoy our life as a couple? All my friends have already been to so many places. Our son also feels left out when his friends boast of all the fun they've had on their vacations," she complained.

My head began throbbing. It was not like I didn't take them on nice family vacations. Every alternate year, we went someplace abroad. But in her friends' circle, vacations were something you took thrice a year. And it was a matter of deep sorrow for my dear wife that she couldn't match their boast for boast.

"Well, I am not letting you go to meet that mother of yours. It's not like she's going anywhere else. Jaipur can wait. She can wait, but this great deal that I have managed to swing is hard to come by," she said with determination.

She fished out the tickets from her dressing table drawer. My heart sank. She wasn't bluffing; the tickets had been bought, and they were non-refundable.

I consoled myself that I would meet my folks three months

later—there was a long weekend coming up—and Shreya wouldn't be able to complain after she'd enjoyed her precious trip.

Anyway, both Shreya and Mohit had a whale of a time on the trip. What more could a man possibly want?

***

It was the last Friday of June. I was planning to finish my work and quarterly report. The target date mentioned on our report looked achievable. It was time to work out a strategy for the next quarter.

At around 4:00 p.m., my sister Khushi called. I disconnected the call, thinking of calling her back, as I was on the other phone. And this stuff I had to complete was important.

After about a minute, Khushi called again. I disconnected again. Being the younger sister, she enjoyed taking my case as she found such games particularly hilarious. The two of us enjoyed a special bond, very different from what I shared with my older sisters. But today was not the right time for such things.

The blinking on my phone told me I had a new message. I checked it out and my heart skipped a beat. Khushi wanted me to call back immediately. It was an emergency. Something told me this wasn't one of her pranks.

Sure, enough she was weeping inconsolably. "What happened?" I asked, frightened.

"Mummy, Mummy," was all she could manage.

I said, "Please stop crying, Khushi, and tell me what it is. Is everything all right?"

"Mummy is no more," she said almost in a whisper.

The ground sank beneath my feet. In one decisive moment, my world had changed forever. "I am on my way," was all I could say.

I called Shreya and told her to send my bag with the driver, as I needed to go to Jaipur. Would she, as the only *bahu* (daughter-in-law), accompany me to the funeral?

As usual, she refused. Our son was to start school for the first time and besides, her mom wasn't feeling too well. I didn't force her. But I was hurt, deeply hurt by this blatant indifference towards my family and their needs.

I informed my boss and waited for the driver to bring my bags.

Within thirty minutes, I was on the way to Jaipur.

***

Shame, regret, and grief intermingled into one as I thought of the poor mother who I hadn't been able to visit in over two years, despite living a stone's throw away. *What kind of life am I leading?* I thought bitterly. I had lost all semblance of personal freedom to visit my friends and family. I had no say in what happened in my house or in my kid's life. My son was three years old and followed his mother around like a shadow. But his dad, he had little time for.

I had lost contact with all my siblings; my presence rarely registered in their lives. We had been such an inseparable unit before I got married. But Shreya had done such an efficient job of distancing everyone and it was difficult for me to make amends.

Luckily, two of my sisters had married local boys and stayed back in Jaipur, even after their nuptials. This had proven to be a huge blessing, as they had been able to take turns caring for my parents.

Khushi had shifted to Indore after her marriage. But she would often visit my parents and other sisters as well. All three sisters had maintained their relationships, even after they were married. But despite their closeness, my parents, in keeping with their ideals, would not even entertain the idea of staying with their girls. As per tradition, it was the son's duty to care for them, but I had dashed their hopes.

I had failed them on so many counts. I felt guilty about breaking my mother's heart time and again by cancelling my plans to visit her. Over the last five years, I had spent almost no quality time with her, nor had I managed to bring my son to her, despite knowing she would have loved to form a close bond with her grandson. The list of my sins was endless. I found myself choking on the tears, unable to come to terms with the fact that I would never hear her voice again.

As was her way, Ma had never complained or demanded a thing. However disappointed she was, she would keep her feelings to herself. Not only that, she would hold my sisters back from complaining or demanding anything from me in terms of material or emotional support or even my presence in their social life.

Mothers sacrifice so much for their children, a blessing they value only when it is too late.

There was so much I could have done to make her feel special and cherished in her last days, but it was all over now.

***

When I reached Jaipur, it was nearly 8:00 p.m. It was a humid July evening but bearable nevertheless.

Nothing was on my mind except my mom and her memories. Khushi flew into my arms. We clung to each other as if that simple, fervent, act would recreate our childhood and bring our mother back.

Together, we entered the living room, where silence reigned supreme in a shroud of white. Ma lay on the floor, as peaceful in death as she had been in life. I never imagined that I could see her in that motionless state. Was she really gone? Perhaps she was only sleeping. She was too active to lie there for long. Presently, she would be up and about, doing this, that, and the other.

But the once busy hands were still forever. There was no turning back the clock.

My father and sisters were trying their best to cope, busying themselves with the funeral arrangements, attending to the visitors, as if the comfort of activity would lessen the pain in their hearts.

I left immediately after cremation the next morning. Was it only because I had exhausted my leave quota and needed to return for the all-important thirteenth day post-demise rituals as per Hindu religion? Or was it an unwillingness to engage in deep conversation with Papa? I was avoiding everyone, their possible questions, and their interest in my life. Actually, it was a time we could have shared our life, memories of Ma, and carved some of the unknown facts from other sibling. Alas…

My mother's life flashed before my eyes. Married off at the age of sixteen, she had accepted her lot in life with dignity and grace. Irrespective of the hurdles that came her way, she had been a focused woman.

It was with sheer dogged persistence that she managed to complete her schooling in an era when women's education was frowned upon. I wondered how on earth she had managed to juggle her household responsibilities with her studies, but she had.

After successful completion of her courses, she had joined the local college to teach junior college students. Teaching was in her blood, a skill she had inherited from her father, and she poured herself into it.

Ma had been the living embodiment of simple living, and high thinking. She had been my ideal.

But what had I done for her?

I had so many regrets about every single relationship in my life. What had I given to them except pain? Like Ma, they too would be gone, and I would not be able to do much about it.

***

"So sorry to hear about your mom; you must be tired," was the sum total of Shreya's response when I got home.

Realization hit me at this point. There was just no way of sharing my life or my feelings with this woman, as she did not get me. Nor did I get her. So what was I doing with her?

A few days passed in a blur. One evening, approximately six days after mother's death, I decided to come home early to take a conference call from the United States. It was scheduled for 7:00 p.m., and I had to be well in time to prepare myself for it.

The house was empty; everyone had gone out. Sonny boy was with his friends, while Shreya was with her kitty group. *Great,* I thought bitterly. What a beautiful family life. Perfect. How concerned she is about me. It can't get better than this.

I couldn't fathom the reasons of her going out with her kitty party so soon after her mother-in-law's death. Shouldn't she be mourning? Unable to react to her insensitivity, I just finished my conference call and fell asleep in the study. It was simpler this way. If I didn't see her, I could avoid our usual pattern of harsh words.

I had given her access to every aspect of my life, including my bank account for home expenses. Funny that she called it that, given that home was missing from every part of my life.

She had tried to change every aspect of my personality to suit hers. As to who I really was, Shreya couldn't care less. Her life revolved around our son, her parties, her friends' gossip, her parents, jewelry, and retail therapy.

Shopping was an important aspect of Shreya's life; something that defined her as a person. Having been an only child, her parents had given in to her every demand, and I had been expected to continue doing the same. But I had neither the time, patience, nor the money to cope with this mindless activity. Heart-to-heart adult talks with her about the state of our finances would only result in tears and tantrums. After all, she had never worked a day in her life. How on earth could she respect the value of money?

Grand plans to take up a meaningful hobby and do something with her life would fail to materialize into reality. Shreya had neither the commitment nor the responsibility to see them through. Her entire focus was on competing with friends, outdoing them in petty matters.

The kitchen and the home were practically run by the maid. For her part, Shreya had far better things to do with her time. To all outward appearances, I was living with family, but I felt more isolated by the minute.

There was one connection left—that was with our son when we had time, but the poor kiddo was too busy with his pre-school and post-school activities. Thus, he was hardly around. As was her way, Shreya was obsessed with the kid knowing everything. It was an important part of her ongoing one-upmanship with her so-called friends. Whose kids are smarter? Who fetched better marks? Who has better dancing skills or who is going for better drawing classes? All that too, in the pre-primary section. Oh God! What would happen to my boy when he got into high school?

It sure looked like a maddening race to me, and I wasn't sure the kid was enjoying the process. Learning was meant to be a happy journey, but try telling Shreya that.

She didn't have too many relatives and she didn't accept my family. The one thing she was consistent about was avoiding all family functions in the name of the kid's school and other pressing commitments. On most occasions, I had no choice but to attend family dos alone. For her part, she didn't ask me to attend any of her parties.

How different she was from Avantika, who had been a giver and nurturer in every relationship. Whereas Shreya was childish and selfish, Avi would go out on a limb for the people in her orbit. She gave without counting the cost, and she gave without a selfish thought. This innate goodness permeated every aspect of her life, both personal and professional. As for Aarav, no matter how tired she was, she had a loving word for him. Despite being so busy, she would take time off from her schedule to attend events and social functions important to her team. And when she smiled at me, I felt like nothing else mattered.

But I had lost her. The one woman I had truly cared for and respected. Did I deserve any better, though?

When one is lonely, one tends to think of the person closest to one's heart. No matter what I did, thoughts of Avantika haunted me night and day. What I wouldn't give for a glimpse of her? What I wouldn't do to spend some time with her, and have her back in my life?

CHAPTER FOURTEEN

Avantika

I was sitting in the cafeteria, absorbed in my thoughts, even as I heard Steve call out my name. Lulled out of my reverie, I gave him a broad smile. "Can I join you?" he asked.

"What a question," I mock-scolded him. "Just sit, will you?"

He placed a brown paper package on the table. Evidently, it was a hearty lunch that he had not yet found the time to tackle.

"Who eats lunch at 4:00 p.m., Steve?" I asked him.

"Yea, well, I couldn't get time to fix my food, since I got up at 1:00 p.m. after my night shift. So I kind of picked up a pizza from that new joint outside the college gates. I managed to get some breathing space only now," he said.

"I see. It must be tough on you to work in shifts," I said.

"It's okay when we aren't chasing the bad guys," he said. "But on the days we're busy rounding them up, we just subsist on cups of black coffee." He took a big bite of his pepperoni pizza. He evidently loved the stuff.

I stared, mesmerized at the sheer joy on his face.

"You wanna share, Avi?" he asked me.

"Well, I wish I could, but I can't. I am a vegetarian," I said.

"Oh, come on; veggies won't make you strong. You need real stuff," he said. Typical American. I smiled to myself.

"Well, macho man; for me, veggies are good enough. Besides, I don't believe in killing living things to make my food," I said carelessly.

He put his half-eaten pizza down on the plate and stared at me.

"I am so sorry." My hand flew to my mouth. "I didn't mean to hurt you. It is your choice and it is fine. Please go ahead. I am sorry." I was sounding desperate.

Finally, he laughed at my clumsiness and said, "Hey, that's okay; no worries!"

He continued with his meal, apprising me between mouthfuls of his journey from good ol' Steve to mighty cop.

"You know I joined as 911 dispatcher. I did this job for about two years. I was good at it."

"What is a 911 dispatcher, Steve? Sorry, new terminology for me," I interrupted.

"Oh, apology; I forget you are unfamiliar with these terms. Actually, 911, as you already know, is an emergency number in the United States and Canada. These calls are received at a centralized location in a county."

He sipped water and continued his explanation.

"The dispatchers are communications personnel. They are responsible for receiving and transmitting pure and reliable messages. In addition, they track vehicles and equipment, and record other important information. They take down the details of the complaint and rate the emergencies before dispatching the force to the complainant.

"By starting my career as a 911 dispatcher, I had managed to get a good taste of what a policeman's life and role would be like; thus, I appreciate my responsibilities better."

He completed his explanation and took a last bite of his food.

I couldn't help but marvel at the meticulous selection process that formed the base of their super-efficient police force. "These days, it's my kid sis who is a dispatcher with the county police. Who knows where it could lead? Perhaps there will be two cops in the family. In any case, it's a great learning experience for a youngster," he said.

Fascinated, I couldn't help but compare the American system with the one that existed back home.

He laughed heartily as I described how it worked in India; the never-ending queues on an open ground and the kind of questions and experiences the candidates are put through.

On that light note, we both got up and walked toward the parking lot.

As I was about to get into my car, Steve fished out a card for me. "Here; keep this," he said.

"What is this?" I asked, surprised.

"Well, this is a card you can show the cops if they stop you any time. I wrote your name and expiry date of the card's validity," he said.

He further explained that cops like him were authorized to hand out cards to relatives and friends, so other cops went easy on them in case they got into minor trouble. Proudly showing me his badge, he stressed its importance. "You can donate some money to the police department and get one for yourself. Avi, you've got lots of money. You can buy one," he said.

"Well, I do not intend to get into any trouble. So I can save my money." I laughed.

He joined in; although something told me it wasn't whole hearted.

I thanked him and shook his hand before I got into my car. As I reversed the car, I saw Steve watching me.

***

I kept bumping into Steve every now and then, especially in the library.

One day, he handed over some movie tickets to me and asked if I wanted to take my son to the show.

"I couldn't cancel it. My ex-wife changed the plan and I've got to rush to work in an hour. I will be filling in for a colleague," he said.

I accepted the tickets and reached for my handbag.

He protested loudly. "Hey, no, Avi; don't do that. I will be very sad if you do," he said simply.

I nodded, but added for good measure, "I will take them only if I can buy you lunch sometime. Say, how about next Saturday?"

"Deal," he said, giving me a thumbs-up.

***

Steve was a friendly and attractive man of German origin; he stood a whopping six foot two in his socks. Fit and handsome, he was a knockout in his uniform. His profession gave him that extra edge. Polished and refined, he was the perfect gentleman. And it seemed like he had feelings for me. So why couldn't I place him anywhere in my life?

It wasn't rocket science to figure out the answer—Rohan. Despite the passing of the years, the wounds had not healed. Whether I liked it or not, he was the love of my life. And I had no choice in the matter.

No matter what I did, or how busy I kept myself, I couldn't get over him.

By now, I had become calmer and less emotional about him. But the hurt was still there. The vacuum was there and, moreover, he was still there as a part of me.

***

Steve and Amanda, his daughter, who Aarav hated at first over sharing their toys and space, and their perception, became regular visitors at my place. We started going out frequently for movies, games, and school activities. Although Steve's ex-wife was initially reluctant to let their daughter be in my company, she relaxed after meeting me. In fact, with typical feminine shrewdness, she'd figured out that Steve had developed a soft corner for me long before it hit me.

Life is complicated and uncertain, and there was a lot more that would unfold in the days to come.

One day, as I was pouring over my research material in the library, Steve leaned over me from the front side, casually. As a reflex action, I bent backwards. I saw the glimmer of hurt in his eyes, but he hastily covered it up with a broad grin. Dressed in a black t-shirt and khaki shorts, he reminded me so much of Rohan.

"Hey, Avi, I wanted to ask you out on a date," he said.

"You mean dinner, not date, right?" I gently corrected him.

"Well, what is it with you? Saint Aaavaaaantikka won't go on a date?" he said, annoyed.

"It is not what you think." For once, I was at a loss for words. How could I tell this nice man that I cared for him, but not in the way he wanted me to?

The little boy vulnerability on his face was touching. "Then, what is it? I care for you."

"I know. And I appreciate that, but I can't walk that path anymore," I said.

"Huh? Are you telling me you don't like me?" he said softly.

"No, of course I like you. Who wouldn't? You are the nicest guy I know. Believe me, you deserve someone very special indeed," I said.

"Well, that sure is a nice way of turning someone down." He laughed, trying to hang on to his pride. "By the way, you sure are good for me." Touching my arm lightly, he said softly, "Learn to enjoy life, Avi. God has given us such a beautiful life; make the most of it." This spiritual, reflective Steve was a new person.

I just smiled. I didn't say much.

But I was sure I didn't want to get hurt. And there was no way I could be unfair to a loving person like Steve. I wasn't kidding or exaggerating when I called Steve the nicest guy ever. I meant every word. But the heart has a logic all its own. Rohan was the only one for me; there could be no substitute ever.

A bizarre truth I discovered was this: *If you love until it hurts, there can be no more hurt. Once we cross the deepest part of hurt, it doesn't hurt anymore. You become part of the eternal journey of love…no hurt, no worries, and one just prays for the wellbeing of other person —that's true love for you. Innumerable poets and philosophers throughout history have tried to figure it out — partially or incompletely.*

Love is a destined journey.

***

Come summer, Steve and I planned a trip with the kids to Ocean City. It was a hectic time, but well worth the effort to see the sheer joy on the kiddos' faces. Each sunshine-filled day of that long weekend was choc-a-bloc with sand castles, ice cream buckets, cycling, and boardwalk shopping. Except for sleep time, we were together every moment.

Steve and I took a leisurely stroll around the boardwalk. By now, we had overcome the awkwardness caused by my refusal, and had become even closer. I felt comfortable enough to tell him all about Rohan.

"Well, he didn't understand your love," said Steve at the end of my narration. "Despite being a third person, I can feel, sense, and experience your love for him. How come he didn't?" he wondered. "As for you, I just can't see the point of you wasting your life pining for him when he was never truly a part of it. Forgive me, Avi, but I don't think he cared for you."

I tried to justify my viewpoint, "Hey, it is like someone once said, 'Perfect maturity is to understand why your loved one did what they did, although their actions hurt you. Hurting them back is not an option.' You just need to understand their decisions and gracefully accept the fact that they can never be yours." I looked Steve in the eye and said softly, "I am fine. I truly do not think I can love anyone anymore. I have made my peace with God and I will live with it. If Rohan is written in my destiny, he will come back. If not, he will not, and believe me, as a practicing Hindu, I am a firm believer in my karma and my destiny."

"Tell me more," said Steve, fascinated.

"Our way of life decrees that everyone is born with a pre-determined destiny. With good karma, one can try to make the most of one's circumstances. But that's all. There is a lot that is beyond the power of mere humans; the future unfolds the way it is meant to. Everyone acts the way they are meant to and lives as they are meant to; not a moment more, not a moment less. Each person that you meet has a role to play and nothing can alter that. The relationship they share with you, the duration of their presence in your life, all of it is ordained."

There was a stoic silence for a few minutes.

"I am still not sure what you are doing is right," Steve said slowly. "In any case, I guess I'm not in a position to judge, since I wasn't around when you guys were going around or seeing each other."

"Well, we actually never went around. We worked together, struggled through the corporate maze, shared our dreams, and, somewhere along the way, we came closer to each other. At the end, we touched each other's heart. The impact was profound, much more than I thought it was initially," I said.

"See; that's my point. If you never went around, how then could you call it a true relationship? And to spend your time pining over him? This is not practical, Avi," he said with a worried look.

"Let us not talk about it," I said.

"You are running away from the situation," he said wryly. "Accept the fact that he can't be yours."

Steve had no intention of giving up on me so easily. His concern and his unconditional love were saying it all. But my mind was adamant in its outright rejection of anyone apart from Rohan.

***

The next day, we spent time together while the kids were busy in building their sandcastle. Steve and I had a lovely day, sharing many memories of our lives. He shared his concern over his daughter. He talked about his risky profession and its possible effect on Amanda's future.

He told me his funny stories - how he first met his wife on the road and they fought with each other. Then they again met in a local park. And, then again in a local bar.

He asked to buy her a drink. She agreed, along with her friends. I almost broke up when he told me how her five friends drank until morning on his credit card.

I shared my first meeting and heated exchange of words with Rohan. And, his unexpected reentry into my life the next day.

***

Steve was a dear friend, a sounding board for my deepest thoughts, even a soul mate. His presence in my life was welcome.

His daughter and he were now a part of our lives. But, I was not the lady for him.

I would try to encourage Steve to go out and meet new girls, and to go on dates. I would take care of his little girl so he could not have an excuse to refuse.

My life was again on auto-mode for the second time in my life. I settled into work and personal life. Apart from work at the office and the university, I was going for regular walks, while my reading and writing habits acquired a new pace. My writing consisted of—a weekly column in newspaper, research papers, blogs and books. Most of the writing revolved around youth and spirituality.

Once in a while, whenever my stomach permitted, I would cook something interesting. I had stopped eating garlic and onion as a part of my spiritual beliefs. However, it didn't stop me experimenting new cuisines with different flavors and different cultural background.

Weekdays were for colleagues in the office and students in the university while my weekends were reserved for either Steve or Rhea, my cousin Prasad's "adopted" daughter. She would visit us at least once a month. During her visit, I would put aside a special time for her and her parents, whenever they came along. Adopted by my cousin and his wife as a four-month-old baby, Rhea was a much-loved figure in my life. I enjoyed her visits. I cherished every moment. It was always an emotional reunion.

CHAPTER FIFTEEN

Rohan

It was a late Monday afternoon in summer. But instead of going back home, I was scheduled to help my American client with his shopping. The shops around him were very attractive, he said, but he was hard put to make the correct choice. "It would be nice to have a local around, Rohan," he said. "Otherwise, these fellas take us for a ride."

I decided to take him to DHL Empirio and other adjacent malls, as there were lots of options for him to choose from. From international luxury brands to the local equivalents of the ma and pa shops, he would be able to select something for his girlfriend back home.

I was a little early and he had yet to arrive. The attractive decor of the Dior shop caught my eye and I decided to take a closer look. Mind you, I was entering the shop only because I happened to be here for work-related activities. Normally, I wouldn't even bother to go in, as their merchandise was way beyond my reach. Contrary to this, Shreya was ever-willing to try out their stuff, irrespective of the fact that I didn't earn enough to afford even their cheapest baubles. In this, she had the tacit support of her parents, grandparents, cousins, and her rich friends. Now you know why I felt left out of this gang.

Nevertheless, I came out as quickly as I entered the store after one look at the price tags.

I was trying to figure out a comfy place to wait for my client, when I spotted Shreya. Wait a minute. Was it a mistake? Why would she be here at this time? I looked again. Yes, it was her, all right.

There she was, sharing a cup of coffee in the cafeteria with a male friend. She was smiling and relaxed in a way she never was with me. She was wearing a short, floral print dress with a deep neck, something I didn't know she possessed. Both of them looked very comfortable with each other. They seemed to be so preoccupied in their intimate conversation that they had forgotten the rest of the world.

It appeared to me that she had known that man for ages and he was more than a friend. Obviously, Shreya had chosen the location with some thought, given the remote chances of me ever entering a mall on a working day.

Numb with shock, I nevertheless thought it would be a good idea to observe them a little longer before jumping to any conclusions. Just then, a text message informed me that my client was stuck in traffic and wouldn't be able to reach the mall for another half an hour or so.

I actually thanked my luck for the delay that gave me enough time to figure out the real scene, which was an eye-opener in more ways than one.

Shreya's girlish, open laughter, her sexy little dress, and wistful expression—these were sides of her I had never seen before, not even in the early days of our marriage. It just boggled my mind.

She drained her cup of coffee, and her friend signaled at his watch. Reluctantly, they got up, holding each other's hand automatically. But Shreya realized soon enough that they were in a public place where she could be spotted and withdrew her hand. Her friend seemed to be most understanding about that, and they walked out of the mall together. He called his driver over the cell phone and, in a few moments, a swanky blue BMW opened its doors to the couple.

I didn't feel sad or hurt. I was numb—very contrary to feelings of outrage over this scene. Shreya had hurt me so much in recent years that I just couldn't feel any hurt. I didn't feel I possessed her in any way—emotionally or physically. I just felt the roadmap I had chosen was so wrong. I had wasted precious years on a woman like Shreya, who in turn had never considered me a part of her life or heart.

Something told me our relationship was over and that the end would come soon. All I had to do was to prepare for it. It was just a matter of time.

***

Back home, Shreya was her own self-absorbed self. She neither noticed my absolute silence nor did she care. It was amazing, the cold precision that dominated her life and actions.

One evening, I was relaxing over a cup of coffee after a hard day's work. Calmly, Shreya asked if we could talk. My heart sank, even though I kind of had an idea what it was all about. She glanced at the bedroom door; her bedroom, to be exact. We would not be disturbed there. Obediently, I entered the room. She shut the door and sat on her favorite chair and pointed me toward the couch.

Without preamble or any attempt to soften the blow, she came straight to the point. "I think we need to go our own separate ways," she said with a deep breath.

A few moments passed in utter silence before she dropped the bombshell. "I want a divorce."

I stared at her in disbelief. Sure, in my heart of hearts, I was expecting something like this, but show me anyone who can accept the "D" word with grace. Anyone remotely human, I mean. Shreya, well, she was in a class by herself.

"Any reason you wish to let me know?" I asked. I was an idiot as well as a loser. Where on earth was my self-esteem? I just wanted to cling to this lifeless relationship for the sake of our son. Now there was no more pressure to remain in the relationship from my family. My mother, who had fiercely protected my interests, was no more.

"There is no reason. But there is no spark left in this relationship; actually, there never was any." She shrugged.

"So when did you come to this great realization?" I asked bitterly. There was no concealing the raw hurt in my voice.

She kept quiet.

"So when did your lover propose to you?" I asked.

To her credit, or her shame—whichever way you choose to look at it—Shreya did not bother to feign surprise at my question.

She knew I knew. We both knew the other knew. Mutual understanding at last.

"Well, Adi was a childhood friend of mine. Before we knew it, we were in love. We were to get married, but unfortunately, things didn't work out between us. But I now feel that he was the only one who made me happy and I wish to go back to him," was her blunt explanation. No messy emotions for our Shreya.

Suddenly, the six months that her parents had taken to come back to us with an answer began to add up. Madam Shreya had been hoping that the great love of her life would ask for her. But he didn't, and guess who the all-around fool was?

I blew up. "Wow! You guys fought and tried to patch up, which didn't work out. So what did you do? You got married to me to get your revenge on him. Now, after all these years, he realized your love. He comes back with that big sorry face and well-rehearsed drama to suit your ego. And now you want to leave me for him. Where do you fit in my feelings or our son in this mess, pray tell me?" I shouted.

Her stoic silence got my goat. I grabbed her arm. "Do you think it is child's play to break up a marriage? I saw you and your boyfriend in the DHL mall, but I kept quiet for the sake of our child. Do you think it didn't hurt my self-respect to do so? That I did not have to swallow the humiliation you had dished out? But I forget. You are Shreya, the great Shreya without a heart or a conscience," I bit out.

To my satisfaction, I saw her flinch. "I didn't know you. Ours was an arranged marriage. You were just another face to me. You guys had taken your own sweet time accepting our proposal. If I wanted, I could have broken the engagement. But I valued my parents' word, then and now," I pointed out. "I married you, and no matter how hard it was, I tried to keep my promises to you.

"No matter how humiliated I felt in this house of yours, how humiliated and hurt I felt after seeing all my relatives leaving me slowly, I quietly drowned myself in my work and didn't utter a word.

"Your kitty parties, your friends, your parents; there was no place for me in your life. Our maid took care of me more than you did. At least she would ask if I had eaten or whether I was hungry or, for that matter, if I was not well. You never knew when I took medicine, when I ate, or what was happening to me.

"How could there be any so-called spark between us when I was never part of your priority list? One has to create that spark by understanding each other, spending time with each other, by sharing our lives, laughter, and sorrow. By getting angry, by fighting, by loving.

"Moreover, it is a two-way process, Shreya. We have to create that 'spark.' No matter who is part of your life, it will be the same if you do not change your attitude toward life toward people."

Suddenly, I felt exhausted. I rarely spoke so much or with such intensity. All the bottled up hurt of so many years had come gushing out. It was a slap in Shreya's face.

Suddenly, tears were rolling down her cheeks. I tried to wipe them off. She stepped back so that I couldn't reach her. "Stay away from me," she said sharply.

Composing herself, she faced me squarely. "How judgmental you sound, Rohan. And how very self-righteous. But you loved a woman before our marriage and not for one minute did you allow me to take her place. How then will you rate your own behavior?"

She went up to the window and looked out. A proud creature at all times, she did not want me to see her tears. "Don't ask me how I know. But I do. I am a woman and I can make it out. You don't have to compromise this relationship any further," she said softly.

Shell-shocked, I stared at her in disbelief. Shreya; self-serving, superficial, I-don't-care Shreya knew all along. And I thought she had no perception.

She continued, "Initially, I thought I would love you more and make you forget her. I tried everything within my reach to make you love me."

Her face was turned away from me, but I could sense the pain as she almost whispered, "I have lost it. I was keeping myself busy in this relationship. I guess it is a big shortcoming to be a loner, but then this is how I grew up, surrounded by just a select group of people. I am not used to constant intrusion; I can't stand noise. I can only stand the company of one or two people at a time, but you didn't understand my need. Now Adi is back in my life and I do not need to stay in this loveless marriage."

A few minutes later, she came back and sat on the corner of the bed. She started playing with her bracelet.

There was silence. Deafening, ear-shattering silence.

I knew it was the end and there didn't seem to be any reconciliation in sight.

"So what is your plan for our son?" I asked practically. No point in shedding tears. There was a future that lay ahead, a future that needed planning.

"Adi wants to adopt him and we intend to settle down in Sydney," she said.

Well, well, well. So she had a neat little plan in place and was just informing me. So why were there so many crocodile tears? I decided not to probe further and maintain a dignified silence.

The very thought of losing my little boy to a stranger was killing me. But he was young and no matter what I did, I would never get custody of a child below five.

I had to let go of everything, as I had no option. Looking at the determined tilt of her chin, I decided not to stretch it further. "Don't worry. I will leave the house by tomorrow evening," I told her plainly. "Aunty will pack my suitcases and I will pick them up by evening. By the way, I will sign the divorce papers whenever they are ready."

More than grief over losing Shreya, it was Avi who dominated my thoughts, even at that decisive moment.

I had left a precious gem for a fake one. Avantika was incomparable; she was invaluable.

Shreya was not at the breakfast table the next morning. Our maid told me that madam had gone out and would be returning in the evening. But she had left a letter for me.

I finished my breakfast and called for the driver. He asked where I wanted to go. To the office, or someplace else?

Yes, we both were never sure where to head to in the morning. But today, with Shreya out of my life, things looked oddly simple. I told him to go to the office. Once I had settled in the back seat, I opened the letter.

Dear Rohan,

As mentioned, I have tried my hardest to make it work. Unfortunately, it didn't work out. All I wanted was a few happy moments together. But your work took up all your time. I have a feeling that you were running away from me, running away from any emotional bonding, and work was your only recourse. A convenient alibi.

I had sensed your broken heart at the very beginning of our marriage. I did my best to create new dreams for you—a real, warm marriage that would heal all your wounds. How naïve I was. There was just no way I could have succeeded.

For our son's sake, I have compromised all these days. Now I want to quit.

Please collect your belongings before I come back late this evening.

Shreya

A short break-up of a long relationship; a marriage of almost six years. I came back home early that evening. It was around five o'clock. I had never seen the evening sun's rays in the house for all these years. The house was illuminated now with the sunset's gold light and everything was bathed in the bright yellow glow. How I had missed these small things in life.

I went to the study to pick up all my stuff. After my son's birth, it was my haven. The place where I read, worked, and slept. It was almost four years now since I had been to my bedroom. Our little boy would refer to the master bedroom as mom's room and the study as papa's room. Our lives had been divided long before this day, only we had yet to put a formal stamp on it. Shreya was only involved in the child, the home, and her friends' circle. Her kitty parties, her jewelry, and her dresses were her main interests. She was never keen on reading or any other intellectual activities.

Shreya and Avantika. Could there be a greater contrast between two personalities?

Shreya was a happy-go-lucky kind of person and had never been serious about her career. But she wasn't a homebound woman whose life revolved around the kitchen. She participated in all my son's activities at home and at school. She took pride his little achievements and kept encouraging him all along.

In her spare time, if she had any, she would be busy thumbing through magazines like *Vogue, Femina,* or *People*. Shreya had a great interest in movies, mainly Bollywood. Her friend circle mostly consisted of other women living in our colony and the neighboring society of four- hundred-odd luxury apartments.

Her appointments were mainly with doctors, beauty salon professionals, fashion designers, or her friends. This was my wife.

She had carved a niche look for herself that more or less remained the same, irrespective of the occasion. She rarely experimented with clothes.

This was Shreya, now my ex-wife.

***

In contrast, Avantika was full of life and ideas. Her passion for exploring a new subject and commanding discussions was commendable. It was precisely this mix of the contemporary and the unpredictable that reflected in her sense of style. In fact, when working with her, I'd find myself looking forward to seeing what she would be wearing that particular day. Some days, she was an earthy, ethnic daughter of the soil; on others, the quintessential global, corporate czarina. She'd start the week in a no-nonsense business suit, then go on to dazzle us with a profusion of colorful saris teamed with silver jewelry. Other times, it was a fusion of Indo-Western clothing, and, on weekends, something classy yet casual. The best part was she carried off almost anything with poise and élan, except maybe the *salwar-kameez*. I don't know what it was about Avi and *salwars*—maybe her choice was poor, maybe the inherently staid outfit did nothing for her eclectic personality. When I had told her that, she had thrown her head back and laughed her open, unrestrained laugh.

I forced myself to pay attention to my packing. I had to get out of here, and fast.

That night, I shifted to my own apartment, the one that had been locked up when Shreya had decided to move us to her grandpa's bungalow.

Entering an empty two-bedroom apartment was a bit strange, but it was peaceful. Luckily, I had the foresight to buy this apartment with the annual bonus I had received in the last six years along with some previous savings. Of course, madam Shreya had taken an instant dislike to this tiny little home, but for once, I had put my foot down. Had it not been for that defiant act, I would have been on the streets.

It took me a couple of hours to complete the necessary arrangements to make it livable. My driver helped me set up a few essentials we bought along the way in the kitchen and living room, while I arranged my clothes in the wardrobe.

That done, I made myself a drink. Vodka and Sprite. Wait a minute. The CD player with its collection of old numbers was in my bag. In about a minute, I had it set up. Ah, perfect.

I hadn't heard these old, sentimental numbers in how many years now? How melodious they sounded, how real, unlike today's cloying, plastic compositions. It was sheer bliss soaking in those tunes.

I felt strangely relaxed and peaceful. No wife, no baggage, no responsibilities.

It was like reliving my old college days. The drink helped me return to my imaginary world with Avantika.

I scribbled something in Avantika's memory…

Waiting the return of the "fragrance" of that morning,
Whose presence is missing in "every morning";
Agreed that - "destiny" has betrayed me today,
but, with power of my prayers,
I shall feel you in tomorrow's morning…

Life as a divorced bachelor was a mixed bag. Things had happened so fast that I had no time to consider the challenges of this new life. For whatever it was worth, I had been surrounded by people as a family man. Shreya, our son, her parents, and even the servants had been part of the surroundings.

Despite my enforced isolation, things weren't bad. I was at peace. Work and reading in my free time took up a major chunk of my day. Whatever socializing I did was work-related. I missed my little boy, though. His childish gurgles of laughter had a way of lifting my spirits in an instant.

But he would be better off with Shreya. I couldn't be selfish on that score. As it was, there had been so much turmoil in his little life that making further changes would be cruel.

Shreya let him visit me on some weekends, and I either took him out or played a game of cricket with him. But this would soon end, as she would be shifting to Sydney with her precious Adi.

My father and my three sisters did their bit of counseling to avoid divorce for the sake of my son, Mohit. My father did his talking over the role of father in child's upbringing. But I couldn't share my humiliation and presence of another man in Shreya's life. Human "self" is so fragile and fake sometimes that we are terrified in sharing our worst humiliations with anyone. What we fear by others, especially close family members, is being judged. However, it is only one aspect as being feared of getting exposed or being misquoted in the incidents in the future by others are our major concerns.

There were some changes in my career as well, but luckily, they were positive ones. I had bagged a job with one of the top information technology companies as the business development head for their banking division. It was a great new challenge and I could use my marketing as well as banking knowledge to create a niche for myself. I was excited about it.

And so, life started all over again.

***

It was almost over a year since I had parted ways with Shreya. Strangely enough, it hadn't been a bad year.

Over the last few months, I had plenty of time to confront the sheer depth of my loneliness as a married man. There was little in life that could match the claustrophobia generated by a loveless marital arrangement. Little dreams crushed, tender hopes brushed aside, and so many moments lost. Before I knew it, the years had passed by in a stupor. Worst of all, I tended to accept things the way they were. All this for what, exactly?

At least the life I was leading now was more honest. I lived for myself, fearing nothing, holding back for no one.

I'll be honest. The idea of contacting Avi was tempting, but I didn't dare. I had inflicted the worst kind of hurt on her, somewhere deep down, I feared—I might have messed up her life; in short, my actions had been unpardonable.

Even so, I couldn't resist the temptation of searching for Avi on Facebook. I found her profile and recognized her picture instantly, even though the photograph was clearly an old one, taken when she had been younger. There was some information she had shared for everyone. Most of it was related to financial management and spirituality. Her location was not mentioned, but it appeared to me that she was back in the United States. I searched through her friends to check if the list included anyone I knew. Not much luck at first. Most of them were from her college and work life in the United States. Wait a sec; here, at last, was good old Wendy.

I immediately send a friendship request to Wendy with the ulterior motive of finding out a bit more about Avantika.

I received Wendy's friendship confirmation in five minutes. It looked like she was one of those souls who were forever online via her smart phone.

Presently, a chat bubble showed up. Her cheeky irreverence had not changed one bit.

"Hi, handsome! Where have you been all these years? No news?"

I blushed. Even after all these years.

"Well, I settled in Delhi after I left the job. What about you?" I replied.

"You know very well I am at the same place. Ha," she said.

"Good for you," I said.

"How are things? How about others in the bank?" I asked. Actually, I wanted to ask her about Avantika, but could not do so directly.

"You mean Avantika?" she started teasing me.

"Well, you can say so, but I mean everyone." I tried to hide my embarrassment. But Wendy was way smarter than I was and way more mature. Besides, she had a disconcerting way of seeing through you.

"Well, let me think if you were friendly with anyone else those days. I can think of no one. Right, handsome?" she wrote with a wink. How much did Wendy know anyway?

There was a pause as I struggled to come up with an appropriate answer.

"Hey, there. I was just teasing you. Honestly, I missed teasing you and making you blush all these years," she answered. The next bit of information, however, had me cringing.

"Avantika took a transfer to St. Louis, Missouri immediately after you left. She couldn't cope after your abrupt departure. She was heartbroken," said Wendy.

Plain speak was Wendy's forte whether you liked it or not. There was no point pretending with her, so I kept quiet.

"She tried her best to continue with work as usual, but clearly, the pain was too much to bear. So she gave it all up and shifted to a low-profile job in the United States. She is heading the research and development team there. It is a very boring job, worlds apart from the glamorous, exciting life she was leading here. I tried to talk her out of it, and so did her dad, but she was firm in her decision."

Finally, my worst fear came true. Guilt and regret lashed over me in a relentless tide. Was there no end to the damage I had done? So Avi had left a lucrative career that would have taken her to even greater heights as the Asia-Pacific head, and later as global head, because she couldn't handle the hurt I had dished out? Why, Avi, why? I never meant for this to happen.

Finally, the gentle voice of reason made itself heard. Sure, I had hurt her immeasurably. Sure, the humiliation of being dumped in a hotel room would have been too much for any woman to bear, but Avi was way too strong a person to abandon her high-profile career simply for a man. Perhaps there was more to it than I knew.

"Are you in touch with Avantika now?" I asked, not caring what Wendy would think.

"Well, I recently connected with her on Facebook. But she has changed so much. It seems to me that she has turned into some kind of modern-day saint. Spirituality and teaching are her new interests, and honestly, Rohan, I found it hard to accept," said Wendy. *"She didn't reply to the last note I sent her, but you can check out her son's progress through the Facebook uploads."* Wendy concluded her update on Avantika.

After my message in FB chat to Wendy, I explored Avantika's profile once again.

This time around, I could see many more updates posted under the friend's friend's category.

Ah, here was Avantika's son, Aarav. My, he had grown into a handsome and confident teenager in the last seven years. He looked so much like his mom, at least his eyes were hers, and he was lucky in that.

Was there a man in Avi's life? On the face of it, there was no post that mentioned a partner or boyfriend, nor did I see any particular guy featured regularly in her pictures.

I also explored her writings on her website and Facebook. They mostly dealt with modern-day management and spirituality. I skimmed through them and, as they were heavy reading, I planned to come back to them later.

****

It was early fall. My client from Simi Valley, California, whose account was the biggest in my kitty, called me to report a major problem. There was a big disconnect between what they expected in terms of the project we were developing for them and what had been delivered by my team in India.

After a couple of rounds of heated discussions, we arrived at the conclusion that I needed to shift to California for a month or maybe more to resolve the issues and coordinate with the technical team from the client's side until the problems were taken care of.

My colleagues assured me this was the perfect time to visit Simi Valley, as it was spring time there.

****

A couple of weeks later, I was on a plane. Although this was my first trip to the United States, I had already been given a conducted tour of the country by Avantika through her long descriptions of her fast-paced life in Manhattan and equally hectic nightlife. Like millions of others, I had always looked forward to visiting the U.S. someday. And no matter what anyone said about economic downturns and such, America would always represent to me, and many others, the land of milk and honey. The land of plenty. The home of dreams.

Now the time had come to behold its beauty and observe it firsthand. I deserved this little treat after all I had been through.

Before leaving, I read about Simi Valley on Wikipedia. It seemed the place got its name from the word Shimiyi, which refers to the stringy, thread-like clouds that typify the region.

It was further mentioned that it was once inhabited by the Chumash Indians, who also settled much of the region from the Salinas Valley to the Santa Monica Mountains, with their presence dating back thousands of years.

But today, this once-ancient civilization represented the heart of information technology and business.

***

My client had booked me into the Sheraton in Simi Valley, which was supposed to be the best place available in that vicinity. It was a thoroughly enjoyable location that was convenient to shopping malls and grocery stores. A rental car would help me commute to work, and I was sure I would enjoy the drive.

Unlike India, everyone in the office would leave by 6:00 p.m. or, at the latest, 7:00 p.m. if they had some additional work. Keeping this work culture in mind, I had to leave the office at 6:00 p.m. and return to the hotel room. The days weren't really long, and it was a bit funny to see daylight after office hours.

My client was considerate and, after work, I had enough time to shop, explore the beaches, and visit tourist destinations like Hollywood Boulevard and Universal Studios.

A veritable melting pot of all kinds of cultures, from Native American to European and Mexican, Simi Valley was a foodie's paradise. And I went mad, experimenting with all kinds of cuisines. But in about two weeks' time, I was kind of tired of the routine. The project seemed to go on forever with no end in sight. The client and I had mutually agreed to add some extra features to the project, given the fact that I was already in the country. Even so, the work took up only a few hours a day, and the rest of my time was relatively free. Naturally, the Internet was a favorite pastime.

One lazy Sunday morning, I happened to stumble upon one of Avantika's spirituality-themed articles. To my surprise, I quite enjoyed it, though the subject matter was heavy duty. She had broken down a seemingly complex issue into a practical, livable philosophy. How typical of Avi to do exactly what she had promised. But while I knew of her interest in the subject from the very beginning, I couldn't help but wonder if she had been fast-tracked on this path due to her experience with me.

I found myself missing her more than ever. Perhaps it had to do with the loneliness, perhaps with the knowledge that she was here in this country. I read as many of her articles as were uploaded on the net and published in various publications. It gave me a crucial glimpse into her life.

A few days later, I was asked to report to the Los Angeles office for a meeting. It was a hair-splitting day, as we carried out a detailed analysis of what exactly was going wrong with the project. Finally, it was decided that a major portion of the work from hereon would be monitored from Los Angeles. This would ensure that the technical team stayed focused. Great, I thought to myself. The project was finally on track and would progress smoothly from this point. In a short while, I would be able to return home.

The timing was just right. My son would soon have his school vacation and I would be able to have him over. Since their move to Sydney, I rarely got to see my boy.

Just then, I happened to spy another of Avi's articles in the local paper. It was a beautifully written piece on the power of thought and the importance of achieving objectivity in every situation. From the article, I could make out that she was practicing *vipassana*, a meditation technique said to have originated from the Lord Buddha.

For some reason, I felt compelled to share my feelings on the article with her. Not that she needed my compliments. She was an established and widely read author by now, but even so.

Despite my nervousness, I could not stop myself from composing a short message and sending it to the email address mentioned at the end of the article. I congratulated on her easy, lucid style and mentioned how I was sure to read as much of her writing as I could lay my hands on.

Honestly, I had no idea what to expect. I wondered how she

would react. Would she be upset with my audacity or would she simply ignore my email? There was also a good chance that she would not even notice my message, given the sheer number of people who must be writing to her.

By the end of the day, surprisingly, I got a two-line reply from her.

Dear Rohan,
Thanks for the compliments.
Take care.

After couple of days, I wrote back.

Dear Avantika,
I am in LA on a client visit. I would love to talk if this does not disturb your schedule or life.
Thanks.

Obviously, there was no reply for a week. I busied myself with work, or whatever was left of it, given that we were at the fag end of our project. How stupid of me to even ask such a thing of her. Why would she want to meet me anyway?

But, as usual, I was dead wrong when it came to Avi.

There was an email in my inbox after a week.

Not sure, as I am busy for the next couple of days with a conference paper.

At least it wasn't an outright rejection. Who could blame her, even if she were acting pricey?

Four days later, I sent her another email, asking for her number.

Her reply was to the point.

My number is 912-485-9876.
Please call me after 7:00 p.m.

I called her at 8:00 p.m., after dinner. I was scared, more scared than I had been in years. My heart was beating faster than usual. At forty, I felt like a teenager calling up the girl of his dreams.

Four endless rings later, she finally picked up the call. "Hello?" said a soft voice at the end of the receiver. I gulped. How different she sounded and yet, it was her all right.

"Hello, Avantika here," she repeated.

"Good evening. This is Rohan here," I said carefully.

"How are you, Rohan?" she asked in her usual warm and caring tone. My God. I had missed her so much, and she, she could still find it in her heart to speak nicely to me. Hope, Bright hope, at last. Maybe she didn't hate me as much as I thought she would.

"I, uh…" I found myself fumbling for words. Nothing had changed on this score at least. Even today, I was as overwhelmed by her persona as I had been on that first meeting with her almost a lifetime ago.

"Well, I didn't expect your email. What a pleasant surprise," she said.

"Yeah, I always wanted to connect with you, but couldn't," I replied.

"Why? Were you scared?" She giggled. This was vintage Avantika, making light of the most serious issues, just like that. "So how is your family? Your wife and any kids?' she inquired.

"Well, I was married for almost six years, but things didn't work out between us. My former wife lives with our son in Sydney, and I get to see him off and on."

"I am very sorry to hear this." She sounded genuinely sorry.

"Well, it was not working. I did try, but Shreya, my wife, didn't want to. I have no regrets, though," I said flatly.

There was absolute silence for a few seconds.

"How is your family?" I asked Avantika.

"My son is in middle school and hoping to get into Harvard for his undergraduate degree. My father expired about two years ago," said Avantika. The emotion in her voice was evident when she mentioned her beloved dad.

"My both aunts have also left for a better world and Baku now takes care of Prasanna's mother. And that's about it," she concluded.

She spoke to me without any anger or apprehension. She was such a patient, loving, and forgiving person toward all the people in her inner circle. In many ways, it was a weakness. Her circle was shrinking and she hardly made any attempt to connect with new people. But whoever she was connected with, she was way too giving, thus she was often taken for a ride. Who would know this better than I?

I mentioned some of her work that I had managed to read. She was humble and graceful in accepting my rave reviews, and I was so grateful that we were finally talking.

We spoke for about thirty minutes, before I managed to muster up the courage to ask her if I could call her more often.

She agreed, to my infinite joy. She always enjoyed intellectual talks; sharing ideas, issues, and analyses. She would have been a good news analyst.

We spoke for almost an hour every night for the rest of the week. I wanted to see her, wanted to meet with her.

I wanted to call her to LA. I knew she was living in a small town and my presence would cause comments.

"Can I ask you something if you won't feel bad?" I inquired hesitantly.

"Shoot," she said.

"I would like to see you," I murmured.

"Why do you want to see me? To abandon me again?" After all the warmth she had displayed toward me, the raw hurt and bitterness came as a rude shock.

I was speechless. I knew I was guilty. I knew I had made the biggest mistake in my life when I left without talking to her, without any explanation, and I was paying for those actions to this day.

It was time to tell her what was foremost on my mind.

"I have no words to apologize for what I did to you that day; no explanation could condone my stupid act and nothing can alter it now. But, for whatever it is worth, the guilt has haunted me day and night without letting up for one minute," I said, trying to control my tears. "But, Avi, please believe me when I say this. I loved you truly. I would have loved to take care of you, be there for you. But when I finally made up my mind to go with you, destiny played a cruel joke on me. I was forced to go ahead with the wedding, as my parents had already given their word to Shreya's folks. And to break their word would mean killing them with my own hands." It was such a relief, at long last, to tell her how I felt. "Yes, Avi, I was a total coward. I did not have the courage to fight for you, for us," I finished tiredly.

At forty, it was still difficult for me to say all these things. I was an introvert, and expressing my feelings had never been a strong point with me.

"Avi, Avi? Hello? Are you still there?" I shouted into the receiver.

After two minutes, I heard some noise of picking up the phone.

"Sorry. I was away; someone was at the door," she said. "Steve had to drop off his daughter, as he had to go on an emergency call. I guess it is late now. We will talk later," she said calmly.

Huh? Had she heard anything at all? Maybe she had, but didn't want to take the trouble of reacting to it. One thing was clear, though. She was not willing to wear her heart on her sleeve and get hurt again. She was running away from me and did not wish to give me a second chance.

Before I could say anything, she disconnected the phone line with a terse "Good night."

I deserved every bit of this treatment. But this time around, I was not willing to give up without a fight.

I called her every day for a week. She didn't answer. On

Saturday, Aarav answered her phone. He handed over the phone to Avantika.

Finally, she gave in.

CHAPTER SIXTEEN

Avantika

Steve and I were meeting up for our Saturday lunch as usual. It was a weekly ritual we strictly adhered to. Two buddies catching up at the end of the week.

On the face of it, Steve had a class every Saturday. But I soon figured out that he would make the trip even if the class were cancelled.

This morning, he seemed particularly disturbed. Little wonder, given the fact that he was in charge of a brutal murder case. The murderer had shot his victims in cold blood before fleeing the scene of crime. Steve, as a cop on duty in that particular area, had witnessed all this, but could not give chase to the murderer as he had to get the victims to the hospital in time. Unfortunately, both were declared dead on arrival by the doctor on duty.

Despite his years of training and experience, Steve was still vulnerable enough, or should I say human enough to be affected by the sheer destructiveness of any such act. There was little I could do to help except listen to him as he expressed his feelings about the situation.

I held his hand. "Steve, we Hindus believe that every person has his or her karma, or destiny, and life goes on as planned in the destiny. Almost everything that is going to happen is pre-determined, even as the soul takes seed in an expectant mother's womb," I said. "If a violent end is written in one's destiny, there's no escaping it. No one can change it. But for your part, Steve, you have to live up to your dharma, your duty as a cop, without letting emotion cloud your judgment," I finished.

He nodded slowly, but was far from consoled.

So I drew out a gem from my bag of precious stories. I consider them precious, for they contain priceless nuggets of wisdom on life and living.

This particular piece had been narrated to me by my granny when I was just a girl of ten. Despite the march of time, the message had stayed with me, as I hoped it would with Steve.

"Long years ago, there lived a rich and powerful merchant who liked to stay on top of the game in every possible way. And so, he approached a saint to predict what the future held for him. The saint, a highly spiritual person, looked straight into his eyes and replied that the merchant was destined to the die the very next day. Shell-shocked, the merchant asked the saint if he had possibly made a mistake. The saint shook his head.

"*Well*, thought the merchant, *the saint is talking rubbish. I am meant to achieve great heights in life; a young death is only meant for the common man, not an important fellow like me. But I must take every precaution, just in case. It will be great fun to prove the saint wrong, and expose him for a charlatan.*

"And so, he locked himself indoors, and asked his henchmen to guard the house zealously. He had no less a person than the king's poison-taster to ensure his food was safe for consumption and he left no stone unturned. In his heart of hearts, he was trembling.

"In due course, the morning hours gave way to noon, then sunset, then nightfall. Triumphant at having gone through the day safely, the merchant prepared for a good night's sleep. But just before going to bed, he decided it was time for a little snack. The food-taster had gone home, but the merchant thought to himself, what harm can an apple do?

"As he bit into the apple, he felt an insect crawling out from it. Before he could react, the insect had turned into a snake, and it bit him. The bite proved to be fatal and the merchant died on the spot.

"The moral of the story is simple enough, Steve. Birth, death, and all major incidents are pre-determined. You just have to be humble enough to accept this fact."

Steve didn't say much. He just squeezed my hand and left. He was too upset to say anything. But I was sure that he would calm down in a while.

Sure enough, in about an hour, there was a thank-you text message from Steve.

It made me feel better.

CHAPTER SEVENTEEN

Rohan

It was about 2:30 p.m. on Wednesday, and I was rushing back to work after a leisurely lunch with a friend and his wife. It had been a long-pending commitment, one I could postpone no longer. As it was, they were furious about the fact that I had been in the States this long without attempting to contact them. The meeting had been a cheerful one, and we had a whale of a time, catching up. But it was a work day, and I had to drive back to the office, no matter how much I wished to linger.

Meeting up with my old buddies had been so much fun that I had completely lost track of time. As it was, I was running late by fifteen minutes. Had I been in India, it wouldn't have mattered so much, but here in America, they were most particular about doing things by the clock.

To make up for lost time, I tried to speed as much as I possibly could. Luck wasn't on my side. I had to stop at almost every blessed signal, and the traffic that day was just impossible. I muttered softly under my breath. Not that I enjoyed speeding. I was a most careful driver, and had never had an accident in my life. Not so far, at least. Although I was unfamiliar with the US roads, I had an International Driver's Permit, and I felt confident enough to drive. After all, I had read up on the local traffic rules.

All through lunch, I was busy texting Avi to tell her all about my plans. I pleaded with her to join me. But there was no way she was going to agree. In fact, her entire tone was that of extreme indifference. The deep-freeze treatment would have deterred any other man, but luckily, I knew her only too well. She was bottling up her feelings and would continue to do so, no matter how much they suffocated her. She was a proud one, my Avi. I had broken her trust once and it had cut her deep. It would take an infinite amount of time, patience, and persistence on my part to break the ice. Even then, I wasn't sure she would agree.

She had feelings for me, but there was no way she was going to let them show. So far, my efforts to discuss personal matters with her hadn't borne fruit, as she would deftly put a stop to any talk in that direction.

I was trying my best to stay calm, but quite frankly, I was getting desperate by now, asking over ten times and insisting on details about the trip. Perhaps calling her over the weekend would be a better idea, as she was likely to be more relaxed then.

I was jolted out of my thoughts by a car taking a left turn from the opposite direction of the intersection. Immediately, I maneuvered away from it, but miscalculated big time. I banged into the passenger side of the car, damaging both the front and rear doors. I heard a sudden loud, thudding noise as the ballooning air bag exploded, putting me in deep shock.

Time seemed to stand still as I was rendered numb.

The car I had hit was a blue Nissan Altima. The passenger side front door was hanging and there was a huge dent on the rear door.

The old lady sitting in the passenger seat was in a state of shock as well.

After about five minutes, I heard the police vehicles approaching us. A lady cop jumped out of her official vehicle, walked to my window, and asked politely, "Sir, are you okay?"

I couldn't answer. The very thought of having murdered the old woman was petrifying. Oh my God! What had I done?

"Sir, you are okay? Are you hurt?" she repeated.

I looked at her slowly, but the words just wouldn't form.

She understood I needed immediate help, and yelled out to her partner to give her a hand with me.

With great difficulty, both the cops helped me get out of the car.

Devastated, I sat quietly on the corner of the road. I felt drained of all energy and my legs seemed to have no sensation.

The lady cop remarked on a wound on my left leg, just below the knee. There was a tear in my trousers, and there was blood. On spotting the blood, I suddenly began to feel pain. Was it a deep wound or a light one? I couldn't figure it out, but at least the sensation was returning.

The cops went through my phone to come to the last dialed number. Sure enough, thanks to the calls and messages I had sent her, the entire log for the day was filled with Avantika's number.

Talking to me gently as if I were an injured child, the lady cop asked me if they could call Avi.

I nodded. I didn't think much about it. I couldn't. I was just too worn out.

The other cop dialed her number, and said something to her in a very soft tones. A few minutes later, he handed over the phone to me.

"Hello? Rohan? Are you aright? What on earth has happened? Are you okay, Rohan? Please, say something." There was a sea-change in Avi's stance. Her voice was tearful. She was dead worried about me and, despite the pain, I felt my heart lighten. So she still loved me. She had to. Why else would she react this way?

"Avi, I am hurt. But it is not a big thing. It's just a small accident. But I will go to the hospital and call you back," I mumbled.

"Rohan, how serious is the injury? Are you really okay? The cop had me all shaken up when she told me that you weren't talking coherently. Oh God, what a thing to happen. Why are you driving a car here anyway? You men... and your over-confidence!" I loved it when she scolded me like that.

Presently, she calmed down. "Tell me, honestly, are you really okay?" she asked.

"I think so. But I am frightened, Avi, because the old lady, a passenger in other car, isn't speaking. I am new here. I am scared of everything: the accident, the badly damaged car, and the old lady. I am not sure if something is wrong with her," I said in a whisper.

"No worries. I will have my friend call you up. He is a cop and will be in a better position to guide you," she replied.

"Thanks, Avi. Please tell him to call these guys right away."

"I will. You call me back once you finish with the doctor. I will be worried otherwise," she said before hanging up. I was not sure what she wanted to say, but I had a feeling there was a lot more left unsaid between us.

For their part, the cops were trying to make a *prima facie* record of my state of mind. Politely yet firmly, they asked me to identify the roadside signals for them. Was it a green light or green arrow? I didn't know the right of way and the difference between these two lights. Actually, the "right of way" concept never existed in India…even if it was in the rulebook, at least I wasn't aware of it.

I had no idea. My mind was still not working.

CHAPTER EIGHTEEN

Avantika

I was not able to concentrate after the call from the cops in Simi Valley.

Although I had managed to have a word with Rohan, I was not at peace. As promised, I called Steve to explain the situation. "Hey, can you do me a favor, please?" I asked without preamble.

"Shoot," said Steve.

"My friend was involved in an accident. I need you to talk to him and the cops on the spot. I will text you the number," I said as briefly as possible.

"Avi, I am not sure I can do much in this case. Besides, it is a minor accident. The cops over there will follow the procedure," he said.

"But he is frightened and needs help. Please." I was getting desperate.

"I mean it, Avi. I am not sure if anything will change with the call. But I'll call your friend anyway. Send me his number." Steve knew me well enough by now to know that I wouldn't let him have any peace until he had done as I requested.

I sent him the number.

In a while, I got a call from Rohan. He was fine, he said. The doctors at the hospital had examined him thoroughly and allowed him to return to the hotel, provided he took good care of himself. They further told him that he would be functional the next day.

That night, I found myself tossing and turning in bed. I just couldn't put Rohan or the accident out of my mind. Thank God, he was okay. But what if he had been hurt or handicapped in any way? The very notion was just too awful to contemplate.

The inner reserve of calm that I had managed to build over the years seemed to disappear, in a whiff.

* * *

The next day was Thursday. A day reserved to go to the library to return and borrow journals.

I got to my usual desk in the library. Although I was trying to concentrate on my research paper, I just could not come up with conclusive logic to validate my findings. How could I anyway? My mind was not at peace.

Steve entered the library and walked up to my desk. But today, he was not his usual friendly self; he looked angry and disturbed. He barely acknowledged my cheery "hi" and studied me closely.

The fury in his eyes was positively volcanic; he looked like he was about to erupt.

He came straight to the point. "So, tell me, Avi, is he your guy?"

I gasped. The question was direct, no-nonsense. For the first time ever, I saw my good buddy in the role of a policeman, and it wasn't a pleasant feeling.

I should have known better than to beat around the bush with Steve, but I just could not bring myself to answer him. "What do you mean?" I countered, avoiding his gaze.

"Stop pretending. You very well know I what I mean, Avi!" he said bluntly.

How could I when I had spent years trying to deny Rohan's continuing effect on my life?

I just nodded silently, trying to avoid his glare.

Unexpectedly, that very moment, the phone started ringing. It was Rohan. I disconnected the call. *What rotten timing*, I thought as I just sat there, squirming under Steve's relentless, interrogating gaze.

There was absolute silence for a couple of minutes before a beep announced a text message. Thanks to the big fonts I preferred, Steve could read Rohan's name. I sighed. There was no point denying it. My eyes, I guessed, told Steve all he needed to know.

He asked me to go ahead and check my message. I did. Rohan had asked me to call him; he wanted me to seriously consider a weekend trip to Simi Valley in California.

I finally informed Steve of the entire episode of our reconnection, which had started about a month ago.

"Rohan is insisting that I visit him in California...." I paused there.

"I guess you ought to go," said Steve. "Not many people are given a second chance in life to get their lost love back. No, don't bother denying it; you still love him. Your phone call to me yesterday told me everything I needed to know. Don't let pride hold you back. At the end of the day, you need the warmth of love," he said.

Tears welled up in my eyes. I nodded. There was no arguing with Steve. He was right.

He squeezed my hand. "If I were you, I wouldn't hesitate to take that trip," he said. "He is the only one who can make you happy."

As I wept softly, he fetched me face tissues from the reception to wipe my tears.

"I had a word with him last evening and assured him he was off the hook as far as the old lady was concerned. She was out of shock and she wouldn't be pressing any charges. Rohan's rental company insurance would take care of her damages. He was relieved to hear that," he said.

As I muttered a silent prayer of thanks for the fact that Rohan was not in trouble, Steve looked at me closely. "He is a nice guy. I sensed he truly cares for you. He loves you," he said. "Avi, you are the most important person to me now. You know I love you. I have seen your struggle to be happy without Rohan and also your efforts to pretend to live your life without that love.

"In darkness, you will find many stars shining in the sky. You will feel one of them is yours and yours alone. Well, as soon as the sun comes out, all of the stars disappear. I am just that, one of those stars in the sky in your darkness. I am always with you, but when the sun comes out, I must hide. So, my love, I am always for you, but you must go for sunshine."

These were the most touching words I'd ever heard. It was quite unexpected from an American cop at any rate. But knowing Steve and his tenderness, I wasn't surprised. Now, I realized why I made choices the way I did with Rohan or Steve or Wendy; every person mattered to me and they reciprocated that love.

It was a true example of selfless love. I couldn't imagine if someone could let the love go so easily, but Steve did it, more gracefully so.

I looked up at him sharply. Despite the magnanimity of his heart, the pain in his eyes was palpable. Steve, that amazingly patient, good-hearted man, who had spent almost three years waiting for me, had let go of me in a few moments. A lesser man would not have been so generous and I felt a sharp pang of guilt.

Steve was a wonderful fellow, despite his hard exterior. Genuine, open, caring, and yes, emotional, even though that side of him was concealed like a nuclear secret.

Steve got up to leave, gave me a gentle squeeze on the shoulder, and left without looking back even once. There was no need, I suppose. His eyes had told me everything.

My heart was in absolute turmoil. Should I? Shouldn't I make that trip? What would be the consequences of letting Rohan back into my life? I had promised myself, after all, that I would move on without him. Yes, I promised. Although I tried, I was unsuccessful by and large. I couldn't disassociate Rohan from my life—he was on my mind; he was in my heart.

It seemed like the many years of a spiritually inclined life had never happened, that I was still the panicky, over-emotional woman who could not come to a decision.

Besides, the thought of meeting Rohan was nerve-wracking. I was just not sure that I'd be able to handle it. Gawd, what was I to do?

I drove back home, lost in my thoughts. There was just no way of facing Rohan with equanimity. Absent-mindedly, I put the books on a table, as Aarav's eyes followed me.

I had forgotten that he had no plans with his buddies this Thursday night and that he would be home. Luckily, he was busy watching TV and didn't pay much attention to me. Or so it seemed.

I always underestimated my son and his shrewd observations.

A little while later, he handed me a cup of coffee. "Here, drink your coffee," he said firmly. "Now, tell me what exactly is bothering you, Mom."

"Nothing, honey; don't be silly." I laughed weakly.

He gave me his favorite wise-teen-knows-much-more-than-Ma look.

"Well, I was kind of wondering whether I ought to make a trip to California. An old buddy is visiting from India and wishes to see me," I said.

"Well, that sounds like a great idea. You go on that trip, and drop me off at Prasad Uncle's place. I'll hang out with Rhea," he said. I smiled. Aarav and Rhea shared a great bond, bullying and pampering each other in turn. Rhea was the closest friend he had and it made sense to drop him off *en route* to Kansas City, even though he was now old enough to stay by himself.

"You do that, sweetie," I said, kissing his forehead.

I set up my laptop and carefully looked up the flights to Los Angeles from Kansas City.

A brief search on orbitz.com threw up what I was looking for. United Airways had a direct flight taking off at 6:00 a.m. to Los Angles. *Good*, I thought, I would be getting there around 9:15 a.m.

Before hitting the select button, I called Rohan.

I had no intention of chasing him anymore. I wanted him to know that I was visiting him only at his behest. This time, someone else was calling the shots and it was restricted to the trip.

And it was best he knew it.

Rohan's reaction was gratifying despite my ice-maiden act. He was as excited as a school boy. Of course, he would pick me up from the airport and drive me up to Simi Valley.

Gawd! The very idea made me nervous.

"You can do the driving if you are scared. You are good, you know," he said mischievously. I ignored the humor.

I booked the ticket and forwarded the confirmation to him.

Carefully, I selected the best outfits from my wardrobe. Simple yet classy stuff that made me feel my best.

I loaded both of our bags—mine as well as Aarav's spunky sports-duffle number—into the boot of the car. The entire routine had to be carefully choreographed, so as to ensure we didn't lose any precious time. The plan was straightforward enough: drive to Kansas City, drop-off Aarav at Prasad's, and head to the airport early the following morning from there.

CHAPTER NINETEEN

Rohan

Finally, the years of waiting were over. This day's morning promised to be the brightest ever. After all these years, I was getting to see the love of my life: Avantika, my Avi!

I just could not wait to start for the airport and waited impatiently for the minutes to tick by.

It was a beautiful morning, the perfect weather for romance. *Don't get too carried away, Rohan,* I told myself. *She is visiting you, that's all.* I checked her flight times repeatedly, so as to ensure I would be on time. I had given myself a whopper of a buffer time, in case traffic got in the way.

It was more than just excitement that made me check the time and details again and again. Avantika was a stickler for punctuality and hated anyone delaying her. I was sure this was one habit that had not changed over time. In fact, a lot of her writing was devoted to the importance of punctuality and promptness in thought, speech, and action.

I reassured myself that it was just a meeting.

I went back and checked myself. I had worn a blue Tommy-Hilfiger t-shirt. I looked at myself. "Hmm...a little paunch...No, let me change into something better," I said to myself. I removed other t-shirts. I tried one after another. I wasn't happy with the look.

I took out my check-in big bag and removed an olive-green casual shirt with small maroon and white checks. I tucked it in neatly and rolled the sleeves at the elbow. I loved the look. It was perfect for hiding my little secret and it also gave a fresh look.

I again checked the time. I was five minutes late in leaving the room. I picked up the t-shirts, which I had thrown on bed after trying them on. Since there was no time to fold them, I stuffed them into the wardrobe after bundling them together. I hurried and went into bathroom, spread the deodorant under my both arms, and squeezed some body lotion on my hand. They shouldn't feel rough.

Just before turning my face from the mirror, I again reassured myself stupidly that it was just a meeting.

I hummed to myself with the song on the soundtrack. The drive to the airport on Highway 1 was breathtaking, as always. The hills, clouds, and ocean… Could there be a more beautiful place on earth than this?

I entered the airport and checked my wristwatch. It was 9:00 a.m. Her flight was to land soon. I knew she would be out any moment from the departure gate.

I couldn't afford to be late by even a second. I just couldn't risk anything going wrong today. Unknowingly, my pace quickened. I bumped into a pretty young girl and she gave me a furious look. I apologized profusely and moved on. She was far from mollified, but I really didn't care. If only she knew there was but one woman who interested me.

My eyes searched for Avantika and, luckily, I didn't have to wait long.

There she was, holding on to her favorite cabin baggage. Time seemed to have stood still for both of them, her and that bag.

She was still on the slender side, and despite appearing a bit tired, she looked fit, radiant, and composed. Avantika looked pleasant and peaceful with her rhythmic pace. She hadn't changed from how I'd seen her last. The only change was that she looked classier now with her attire. She had on an off-white expensive top teamed with a dark brown equally expensive knee-length skirt and a multicolored silk scarf, nice dark brown pumps with some brass work, and pearl jewelry that complemented the outfit. No doubt about it, she hadn't lost her flair for putting an outfit together. She had her sunglasses on the top of her head.

I was amused to see the continuing presence of the cabin bag, the same one she had taken to Hyderabad all those years ago. Trust Avi never to abandon anyone—not people, not things.

She looked at me and it looked like she was under great pressure, unsure how to deal with the conflicting emotions of her heart. I took her hand in mine and squeezed it gently. Honestly, I just wanted to junk all the formalities and sweep her in a tight bear hug, but I didn't dare.

But then she smiled, that heartbreaking, no-holds-barred smile, and opened her arms to me. I didn't resist the invitation for even a second, and I held her close. All the pain, heartbreak, and hurt seemed to heal in those few seconds. How had I ever let this woman go? She was everything to me.

Sure, there were plenty of differences between us, but it didn't bother either of us. She bullied me; I enjoyed it. She pampered me; I loved it. It was wonderful to be cared for by a person who had seen so much of the world, a woman who could help me see the difference between right and wrong, and laugh at my naiveté.

In short, there was one Super Glue holding us together: love. Nothing mattered when we were together.

I held her bag in one hand and her hand in another. We walked in companionable silence to the parking lot. Luckily, there wasn't much of a crowd and I was able to figure out my parking slot quickly. Removing the keys from my trouser pockets, I opened the car with a click. I picked up her bag and put it inside.

She was smiling at me; blushing, actually. I realized that I had been up to quite a circus, not letting go of her hand for even a second.

Releasing her hand, I opened the car door for her. She got in.

If driving to the airport was fun, driving back was pure heaven. She was wearing her signature Dior *J'adore*. I could drown in that scent for all eternity.

I was thrilled to see that she hadn't lost any of her sense of fun. In fact, she insisted I keep the windows down to better enjoy the gorgeous scenery. In one deft motion, she had the scarf around her head and put on her sunglasses. Worn that way, she looked even more chic and was reminiscent of that amazing Hollywood style icon, Audrey Hepburn.

From LAX, we took Highway Route 1 towards Simi Valley. I deliberately went that way because it had beautiful Malibu Beach scenic views along the way.

While we passed through the Solstice Canyon view and waterfall area, Avantika made a request to slow down. The rocky area was quite an engaging one.

She giggled girlishly as the wind brushed against her face, making a lock of hair fall over her forehead. "Oh my Lord, this is so beau-ty-full," she yelled, opening her arms wide, as if to embrace life and all the pleasures it held.

That was what made my Avi so special; this untiring zest for life, the unabashed joy in little, little things. Here was a woman who had the world at her feet and, despite the detour in her career, still commanded immense respect. But the tiny pleasures that life had to offer moved her and made her happy. There was poetry in her soul, and that was what kept her so young. In fact, she was the embodiment of what Deepak Chopra terms an ageless mind in a timeless body.

I stopped the car almost five times so Avi could admire some wildflowers or click a few pictures along the way. I loved it that she was enjoying herself so much.

She gave me a look of gratitude. "Rohan, you have not changed a bit. You have always had a way of reading my mind. I mean, I haven't said much, but you know just where to stop. How do you do it?" she asked wonderingly.

I grinned at her. "Call it love, or good old connection."

She gave me her trademark punch and laughed off that remark. I wished she hadn't. I wished she would take me seriously. *Be patient, Rohan, I told myself. At least she hasn't rebuffed you.*

It took us a couple of hours to reach the hotel. I didn't intend to go back to my client's office as I wasn't sure of my schedule and my mood after meeting Avantika.

It was past 2:00 p.m. How silly of me. She would be hungry. "What would you like, Avi? Pizza, pasta, burger, or meal at the Chinese restaurant a block away?" I asked.

"Rohan, I have not eaten onions and garlic after I turned spiritual a few years ago, so I have very limited options," she said.

I was puzzled.

"Rohan, you know 'sattvik' the food, which means the food that is based on freshness, purity, and lightness, and it is now part of my new lifestyle. Whereas onion and garlic are 'tamasic', which means they are smelly and bring lethargy and darkness through desire."

With her explanation, I knew she wouldn't break her rule. I was a bit confused about choosing the cuisine. "So tell me, what would you like?" I asked. Knowing her finicky nature, I was prepared to be patient.

"We can walk down and ask those Chinese guys to prepare something without onion and garlic," she said. This was the famous Szechuan Garden Restaurant in shopping center, a block away from hotel.

I was in a mild state of shock. Only Avi could ask for a Chinese dish without onion and garlic, the mainstay of the cuisine's flavor. And only Avi could pull off such a request.

We freshened up before walking to the restaurant. After some deliberation, we selected a cozy corner table, all the better to sit undisturbed. Carefully, she spelled out her special requirements to the waiter, who slowly nodded in the affirmative.

I filled up my plate from the buffet counter and sat down. I offered her a taste, but she refused. Hungrily, I attacked my food while she sat in silence. Yup, I can be without manners at times, but this was Avi, my Avi. I didn't need to pretend with her or assume any formalities. She loved me. And that was that.

Fortunately, the restaurant staff had her dish ready in about fifteen minutes. As she ate, I quickly scanned over emails to check for any emergencies. It took a couple of seconds to scroll down the list. When I was sure there was nothing important, I filled my plate a second time, all the while savoring the sheer bliss of being with her.

It was a leisurely lunch and we arrived back at the hotel at 4:30 p.m.

I helped her settle down in her room, and could not stop myself from giving her a hug and gently brushing my lips against hers. She hugged me back tightly. This was my Avi; genuine, unrestrained, and real. Nothing put on about her. But I didn't want to rush her in any way.

Reluctantly, I went back to my room and lay down. I couldn't doze-off even for a while. I was just too excited. What a wonderful day it had been!

Around 7:00 p.m., I called her. To my dismay, the phone rang, but no one answered.

I tried a second time. No answer again.

I rushed to her room, only to find the door slightly ajar. There she was, oblivious to her surroundings, standing on the balcony. I hugged her like I would hug a lost child. She looked at me with surprise.

Although it was definitely well past tea time, neither of us was in a mood to go without a cup. I ordered some tea and chocolate cookies from room service. Ah, pure bliss.

She told me all about her new life in St. Louis, her experiences as a professor, her writings, the people she met, and so forth.

Her face lit up when she told me all about Aarav and his achievements. The maternal pride in her eyes was touching as she confided in me all her aspirations for him. I looked at her in silent admiration. If I ever saw Aarav again, I would be sure to tell him that he was a lucky fellow to have a mom like her.

She wanted to know all about my life, personal as well as professional.

I gave her a brief overview of my career and how it had taken shape. She was surprised to know that I had switched tracks from business development to a more technical profile. But this was likely to take me to the higher management levels, so it was a wise career move.

She smiled at my enthusiasm, or rather over-enthusiasm, but I knew she approved of my focused approach.

There was, however, no discussion about our relationship. It was late by now, and she refused any dinner. This was my cue to leave, although I was much more comfortable where I was.

***

We met for breakfast the next morning. She was well-rested and as poised as ever. How I envied her composure. I did not get much sleep the previous night. "So what would you like to do today?" I asked.

"Well, Rohan, I have been to LA several times, but haven't had much time to explore it thoroughly. Visiting the Gaiety Art Center is a big thing on my mind," she said, looking at me for approval.

I would have taken her to the moon had she so desired. "Lead on, madam, to the art center," I said jovially.

A car drive followed by a short train ride took us right to the bottom of the mountain, the top of which was where the art center was located. It was a novel location, and a wonderful way to spend the day together.

I especially enjoyed the train ride with Avi, although I'm not really fond of trains. But her child-like glee and curiosity made the discomfort worthwhile. No matter how old she grew, she would never lose the wonderful quality to appreciate things with the innocence of youth. You could never tire of being around such a person.

We explored the gallery from end to end. She pondered over each and every painting and sculpture, making a comment here and there. Obviously, she knew her art, while I knew very little about the subject; still, I enjoyed the tour. It was educational and entertaining. What added considerably to my joy was her involuntary, almost subconscious grip on my hand. It reminded me of our dinner at Caprice's in Mumbai.

Suddenly, her grip got tighter. I looked at her. Her eyes were moist in appraisal of a beautiful, life-like portrait of a woman with tears in her eyes. I could have cried too. Dear, dear, Avi. So much regret, so many years lost.

She pointed out a world-famous work by Picasso. I was diverted. I had read about this painting. It had been the talking point on the market for some time now.

We lost track of time, so absorbed were we in our beautiful world. But my rumbling tummy soon made its presence felt and we went to the gallery's cafeteria for a meal.

It was well past 3:00 p.m. by the time we returned to the hotel. I walked her to her room.

"Avi, you look tired. Perhaps you'd like to rest?" I asked, concerned.

"Yes, I guess I'll lie down for a bit, but I don't know if I'll manage any sleep. Putting my feet up would be great, though," she said.

I nodded. Boy, she sure looked exhausted. How come? It hadn't been that hectic a day.

Never mind, I thought. Women are more delicate anyway. Let her rest. It would do her good. The trouble was, I couldn't bring myself to leave her alone.

She opened the door and I told her I'd wait outside while she changed.

She looked at me for a moment before finally muttering, "No need for that."

In that one sentence was an implicit acknowledgement of all that we meant to each other, even today. But there was no way we were saying that to each other. Not yet, anyway.

Quietly, she pulled some clothes from her suitcase and went into the bathroom to change.

In a few minutes, she emerged, looking fresh and oddly child-like in pajama pants and t-shirt. She smiled at me, and I marveled at how smooth her face was still, and as she pushed back a lock of hair, I noticed her delicate hands. Come to think of it, her feet were pretty too. They were small and well-formed, with toenails painted a discreet shade of pastel pink.

Climbing into bed, she smiled brightly at me.

On an impulse, I moved my chair closer to the bed and took her hand in mine. She closed her eyes.

Now was the time to tell her how sorry I had been all along. That despite my seeming callousness, I had never stopped respecting or caring for her, but it was already too late.

However, before I could say anything, she said softly, "Rohan, my life has been a roller-coaster ride in more ways than one. The uncertainty of it all was hard to deal with, you know. Changing jobs, bringing up Aarav, trying to keep up with my duties as a daughter and a professional; all of it was taking its toll. And relationships, they were hard to maintain.

"I knew I could not continue this way. So I deliberately moved towards a life of spirituality, of looking at things beyond the surface. It helped, to an extent. These days, the highs and lows of life don't get to me and I wonder if it's acceptance or just indifference. Either way, I don't get too involved in things beyond my control and that includes people. I won't lie to you. Your rejection of me drained me in every way. These days, words like passion, commitment, and forever sound strange to me."

I hung my head in shame. For long years, I had awaited this conversation, and today, when I finally had the chance to talk things out, I felt worse than I imagined I would. How I wished she would rail at me, shout at me, instead of being so nice about it.

But then, Avi moved on to other topics. Her writings. Her friends. Her work. Aarav. Most of all, her life at the university as a professor.

I listened in silence, all the time trying to organize the chaos that reigned in my head. I held her hand again, even as she was mid-sentence. "Avi, listen to me," I said urgently. "You have to know this; indeed, I need to confess I haven't been at peace for one single moment since I left you."

So on and so forth. I was so busy saying my part, I failed to notice she had fallen asleep. I looked up. Maybe she was pretending to be asleep, maybe she wasn't; but then, how could I expect her to be willing to talk of a past that was so painful?

The expression on her face was so peaceful and angelic that I didn't have it in me to wake her up. Avi was no raving beauty, but she had a striking personality and immense grace in whatever she did, be it picking up the shreds of her life or making a friend feel welcome, despite the hurt between us.

To my infinite joy, though, she clearly wasn't letting go of my hand any time soon. Not that I had any intentions of going anywhere. either I could look at her forever and just say:

How could I make you love me now...
until that morning in the Spring,
everything seemed to be going upswing;
after I met you...
there was nothing left as 'mine'...
as my mind went racing without caring,
somewhere I left you, 'promise of sharing'

How could I make you love me now...
as I crushed your dream...when we sailed merrily
shunning turbulences and bumpy sways,
and we merrily sailed through that stormy voyage,
reaching new shores and shunning the scary ledge...

How could I make you love me now...
when, 'Time' forced my feet with an unexpected storm,
before that goodbye, you looked peaceful;
may be thinking of me or a promise of trust,
all crushed with the 'note' that was so deceitful...

How could I make you love me now...
when I left you alone to fight that battle,
breaking your heart and discounting my mettle,

which wasn't less than a million deaths,
maybe you refused to take another breath...

How could I make you love me now...
shattering your dream as I held a stranger's hand,
another tsunami struck far away;
and three lives went separate ways,
when the equation of life could have been straight away...

How could I make you love me now...
thinking, if 'fate' gives us another chance,
will you forgive me now, accept me now;
with promises of love and promises of life,
can I make you love me back now...

I didn't know how, but I fell asleep in my chair, her hand in mine. It felt so natural, it couldn't have been any other way.

Unexpectedly, the grip on my hand became vise-like. I got up with a jerk. Avi's face looked painful as she pressed her heart with her other hand. Clearly, she was in pain. She was actually gasping for breath. Her t-shirt was drenched with sweat. "Avi, oh my God; what's wrong?" I yelled, gathering her close.

With great difficulty, she whispered in my ear, "Rohan, I don't know what's happening to me. I can't breathe, oh, God."

"Avi," I asked, struggling to keep calm, "has this happened before?"

She nodded her head in affirmation.

Quickly, I opened the windows for fresh air before dialing 911. Luckily, they understood the gravity of the situation without me having to break my head. It looked like a heart attack. She needed help, and fast.

Her eyes shut, and breathing unsteadily, Avi was nevertheless disapproving of my move. Despite being in pain, she was upset I had called 911 without asking her.

Well, I had no intention of listening to her on this score

anyway. Avi was stubborn, willful, and totally negligent when it came to her health. Let the paramedics come. They, not Avi, would decide what to do. I held her close, comforting her gently, as there was nothing much else I could do. I felt so helpless. The thought of losing her again was just too much to bear.

A loud knocking on the door informed me that the rescue party had arrived. They were accompanied by a pair of grim-looking cops.

And just in time. She was beginning to turn blue. Without losing a moment, the medical team put an oxygen mask on her. But she seemed to be rejecting it. Oh God, why? Did she know the end was near? Was she so very tired of life?

I ran up to her and whispered in her ear, "Don't give up, Avi, my love. Not now. We both have everything to live for. Don't give up on me, darling. I can't live without you."

I was sobbing loudly by now. The cop put a warning hand on my shoulder. "Sir, please." The disapproval in his tone was obvious. I didn't care, though, just as long as Avi knew how important her life was to me.

"All right; her breathing is steadier. Let's move her now," pronounced the team leader.

In a jiffy, they had her on a stretcher, but Avi held on to my hand tightly. "Can I go with you?" I asked the paramedics. One of them nodded affirmatively.

That was my first ride in an ambulance. And totally my worst nightmare.

Avi's eyes were open now. Despite the mask, they managed to convey a host of feelings. Love, regret, and pain.

She gestured to me to remove the mask; she wanted to talk. Furious, the paramedic took charge. "No, ma'am! You cannot do that," he hissed.

"We will talk later, Avi. When you are well and strong. Please don't resist. Let the doctors help you. Please, Avi," I said, managing a watery smile for her.

Avi seemed to accept the situation for a minute or two. But

then, the ambulance took a turn and Avi tore the mask off her face and flung it away. She lunged for me, taking me in a bear hug. And then, she slumped against me. For a heart-stopping moment, I thought she was gone.

"No! No! What the hell are you playing at, lady?" yelled the paramedic before pulling us apart.

Worn out by her rebellion, Avi slept through the rest of the journey, with a paramedic holding her hand lest she tried to remove the mask again.

At long last, we reached the hospital. I was asked to wait outside the ICU.

Despair, the kind I had never known before, hit me like a fury. Life seemed totally worthless. What was there to live for if I didn't have Avi by my side? The tears flew like a river in a spate. The hospital staff looked at me quizzically, but I was in my own world.

How had I gone so horribly wrong in life? Why had I failed to love and cherish the woman I loved when there was time? Was this heavenly retribution for all that I had done to her? Was this my punishment? Was "time" teaching me a lesson?

Don't do this, I pleaded. *Let her live; let me die. Or give me another chance, God. Let me put things right. I will never hurt her again.* Our elders sure knew what they were talking about when they said that life was too short to hurt anyone, especially the one we loved. I would give the world to be able to push the clock back. *Oh God, Avi. How has it all come to this? You didn't even allow me to say sorry to you, honey. Why? Oh Why? Why did I not fight for you, when we had time? Why did I not stand by my convictions and own you publicly as my woman?* All I could say was that that love is simple, but I had complicated everything. Life is all about "now." The power of "now" is so powerful. If you find love, value it. Go for it. Tomorrow never comes.

I was thinking…

Love is not about age, love is not about marriage, and love is not about society. Love is none of this. Love just means silent acceptance.

Without love, nothing else has meaning; not your professional achievements, not your bank balance, and definitely not the hypocritical need for social acceptance.

The sudden shuffling of footsteps interrupted my thought process. I looked up. There stood the doctor and he was actually smiling. That smile meant everything in the world to me. A thousand promotions or even millions in the bank account couldn't begin to compete with the relief of that moment.

"Hey, come on. She is out of danger now," he said. "In a couple of days, she will be fit for discharge. You can see her tomorrow morning, as she is heavily sedated right now."

Words could not express my gratitude to this good, good soul. I hugged him.

Giving me a friendly pat on the shoulder, he left.

However, there was no way I was leaving without taking one look at my Avi. Luckily, her bed was close to the window of the trauma unit. It was a disturbing sight, all those tubes and wires poking at her. I entered into her room without permission. I could not resist my temptation of reaching out and touching her forehead. Then, her arm. Who knew if she could hear and feel me? A junior doctor on duty shook his head at me. Time to leave; I had work to do.

It was with some difficulty that I convinced my client of the need to extend my two-day leave by another week. He sounded put off, but I would deal with that later. Now it was time to book airline tickets for both Avi and me to St Louis. I also arranged the transportation of her car from Kansas City to St Louis.

Oh, and I better call Aarav. The poor kid would be mad with worry. I had Avi's phone on me, so getting through to him wasn't difficult.

I was worried I would have to deal with hysterics. But Aarav sounded mature beyond his years. After confirming for about the tenth time that his mom was out of danger, he said he would return home with his uncle and prepare it for receiving a patient.

"I'm going to make sure Mom eats well and gets enough rest. I won't listen to any of her excuses now. Now, I will take care of her," he said.

"You do that, son," I said warmly.

How well he had taken the news of his only parent's sickness, how composed he sounded. I had to congratulate Avi on having done such a great job bringing him up.

***

After two days, Avi was discharged from the hospital and we planned our travel.

We had to be extra careful during the flight, but the airline staff was ever so kind. This was another thing I admired about the United States—the tenderness and consideration shown towards the sick.

For her part, Avi seemed to be coping just fine. She held on to my arm, ate from my hands, and rested her head on my shoulders. For once, she let guard was down.

As soon as we cleared the formalities at the St. Louis airport, I hailed us a cab.

It was such a romantic, peaceful ride; this lovely garden city and the woman I loved by my side.

We reached her home and it was love at first sight. She had created the perfect home and it was visibly different from the one she had in Mumbai.

Spacious, uncluttered, elegant, and warm—this lovely abode seemed to reflect the spiritual journey of its owner.

Aarav stood at the doorstep with *aarti ki thali* in hand to perform *aarti*. The ceremony is performed to welcome a new member into the family, such as a daughter-in-law or a newborn infant, who are entering the house for the first time.

When the "*aarati*" is performed, it is believed that the divine blesses the plate and light. That is why the plate is passed around, so that all present can put their hands over the flame and touch it to their eyes. In my case, it signified Avi's victory over death… although hindsight this might sound funny concept to most.

"Welcome home, you guys!" he said cheerfully.

What a thoughtful young boy. How noble his bearing, and what height. He was tall for his age, even by American standards.

He smiled at me. In that one moment, I was sure we would get along just fine. Gently putting a *tilak* (vermilion) on Avi's forehead, he inquired after her health. I felt a lump in my throat. How many teenage boys back home would welcome a sick parent with such dignity and composure?

He pointed us to the bedroom. For all his friendliness, I realized he was sizing me up. I smiled. This kid saw and knew a lot more than most people thought he did. Had he managed to link two and two together—his mom's sudden visit to me along with her equally sudden career move to the States? I was told by friends that kids grew up fast in the U.S., and Aarav was not slow on the uptake, not by a long chalk. He was also hugely protective of mommy dearest. Far from being wary of him, I found myself liking him even more for his concern toward his mother.

"Thank you," said Avi politely as I pulled the quilt over her. I could sense the return of her formal, icy stance. I sighed. I wished she would give up, at least for now.

I fixed all of us a glass of fresh orange juice and ensured Avi finished hers. Aarav cheered her on as I determinedly held the glass to her mouth.

"Mom, can I fix us my famous club sandwich for din-din?" asked Aarav. "Sorry, sir. I don't quite know how to cook a full meal," he said to me in an apologetic voice.

"So why don't I do the honors today?" I asked brightly.

"Oh, we couldn't, sir! You are our guest," he said awkwardly.

"Don't refuse the offer, sonny. I have been told I'm an awesome cook," I said.

"Since you put it that way, then please, sir." He smiled.

With his help, I managed to locate the *dals* (lentil) and veggies. We needed a simple, wholesome, tasty meal for Avi. Something she would not be able to refuse.

So—there it was. *Dal tadaka* (spiced cooked lentil) with *jeera* rice (cumin spiced rice), *aloo ki sabzi* (potato veggie), and *raita* (spicy yogurt made finely chopped cucumber, tomato, and green chili). It was the first time I was cooking for my Avi, and it had to be special.

I set up the pressure cooker with the *dal*, rice, and potatoes. It seemed a little slow, not like the efficient ones we had back home. I made myself a cup of tea as well.

A rapid *thump, thump* sound from the garden made me look out of the window.

There was young Aarav, playing basketball all by himself. Holding my cup of tea in one hand, I pushed open the kitchen door that opened into the backyard. I sat on the steps, admiring his athleticism and grace as he made basket after basket.

Initially, he didn't realize my presence. When he saw me, he grinned at me, but continued playing his game. That reminded me the time when I first visited their home in Mumbai when he was just five years old. So this was his inborn trait, the ability to carry on alone. He was polite and welcoming, but he was not my friend. Not yet, anyway.

After watching Aarav for almost ten minutes, I asked him, "Can I play with you?"

I had played basketball during my school days almost twenty-five years ago. I wasn't sure if I knew the game anymore. It was quite a chance I was taking, letting this fit youngster gauge the extent of my talent.

"You bet," he said.

I was confused. He saw my confusion and quickly appended, "Yeah, sure. I mean, you can," he said.

Boy, this American way of speaking took some getting used to.

I took center-stage on the mini court and tried out a few tricks from my school days. Luckily, Aarav didn't know them, or perhaps he was just being polite to me. But he cheered me on. "That's cool stuff, for sure."

"Sonny, you should try out this one." I got a bit excited and started showing off my dormant skills. I had never been able to play with my own son like this.

Aarav took the ball from me and tried to reach the net. He made the shot. Turning to me with a smile, he said ever so casually, "May I ask you something?"

"Yes, you can," I said, on my guard. I could sense he wanted to know something.

"Hey, were you mom's friend or…" He trailed off, leaving the sentence unfinished.

"I was her colleague. Well, actually, she was my boss's boss, but I was working for her as there was no one in my senior's position," I explained.

Of course, it didn't satisfy him.

"I see. Just checking if that covers everything or whether you guys were closer." My word. This boy. He was as direct as he was sharp. No point beating around the bush with him.

"Yeah, you are right, something more to it. We fell in love," I said. I knew it was better to be honest. And Aarav was mature enough to understand.

His face lit up. He wanted to know more.

"But it didn't work out. I mean, it was my fault. I was young and didn't have the courage to make things work."

Aarav kept looking at me steadily. His mother's gaze: unflinching and demanding.

"I couldn't get over her," I said flatly. "When I was ready, it was too late, as my parents had already arranged my wedding. It would have been extremely difficult for me to break away—the relationship, their reputation—so many things were at stake. But I lived to regret it. I learned the biggest lesson of my life—one should listen to their heart and that inner voice before making such major decisions in life." *Get a grip, Rohan. He's only a teenager. Don't scare him off.*

"I see," was his laconic response. I wondered how much he had understood anyway? However mature he might be, he was still just a kid.

We resumed the game. A couple of rounds later, he was ready with more questions. "How was mom those days? I mean, was she serious, kind, or jovial?" I could sense the need to know his serious, focused mom a bit more.

"She was fun. She was nice, she was caring, but she was a bit of a monster when it came to work." I laughed. "Hey. Don't tell her I said that."

He laughed and agreed with my opinion. "Yeah, I can imagine. Mom is a control freak, a kind of ringmaster when she wants to be," he chortled.

"Oops, you said that right." And we gave each other a high five. "Well, this is between us, you know."

He nodded and we had a tacit, unspoken bond. He had gotten the information he needed about me and he hadn't rejected me outright. Thank God for that.

We moved on to other topics. His school projects, his pals, his potential girlfriends. It was fun talking to this youngster, this odd mix of kid and adult. Despite living in the U.S., there was an odd vulnerability and innocence about him that was touching. How I could grow to love this fellow.

It was close to 6:00 p.m. by the time we finished. "Hey! It's about time we got dinner underway," I said.

"I'll help," he said.

And that was how Avantika saw us, standing by the kitchen counter; laughing, chopping, frying, and mixing. She looked at us for a minute or two, and I knew she was not displeased. Finally, she smiled at me to assure me that she was better.

"Hey, something smells good. What are you up to anyway?" she asked playfully, hands on her hips.

I decided to capitalize on the moment. I went down on bended knee. "I am working on, well, asking you to love me back. Take me back in your life," I said.

This was the proposal I had dreamed of making all those long, lonely years.

"Hey, get up. What are you doing?" she said, visibly

embarrassed, shooting a pained glance at Aarav.

Aarav looked at me, surprised. But his smile told me everything. It was all the encouragement I needed.

"No, not at this juncture of my life," she said, gathering her words and thoughts. That I had caught her off-guard was an understatement. "I mean, I'm not the one who should be part of your life. It is too late," she continued. "You better go from here; you are quite a confused soul."

"Avi, you sound like Annu Kapoor's character in Hindi film, *Vicky Donor*. Remember how he described Anshuman Khurana as a confused sperm?"

My unexpected analogy made Avantika and Aarav burst into peals of laughter. "Mom, he's priceless," screamed Aarav.

"What's the joke? Will someone tell me, please?" The clear, girlish voice had the effect of silencing us all.

I turned to look at the new entrant. A little girl, about six years old, stood looking at us curiously. Her face looked oddly familiar, um, like Khushi. And my other sisters. Perhaps even me.

I looked at Avantika, gob-smacked. She knew what I was thinking and nodded in the affirmative.

My head spun. God! I actually had a daughter with Avi! A daughter whose existence I had been blissfully ignorant of. For a moment or two, I was mad at Avi for hiding something like this, but to be fair, I had given her little reason to trust me.

"She is Rhea, my daughter. She lives with my cousin in Kansas City, as the place has schools that are appropriate for her interests," said Avi.

I was at a loss for words. "Honey, this is Rohan Rana, my former colleague and friend," she told the little girl, who acknowledged me with a cheery, "Hey, how are you?"

"Mom, what else you are forgetting here?" said Aarav, with a hint of steel in his voice. Without awaiting a response, he filled in the blanks. "Rhea, he is your dad!"

"Aarav," Avantika tried to stop him.

"Mom, what is it? Rohan made a mistake. And he truly regrets it. You should forgive him and accept him," said Aarav earnestly.

What a big-hearted boy; how very, very grown up, I thought, moved. Clearly, the absence of a male figure in the house had taught him to shoulder responsibilities beyond his years.

There was a pause for a few seconds.

"Mom, you teach spirituality to others. Can you follow the same?" Aarav pleaded on my behalf. "Please forgive him. He is a nice guy. He really loves you." So on and so forth. I could not have found a more dedicated and fervent advocate than Aarav, even if I had searched all over.

Rhea gaped at us, utterly bewildered. The poor kid was suddenly confronted with her father in the space of a few minutes, and to top it all, Aarav *bhaiyya,* her elder brother, was pleading this strange man's case.

"Avi, why didn't you tell me about her earlier?" I asked Avantika.

"What was there to tell you, Rohan?" she said curtly. "By the time I realized her existence, you were married as per your note. What purpose would it have served me contacting you, apart from wrecking your marriage and causing heartbreak all around? I wanted you to be happy in your chosen life," she said. "Rohan, I am a firm believer in destiny. And I accepted 'my lot' in life with as much grace I could possibly muster. My only regret is that both my kids have suffered in the process."

I held her close and wiped her tears.

She shrugged me off and pulled Rhea closer. "Rohan, I have tried my level best to give them everything except a father's love. I wish I could have changed that. Now it is too late."

"Avi, no, it's not too late. You only have to look into my eyes and see what I feel for you and the kids, our kids," I said softly. "Just give me one chance, will you?"

In response, Avi just stared back, unblinking. She was looking for assurance and commitment. Oh, God. She was just recovering from a heart attack and all this drama would have the docs fuming. But it was now or never.

"Mom, come on; go ahead. You still can be together. I want you to be happy." Aarav's tone bore the desperation of a child who has silently watched a beloved parent suffer over the years.

"You need this love in your life. I have heard his name in your sleep, mom. Please do not turn him away," added Aarav.

"Mom, please don't cry," pleaded Rhea. She was unable to comprehend the situation.

I broke down completely. These poor kids. How much they had experienced beyond their tender age. They sure didn't deserve this. And Rhea; should a six-year-old be talking like this? But they were good children who were sure to grow up as decent people and I would help Avi do that. Bring normalcy into their lives. Couldn't she see that we were a unit that belonged together? Hadn't she punished me enough?

The children's innocent words had the desired effect. Avi's heart was melting despite herself. She looked at Aarav for assurance and he didn't disappoint.

He repeated, "Mom, I want you to be happy. I am sure that Rohan will make you happy. I have seen genuine happiness on your face after so long. He is meant for you. He is the love of your life. Go on, mom; don't you deny it. You think I don't know? That you used to cry into your pillow at night, that you never went out much apart from work? Sure, you managed to conceal the hurt, but it never truly went away, did it?" he asked.

His next few words were the game-changer.

"Parents always think that their sacrifice will bring happiness to their children's lives. It is not true. As your son, I have all your unconditional love, mom. Now, it is your time to go and enjoy your life. Your sacrifice has never made me happy and I am sure it will never make me happy in the future. I will be far happier to see your happy face, your laughter, and your spirit that I saw when I was younger. Trust me, mom, my happiness lies in your happiness. I am sure Rhea will agree." He completed his non-stop argument and looked at Rhea.

Rhea nodded in agreement.

Avantika sat down on the wooden floor and tried to look into my eyes.

She couldn't reach me, as I was still on my knees. I sat down in front of her to align my face with hers. Now she could look into my eyes and find what she had been missing all these years: the assurance of lifelong commitment.

"Avi, I am sorry, really, really sorry for everything. Trust me on this: my cowardly behavior of abandoning you, the only lady I have ever loved, has haunted me day and night. Take me back. Give our life a chance. I will try to make up for everything, including the time taken from you and from us." I was rambling by now.

Fortunately, she understood. At long last, she understood. And she pulled me into her arms.

I held on to her for dear life. We wept in each other's arms as the kids looked on in silence. Finally, Aarav reached out and enfolded both of us in his embrace. Rhea followed suit.

We all hugged...

CHAPTER TWENTY

Avantika

My kids and I hugged Rohan.

Although I understood Rohan and his situation, I was confused. I was unsure of everything.

He, too, was dumbfounded.

I said, "I need little time to decide on this…Please."

He was clearly not anticipating this. He thought that I would probably agree to his proposal right away.

Rohan looked at me and closed his eyes for a second. Was he avoiding his emotions?

He rose on his feet.

He said, "It's too late for you. Let me walk you to your bedroom."

He handed me his right hand for me in support to rise.

We silently walked towards the bedroom.

He helped me to lie in the bed. He sat in the chair next to me.

I was awkward as I lay in front of him. When I tried to pull the tucked quilt, he got up from the chair and helped me with the quilt. He tucked me in. He touched my face with back of his palm. His hand was warm. His touch had a feeling of strange familiarity. That one touch conveyed to me how much he loved me. How much he regretted.

The turmoil was: *But do I need to forgive him? Do I need to accept him? If yes, why now? Is this what Aarav wants?*

Although Aarav argued his case to make me realize what I needed, it only summarized how important was the role of a companion in my life. Or was he feeling pressured from being the man of the house? Or was he concerned who would look after me when he was gone to attend his university? Unknowingly, he did fill in lots of spaces that were not meant for him.

Should I move on in my life?

Now, the medication started working on me. I was bit drowsy and fell asleep with a very indecisive state—to be or not to be.

***

I got up with morning rays in my bed; very unusual of me to sleep until past dawn, let alone getting up at sunrise. On day-to-day basis, I would finish my daily prayers and meditation by this hour of the day. I would be almost at the door in my professional gear to complete some last-minute unfinished chores.

The morning rays in the bed brought warmth and freshness. Although the rays played hide and seek through the leaves of our trees, it brought enough warmth to make me feel better. The tree was changing its color from green to yellow-green. Maybe next week, it would change to another color. Each of our trees in front of the house had different hues in the fall. These vivid colors, along with breakfast over the weekend during almost every fall and spring, inspired us to experience different verve and became the major source of planning for our annual travel.

Rhea stirred in the bed. It brought me back, into my bedroom.

When I glanced over at the sofa that was placed next to the window, I sensed that Rohan spent his night in that, as some part of the quilt was flowing over the sofa and over a small center table.

The thought of Rohan made me feel what I wanted to do. The feelings of "rejection" just evaporated. My pride made peace with his sense of wanting me back. Another thing I realized that his love for me was not worthless, but the most precious one for him and for me. But, when? After all these days… After all that he had put me through…

Where was he when I needed him? Who was with me when I needed him the most? Did I need to be selfish? Did I need to go for the one who was with me? He came back to me when he needed; not when I needed him.

The picture was obscure…

He left me when I needed him the most.

He came back to me when he needed me the most!

Is this "forgiveness" a virtue of women? Go girl, and decide whether you want him or not? You want to forgive him or not?

The turmoil churned my thoughts ups and down, in and out; and the picture was getting clear slowly and steadily—what I wanted for myself.

***

I think I was in my turbulence for a while and only came back to my senses as Rohan walked in. I was gazing out of the window through the tree...at the unknown. Of course, Rohan described this to me in the cab.

Rohan was leaving for the airport in the late afternoon...There was question mark on his face. He was looking for an answer.

I searched for my voice to tell Rohan about my thoughts over him and my hesitance over everything.

Rohan went out for a while before making his grand re-entry. He brought my breakfast and placed it on the center table. He stood in front of the bedroom door, facing me. He declared that he wished to read his mail. But I thought he wanted me to spend some quiet moments to make a decision.

I held his hand and asked him to come and sit next to me while I finished breakfast.

We chatted. We talked about our days at the bank. We talked about our colleagues, our clients, and, of course, about Wendy as well.

I further described some of the hardships I had gone through. About Steve, hilarious moments we spend together, my friendship and my feeling towards Steve. How Steve insisted that I make that trip to Simi Valley.

Slowly and steadily, the thought of me being happy with Steve started sinking into Rohan's brain.

He walked up to the window when I finished talking about Steve. He kept looking out of the window. He was searching for his answers or hiding his emotions or started accepting another man in my life.

After few minutes, he gave me another dose of medication and left the bedroom to complete his unfinished work.

***

It was about three pm; time for Rohan to leave for the airport.

I called Steve. He was surprised to hear from me.

"Hey, Steve, where are you?" I demanded his whereabouts.

"At home! My sexy professor gave me some homework to complete over the weekend. Working on my case study... How is it going with you?" he asked.

"I am good," I replied. "Just checking if you would be dropping Amanda over the weekend?" I made up an excuse to talk to him to know his whereabouts, as I knew it was his routine for a year to drop his daughter to spend some time with Aarav. They loved the latest video games and latest culinary experiments.

"Yeah. Sure. The same plan. Unless you have something else on your mind." He was sad and sounding me out about the development at my front. But, clearly, he didn't get any clue. He was as confused a soul as he was before the call.

"All right then..." I finished my call.

"Hey, Rohan, can you drop me off at Steve's home on your way to the airport?"

"Sure, I can," he said. He sounded defeated.

Rohan picked up his small cabin bag and started walking towards the porch. He just wanted to leave my home as quickly as he could.

I came down wearing one of my best dresses. I was a bit overdressed for the occasion and Rohan saw me admiringly and couldn't say a word. Everything was too late for him. Horribly late!!!

By the time I put my foot on the steps, the cab arrived and took a sharp U-turn in the curve.

Rohan held my hand and helped me settle inside the cab. He picked up his cabin trolley bag and settled that on the front passenger seat.

I sat comfortably and ensured I didn't lean on him. He also sat next to me by adjusting himself and ensuring a "safe" little distance.

The message was clear.

After the cab started, I spoke about my next trip to India and future book. He talked about his work and his travel schedule.

Finally, we reached Steve's home. The cabbie looked at me. He understood unspoken words. He put on a handbrake and told Rohan that he was going to check the engine, as it was making some peculiar noise. Actually it didn't, but he just wished to give us some privacy to say good-bye.

After the cabbie put his head behind the car front bonnet, I felt comfortable to start my unrehearsed speech. I just wanted to pour my heart out genuinely. It wasn't easy.

Ultimately, I broke the ice. It was hard for me, as that ice had hardened over the years…

I spoke whatever came to my mind and whatever was in my heart. "Rohan, it was difficult to know what I wanted. There is no doubt I loved you. There is no doubt I adored you. There is no doubt you were and will be part of me for the rest of my life.

"Today, when I laugh, I share with Steve. When I cry, he shares that with me, as it was he who offered his shoulder every time there were tears in my eyes. He was not only my friend, but also my partner in almost every part of my life. He is even there in my university life as a friend and as a student.

"I think, I breathe… it is Steve who can make me laugh and who can pacify me. He brought the sense and peace into my life. It was Steve who unknowingly filled the vacuum in my life that was created and that part of him completes me. For a very long time, I was living in the past, I was living in memories, and that was not the real world. Those were sweet memories and it was an imaginary, unfulfilled dream. However, it is over now. But the traces of that dream are real. Rhea is real. She is a big part of me and will be even bigger part of you. I hold no negative feelings for you. I understood your decision then and now. I also knew how much your mother and family meant to you. Any dutiful son would have done the same in your situation. I do love you, but now that is because you are Rhea's father, and a part of her. Whenever I embrace her, I feel you.

"I wish to live in today and look forward to life in the future. It is Steve who will give the future, as he knows my past, he knows my present, and he was there every time I needed him. He brought a strange peace in my life. I can't deny that and I can't betray him, as I know what that betrayal or rejection means in real sense. I love him. I adore his selfless love and sacrifice since he is the one who pursued me to take that trip to California. Someone who loves so deeply, so altruistically can only do all that.

"Please, please let me go.

"I want you in my life as my best friend; as my inspiration and as my partner in happiness in Rhea's life...."

Rohan clenched my hand. He looked into my eyes. He wanted to assure me that it was the right decision. He wanted to endorse me. Before he could utter any word, tears appeared in his eyes…

He didn't attempt to hide. He didn't bother to wipe them off.

After he swallowed a lump in his throat, which potentially would have triggered new flow of tears, he said, "You know both the times when I was leaving you, I was in tears. The first time when I was for leaving you in misery and now, when I am leaving you in happiness...but on a very different note."

I hugged him. He hesitantly brought his arms around me. He held me tight.

I released myself from his embrace as I heard the cabbie bring the car bonnet down with a big thud.

I hugged him, gently twisting myself back in the cab, and planted a good-bye kiss on his cheek.

"Take care! Write to me often." These words barely came out of his mouth as I left him.

As the cab pulled out on the road and disappeared, I took out my cell phone to dial Steve's number.

After fourth ring, it got connected.

"Hey, Steve, how is your case study going?" I asked before he even said hello.

"Oh man! These women professors are too hard on us...make us slog so much. I am struggling but I will get there, may be in an hour." He chuckled.

"How about your professor helps you with your case study..." I teased him.

"You're kidding!" He laughed.

"No, I am not. Just open the door...your professor is right here," I said. I was never so excited to see Steve in the past.

Steve opened the door; he was still holding his phone to his ear. He was stunned.

I leaped into his arms. First time. An unexpected act and my weight threw both of us off our feet and we fell on the carpet in his living room. He held my head in his right hand and threw the phone below the sofa.

He held me so tight that I couldn't breathe. I struggled my head up to see his face. There was curiosity in his eyes. He was moving his lips to ask something.

I put my finger on his lips and hugged him back.

Now I never wanted to release myself from his warm, caring, and resilient embrace.

I felt his lips over mine

Life is beautiful. Life is great.

It has no place for confusion, no time for regrets, and no chance for living in the past...just the present and today seem to be "a real present."

Poems inspired by "second Spring..."

मेरा होना तेरे होने का हासिल

तेरे होने में ही मुश्किल बड़ी है

तसव्वुर में ख़ुशी पाने की आदत

बड़ी बेकार ये आदत सी पड़ी है

जुदा वक्त ने तुझसे कर दिया,

पर हमारे बीच लम्हों की लड़ी है

ख़्यालों में तुम्हारा अक्स जैसे

कोई उम्मीद आँखों में जड़ी है

हमारे और उसके दरमियाँ अब

ख़मोशी ही फ़क़त साझा कड़ी है

By - Nandita tiwari
shared these beautiful lines for Avantika,

मृगजळ

एक सुख   एक अंत
तुझ्या आभासाचे   दुःखाच्या धडींची
तू नसताना   सुखाच्या प्रतिक्षेची
मन रिझवण्याचे   मोक्षाच्या क्षणाची

एक दुःख   एक मृगजळ
तु नसण्याच   तुझ्या सहवासाचे
तु नाहिस म्हणुन   डोळ्यांच्या दोषाला
जगत जगत मरण्याच   नशिबा दुषावण्याचा

एक सुरवात   एक अस्तित्व
तुझ्या सोबतीची   अबोल स्वीकारलेले
वाट नेहमीचीच   मोहाच्या क्षणांना
तुझ्या आठवणीची   दुर्दैवात मांडलेले

Girish Morje २३.७.२०१४

Author's Note

This is my debut novel and it turned me philosophical overnight. While portraying the characters, Avantika and Rohan, I had gone through a huge analysis of life from a different perspective.

Avantika was a character inspired by a lady executive whom I noticed while I was working for an investment bank in Manhattan. I never made an attempt to know her name or her role. I just observed her from a distance. As a part of a custom of bringing family members to work on the Friday after Thanksgiving, she brought her young boy (approximately four years old) to the office. While entering her corner office, she said, "This is where your mommy works." Her son went around her glass cabin proudly and fiddled with a few items fondly while she finished her routine work. What fascinated me was the complex life of balancing the mother-son bonds along with her high-profile professional role...

Rohan was a character inspired by my recent interaction with students, most in their late twenties or early thirties. I was astonished by how life had changed for youngsters socially and culturally at home and at work in India. This observation of young professionals in urban India changed many of my age-old perceptions. Youth, in general, know what they want, how they want, sometimes by hook and crook. They are assertive, impatient, and fiercely competitive; but they can be ruthless or dangerously shallow at times. One can't define it in terms of black and white. There are several shades of grey, and some of the shades of grey which are acceptable today were taboos just a decade ago. Some of the trends (liberalization), even unusual to American norms, are gaining foothold here faster than I could imagine.

While putting down my thoughts randomly, Mr Shyam Tare, one of my editors (and an author) for professional writings, suggested to me to convert it into a novel and guided me during the initial phases of the novel.

I also would like to give credit to my editors, Kalyani, Marley, and Beth, who have painstakingly reviewed it several times.

My sincere gratitude to my Facebook friend, Maj Gen Parthasarathi Paul, VSM (Retd), who meticulously reviewed the manuscript and offered many valuable suggestions before I launched it in India.

My special thanks to another Facebook friend and poet, Girish Morje, who was the first one to review and report his feedback on the novel. I will always adore the poem he has written for the characters he loved in the novel.

Facebook has given me wonderful friends and the constant involvement and encouragement that made me start another project.

Acknowledging my niece, Akanksha Kuruvathy, 18 years old, was the first one to tell me if the story was worthy or not; and also to my mother, my husband and my son, who were more excited than I ever was during this venture.

Finally, thanking you, Manish (Pant) for everything!

Hope you all will love this novel of mine; and my future projects as well.

ABOUT THE AUTHOR

With a Master's degree in Information Technologies from the University of Central Missouri, Sandhya Jane has been working for over two decades in the global corporate environment, including for some of the leading investment banks in Manhattan, India, and Hong Kong.

She has traveled widely across the globe for work assignments, giving her a unique look at many different cultures and regions. Currently, she lives in Hong Kong with her husband and son.

In addition to writing fiction, Sandhya also regularly writes on the subjects of technology, management, Vedic science & technology, and other motivational topics for leading websites and an Indian newspaper.

Please visit her Facebook page at: https://www.facebook.com/SandhyaJane or send an email to her at sandhya@sandhyajane.com.